Osborn

The Death of the Automobile

by JOHN JEROME

Illustrations

The Death of the Automobile

The Fatal Effect of the Golden Era, 1955–1970

Osborn

W · W · NORTON & COMPANY · INC · NEW YORK

Copyright © 1972 by John Jerome

FIRST EDITION

Library of Congress Cataloging in Publication Data
Jerome, John.
    The death of the automobile.

    Includes bibliographical references.
        1. Automobiles—Social aspects—United States.
    2. Automobile industry and trade—United States.
    I. Title.
    HE5623.J47   388.34′2′20973   72-4483
    ISBN 0-393-08510-4

Published simultaneously in Canada
by George J. McLeod Limited, Toronto
PRINTED IN THE UNITED STATES OF AMERICA

1 2 3 4 5 6 7 8 9 0

Senator Robert F. Kennedy: What was the profit of General Motors last year?

GM President James Roche: I don't think that has anything to do. . . .

Kennedy: I would like to have that answer if I may. I think I am entitled to know that figure. I think it has been published. You spend a million and a quarter dollars, as I understand it, on this aspect of safety. I would like to know what the profit is.

GM Chairman Frederic Donner: The one aspect we are talking about is safety.

Kennedy: What was the profit of General Motors last year?

Donner: I will have to ask one of my associates.

Kennedy: Could you, please?

Roche: One billion, seven hundred million dollars.

Kennedy: What?

Donner: About a billion and a half, I think.

Kennedy: About a billion and a half?

Donner: Yes.

Kennedy: Or one point seven billion dollars. You made one point seven billion last year?

Donner: That is correct.

Kennedy: And you spent one million dollars on this?

Donner: In this particular facet we are talking about . . .

Kennedy: If you just gave one percent of your profits, that is seventeen million dollars. . . .

> Testimony before the Ribicoff subcommittee on executive reorganization, the United States Senate, July 13, 1965.

For my favorite walking companions:
Katy, Marty, and Julie

Contents

Acknowledgments

Chris Packard (research)
Alan Sherrod
Clem Barnes
Hap Sharp
Jim Hall
Steve Smith
Bruce McCall
Dick Ruopp
Judson Jerome
Bill Ziff
Car and Driver
Brock Yates (stimulation)
David E. Davis Jr. (who got me into this)
Chris McCall (who got me out)

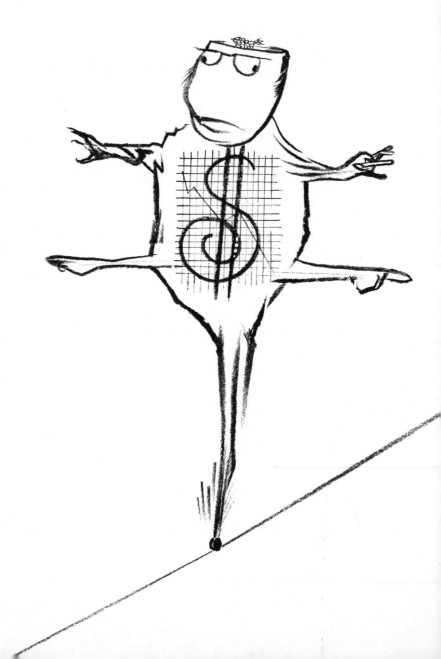

Introduction:
In the Beginning There
Was Mobility . . .

When the history of the automobile is written, scholars will necessarily focus careful attention on the crucial period of the late sixties and early seventies. During that period the largest industry the world had ever known—greater even than the war machineries which fed man's most consuming pastime—peaked out. The automobile industry began to die.

The acceleration of both change and rate of change in our technology is hard on transportation systems. Railroads began in this country in 1830, boomed along magnificently and profitably for about a hundred years, then faded fast. World War II brought one last spurt of furious activity, the railroad system playing a large part in the heightened productive capacity of the period. (In tribute to the importance of transportation to that productivity, we even called the effort "mobilization.") But with the shift to a postwar economy, the railroads became moribund. Intercity passenger miles dropped from 32.5 billion in 1950 to 8.7 billion in 1968. Attempts to prop up the railroads since World War II have usually been couched in terms of "national defense," and it seems likely that the railroads will end up effectively mothballed, as is most of our other obsolete war machinery: an unmaintained, marginally useful, $28-billion capital investment in cold storage, awaiting the moment when war-making again becomes a national enterprise. The railroads are perhaps the ultimate example of a throwaway economy.

13

Introduction

Automobiles have a shorter past and a shorter future. It is un-likely that public control of corporate excess will become power-ful enough to kill the automobile so long as there is any profit-ability to be wrung from it. But as our technology becomes more sophisticated, so does our cost accounting, and new costs—social ones—are being fed into a ledger at a much faster rate than new areas of automotive profitability can be discovered. As long as the industry was keeping its own books, the costs were vir-tually undiscoverable. But the sheer success of the industry has proved—as in cancer—its own undoing. By growing from novelty to pervasive element to absolute necessity in American life, the automobile has effectively rubbed the nose of society in the excesses of the industry. Because the automobile affects us all, its industry has grown into a new kind of supercorporation. And finally, the society has begun auditing the books.

The balance sheet could more accurately describe a war than an industrial success. Automobiles kill almost sixty thousand of us per year and injure 4 million more, pollute the environment more outrageously than any other industrial source, gobble natural resources like cocktail peanuts, destroy the cities, choke off development of more efficient or serviceable transit systems, spread squalor on the land, jam the courts with unnecessarily complex and unwieldy litigation (often as not in violation of the civil rights of the involved), exacerbate our unsolved problems of poverty and race, shift patterns of home ownership and retail trade as casually and whimsically as natural disasters, alter sexual customs, loosen family ties, elbow their way into living space de-spite our best efforts to keep them out, rearrange the very social and moral structure of the nation, and dominate the economy to the point of subverting the hallowed capitalist system.

On balance, the only entries on the credit side of the ledger are an occasionally flourishing—if jittery and hypertensive—economy, and a considerable amount of convenient, comfortable, and sometimes even reliable mobility.

It is the last-mentioned dubious benefit that is wrapped in the most tragic self-delusion. The basis of the appeal of the private automobile has always been a kind of mystically perceived total freedom. In practice, it is the freedom to go wherever one wants to go (wherever the *roads* go, which opens up another socioeconomic can of worms), whenever one desires to go (whenever the car is ready, when one has paid the price in preparation and maintenance, in taxation and legal qualification, whenever one has the wherewithal simply to feed the machine), at whatever rate one desires to go (assuming the traffic will allow, that congestion eases—and at rates up to but not beyond the arbitrary standards established to protect one from the dangers of excessive use of his own freedom).

Never mind the cavils, however; mobility, or the illusion thereof, has indeed been the prime attraction, the dream for which we have so cheerfully paid all those other costs. The tragedy is that if mobility alone had been the single goal in the development of the modern private automobile, we could have achieved a better measure of it for a fraction of a percentage point of the cost we have paid.

The economic effect, in its most directly financial and tightly automotive forms, is totally out of range of the kind of dollars-and-cents sums that have any immediate, personal comprehensibility. The car business produces about 13 percent of the gross national product; approximately one American in six derives his income from an automobile-related business; we spent $93.5 *billion* in 1970 to buy, fuel, clean, insure, repair, park, and build roads for our automobiles. In 1968 we drove 1 trillion miles, finally achieving that magic number for which the road-building and gasoline interests had been straining so long; one can only assume we've improved markedly on the figure since. But no other statistic describes the American involvement with the automobile better, I think, than this: in the years 1955 to 1970, we bought just about 100 million private automobiles.

A hundred million passenger cars would seem to represent a substantial degree of realization of the dream of mobility. But the fascinating aspect of this exercise in industrial overkill has been the rapid diminishment of the significance of mobility, per se. A kind of hipshot Protestant-ethic historical analysis of the rise of the automobile can be keyed to just which factors other than

Introduction

mobility have dominated the concerns of the car builders. Once a faltering mobility had been achieved in the spindly, prepubescent automobile the search was for mobility plus reliability. Once that was achieved, practicality and economy became the goals. In rapid order, in a Bunyanesque route to automotive paradise, the peripheral concerns became speed, safety, comfort, status, luxury, and—all of the foregoing accomplished to what seemed a reasonable degree, and nothing else seeming to offer itself as an additional sales tool—finally, sheer sensation. Moralistic as such an accounting may be, it is nonetheless accurate; what evolution has occurred in American automotive design has clearly been from the essential to the sybaritic.*

A single example demonstrates the evolutionary tendency, and provides as well a somewhat sardonic commentary on the level of industrial planning on which rests the bulk of the economic health of the United States. In the latter half of the sixties the economic and social analysts who guide the fortunes of the domestic automobile industry discovered the Youth Market. The facts of economic life were explained to the industry. In 1965 there were 21 million people in the U.S. between the ages of thirteen and nineteen, controlling $14 billion of the nation's wealth, spending $4 billion of it annually on transportation. By 1970 that segment would grow to 27 million souls. In 1965 it was decided that if the industry was to consolidate its spectacular growth rate of the preceding decade, the means would have to be found to tap the Youth Market.

Social analysis has never been Detroit's long suit, as the city's racial history will attest. The industry's motivational-researched response to the challenge represented by the Youth Market was the "Supercar." The Supercar was a youth-oriented version of just what the industry had been offering the public, basically unchanged, since 1955. It was, in effect, a cosmetically treated, over-

---

* Beginning in the early fifties, and continuing through today, used-car lots label otherwise unsaleable fifty- and one-hundred-dollar junkers as "Transportation Specials." "Here," the dealer seems to be saying, "is a car so worthless that it can be used for nothing but mobility."

16

powered, semiracing version of the conventional American automobile. The Pontiac GTO was first, followed quickly enough by the Plymouth Road Runner, Chevrolet Chevelle SS 396, Dodge Charger, Ford Cobra, Oldsmobile 4-4-2, and the like. These cars offered no technological advancements other than detail refinements. "Performance"—meaning, in Detroit's tunnel-visioned terminology, sheer acceleration—was vastly increased. Lesser gains were made in handling and evasive capability, and braking. Efficiency and economy of operation were, of course, thrown out the window; the Age of Affluence was to go on forever.

The appeal of the Supercar was entirely emotional (and moralistic considerations about just what kind of emotions it appealed to were discounted as somehow antiprogress). It had a youthful image. It also had a gruesome safety record, and abysmal warranty history (when warranties were offered at all—they were drastically reduced or canceled outright on some of the more extreme versions of the Supercar), and resulting soaring insurance rates. Detroit projected a market share of between 15 and 20 percent for its new baby.

By 1970 the Supercar was dead as a marketing phenomenon. It had had the full treatment in ads and editorial coverage; automotive journalism was madly in love with it. It gained a great deal of publicity, some of which may have rubbed off, for good or ill, on the standard products of the industry. But the combination of growing public (i.e. government) concern, skyrocketing insurance rates, and such vagaries as increased draft quotas for Vietnam simply wiped the Supercar out.

The Youth Market, meanwhile, was making its own emphatic statement about automotive transportation. If any one single automotive solution typifies the disaffected youth of the late sixties and early seventies, it is the two-hundred-dollar, clapped-out, fourth-hand, barely mobile, hideously ugly Volkswagen bus. If the Supercar was the accurate translation of Detroit's vision into consumer product, the VW bus became a precise metaphor for changing market reality. It was the absolute antithesis of the Supercar. The kids loved it; it was almost anti-automobile.

The Bad Machine

The premise of this book is that the automobile must go. We can no longer afford it, not because we are so poor but because it carries costs that rise so rapidly they leave us exhausted in the midst of our wealth. The premise is absolutely radical, of course, in the classic sense. The traditional response to radical solutions is to regard them as more or less the product of dementia. We worship, in our American myths, hard-nosed practicality—usually symbolized by the Jeep. But we build Buicks—build them and buy them, in numbers that eloquently demonstrate the distance between our myths and our realities. In any kind of overview of the automobile it soon becomes evident that to abandon the machine is more practical than to keep it. Overviews, however, are as difficult to maintain as accurate mythologies. It certainly doesn't *sound* practical, this talk of quitting automobiles.

In an attempt to tie this larger practicality to the more commonly accepted ones concerning cars and their charms, I have tried to inject as much of my own automotive experience as possible into these pages. That experience is much like that of most other American males coming of age in the fifties: buying cars, selling them, building, racing, wrecking them. Driving them, hundreds of thousands of miles. Surviving them. Really hating a couple, and falling in love with several others. I don't mind being called a car nut because I am one, still apt to succumb to fascination with almost any inane new automotive wrinkle that comes down the pike. I love World War I aircraft, too, but I see in them a satisfactory solution to neither private transportation problems nor international political disputes.

In addition I have been the one in six, earning my living from automobiles for about ten years, in what we self-importantly called automotive journalism. When I quit it was not out of pique or any cold-eyed rational rejection, but because my ardor had simply cooled. It seemed to me that there was still a great deal of personal satisfaction to be derived from avocational car ownership, but the cars, somehow, never seemed to provide it. Car ownership nowadays is too difficult, too expensive. Too hard on the conscience. These discordant feelings of pleasure denied still gnawed at me as I began work on this book.

(I still own a car. I still have to, now, living out of the city. For a few years I didn't, however, and that was a revelation. Perhaps the seed for this book was planted then, in examining that revelation, that freedom.)

If my own automotive experience is offered to inject a note of practical realism, then I suppose my fantasies must counterbalance that cold practicality. Plenty of fantasies are available, and I am a sucker for them, still dreaming of a workable automotive world. I am as susceptible as the next to the kind of pop-sci schemes the mechanically inclined media have been pumping out regularly for several decades. (Originally I included in my research—for laughs—an admittedly light-hearted contest, run by an automotive magazine a few years back, for the design of a disposable car. In the past year I have learned that serious research projects to develop such a car are now being carried forward in Japan and Europe. No more apologies for fantasies.)

Putting aside the mind-sets engendered by current technological considerations, I speculate about slim, spare, human-scaled envelopes that answer our automotive needs without overburdening our planet. The pro-Detroit segment of the media usually refers to such dreams, derisively, as "transportation modules," rejecting them out of hand as sterile, characterless manifestations of a depersonalized computer society. (One wonders about the character the Chevrolet Impala contributes to American life.) Nevertheless, envision, if you will, such a "module," created on the outer fringes of technology.

It would be capable of moving at reasonable speeds—capable, let us say, of breaking every speed limit in the U.S., meaning that it would have a top speed of 76 mph—in almost total silence. It would provide a level of passenger safety at least to current aviation standards. It would have the crushability characteristics of a fiberglass motorcycle crash helmet, might in fact in overall structure be considered a kind of total-body "helmet," although less constricting. It would have the accident-evasion capabilities of a modern Grand Prix car, albeit without the acceleration and top speed, and could be brought to a stop in about one third the distance, from a given speed, that is required by the best present-day domestic sedans.

The power unit of this figment of my imagination would be smaller than an overnight bag, pollution free, light enough in weight to be carried by one man in one hand, designed for replacement on an instant plug-in basis—perhaps maintenance free and sealed for life. Such a power source could go anywhere in the vehicle—front, rear, beneath the floor—that maximum efficiency and safety might require. It could also be joined serially —again on a plug-in basis—to other, similar power units, which I might need when I latched onto additional seating components, or load-carrying modules. Such an arrangement would allow me to avoid hauling around more seating or load space than I needed for the automotive task at hand (and to avoid using up more of the increasingly precious energy supply than needed). I might even rent auxiliary power units, only for those periods when I actually needed them.

Fifteen hundred pounds ought to mark the upper limit of the largest version of such a vehicle, less in one- or two-seat manifestations. (A friend of mine recently heard the chief of engineering for General Motors muse, while gazing at an off-trail motorcycle he had purchased, "That thing will carry two people at seventy-five miles per hour. It weighs three hundred pounds, and costs three hundred dollars. And to overcome its shortcomings as regular transportation right now, we have to go to over two thousand pounds and over two thousand dollars." He was speaking, of course, of Chevrolet's Vega, which makes up less than 10 percent of General Motors' production; the other 90 percent double those minimum figures.) With such a low gross weight this "car" would provide remarkable economy of operation, whatever the fuel, at perhaps triple the longevity of our existing solutions to the problem of private transportation. Tires, for example (if such an obsolete component is still required), might last well over a hundred thousand miles. Road-bed life and that of other automotive ancillaries would be similarly increased, with attendant economic benefit. Such a car would consume much smaller quantities of natural resources, in both manufacture and operation. It would spew less—if any—pollution into the atmosphere, squander much less space in an overcrowded world, cause markedly fewer deaths and injuries on the highways, and exact a smaller psychic toll on owner or driver.

The most bizarre and dreamlike element of such speculation is that the bulk of the technology to accomplish all of the above is available now. We could do it. Given a comfortable five-year lead time, such a car could be in mass production well before the end of this decade. And the rapidly escalating federal safety and pollution standards which the manufacturers claim are stifling technological development at present would be beside the point by the time the vehicle hit the showrooms.

Those who are swept up in that kind of dream of automotive rationality should prepare for disappointment: it isn't going to happen. Such a vehicle wouldn't, in the first place, accelerate at anything approaching the 1-G rate that seems to be the ultimate goal of both American manufacturer and American customer. A more drastic consideration is that such rationality would deny the manufacturer the opportunity to drape his product with the emotional festoonery which provides him with the only sales tool he has yet discovered. The manufacturer won't build it because he is convinced the public won't buy it. He may well be correct.

But it is not just that such a solution won't be built. It *shouldn't* be built, no matter how many automotive problems it seems to solve. Because it won't work. Such a vehicle—safe, economical, nonpolluting—could be made to function, but it won't solve the problems. Designing better cars to solve problems that the automobile has brought us is exactly like building more freeways to reduce traffic congestion. Thirty years of experience has shown us that *that* "solution" only intensifies the problem it is designed to solve.

Technology isn't evil, but the uses of technology often are. The car is a bad machine—and the solution is not to build a better bad machine, but rather not to build bad machines. Yet

Introduction

this huge, wealthy nation is trapped with what is virtually a single transportation system, and to suggest simply abandoning that system is to suggest paralyzing the nation. We have become addicted to automobiles; they have become literally a necessity for sustaining life.

How we became addicted, what the future holds for such an addiction, and how we can escape the trap that that addiction ensures is what this book is about.

PART I

The Car

CHAPTER 1

The Age of
Accessories

Building What America *Wants*

Back in the dim red dawn of time, about 1954, when Chevrolet, Ford, and Plymouth were still referred to as The Low-Priced Three, the golden age of the automobile industry began. It became apparent that the public was capable of buying cars at the altogether luscious rate—for the manufacturers—of perhaps 6 million a year. Chevrolet, Ford, and Plymouth prepared for this opportune moment by bringing into production all-new cars in 1955, virtually for the first time since World War II. Consumer interest in the new cars was positively frenzied: in those days the annual introduction of the new models had become, for most of America, an event ranking with the Homecoming Game of the local high-school football team. (Imagine, if you can, a new-car purchaser nowadays bringing the shiny new purchase home and expecting to give neighbors a ride around the block. That hallowed custom has gone the way of the back-porch ice-cream freezer, and the owner is more likely to slip the new car quietly out of sight in the garage to prevent vandalism.) The customers also had the cash in 1955—or at least the credit— and times were good, the economy hot, Eisenhower's first recession already a memory and the second, more severe one still in the future.

Sales and promotion staffs were geared for the massive push to 6 million; gallons of showroom window paint were stored in readiness, buttons, banners, and brochures already on the road. In the fall of 1954 the doors opened and the frenzy started. One year later, when the machines stopped clanking and the cash registers stopped ringing, when the weary salesmen were sweeping out their empty showrooms to make way for the 1956 models, the total car and truck sales for the 1955 model year came to 9,169,292, of which nearly 8 million were passenger cars. Sales successes would come and go—in spades—in the next decade and a half, but none would match the heady triumph of 1955, for the whole new worlds of possibility it opened to Detroit's view.

If you had asked a car man the reason for the success, he would have answered, simply, "product." Product was all, in 1955, although it is misleading to think of that product as technological wizardry or even substantial engineering advancement. The stodgy car died in 1955. All our clinging Calvinist sensibilities of practicality, economy, simplicity, all the cramped guidelines of American Gothic, were junked. We wanted more. We got it: bigger engines, more "zestful" performance, more options, chrome, jazz, sex. That was the year the "two-tone paint job"—quaint liturgy from our automotive adolescence—was finessed; there was actually a successful Dodge model offered in resplendent black, white, and purple. Gone were the opportunistic little Ford V-8's that were the prewar hotrods, with mud-plain styling, good performance, and solid, if simple, engineering. In their place came Ford

Crown Victorias, with bands of chrome sweeping up the sides and across the top (the model was popular in bright yellow; one observer pointed out that with the "handle" of chrome across the top, it looked like a twenty-foot Easter basket). Enter also the motivational researcher, tooting the horn for automobiles as extensions of sexual peculiarities. (The data banks were already bulging with the bales of misinformation which would bring to fruition in 1957 that cornpone's humiliation of motivational research, the mighty Edsel.) We were building automobiles for the new American voluptuaries. The single central goal was the appearance of luxury, even in the "small" "economy" models.

What every American really wants, automobile executives are fond of reassuring each other, is a Cadillac. The Cadillac is the most expensive American car; ergo, it represents the American Dream. It resides in the language as the *ne plus ultra*—"The Cadillac of carpet sweepers," "the Cadillac of fishing reels." Legendarily it is the first hasty purchase of the extra lucky, the blessed few who somehow stumble into the scattershot bonanzas strewn about the American scene: bonus-baby athletes, gamblers, sudden oilmen, uranium millionaires, entertainment figures who mine pure gold underestimating the taste of the public. It is also the single standard of thousands of middling-successful Middle-American small businessmen who emulate the tastes of those other economic sultans of the domestic midway. The Cadillac has been called, appropriately enough, the essence of all that is avaricious and trivial in our middle-class life style. And so it is a tenet of Detroit's faith that the highest good is served when the industry makes every car an imitation Cadillac, when all automotive design is pushed toward that single standard. Unfortunately, the single standard is expensive, and the only feature that can be duplicated cheaply, that will register on a dim public consciousness as Cadillac-*like*, is size.

The Car

Above all, the 1955 cars were bigger and heavier than ever before.

Bigger cars need bigger engines. Chrysler Corporation kicked off the horsepower race in the early fifties with a then-incredible 160-horsepower "Fire-Dome V-8"; schoolboys struggled with the polysyllabic mystery of "hemispheric combustion chambers." [1] Although it is perfectly possible—still—to provide adequate highway performance in a full-sized car with the 60 to 90 horsepower of pre-World War II and early postwar cars (as the current over-three-thousand-pound, low-pollution, 65-horsepower Mercedes-Benz diesel demonstrates), Detroit was after bigger things. The operative philosophy was clear: trade 'em *up*. No other course seemed workable, in the flowering of the second phase of car marketing.

(Phase I had been all Henry Ford's, with industrial rationalization, durability, economy. The assembly line, replaceable parts, mechanical simplicity, rock-bottom prices. But Phase II was the exclusive property of General Motors: diverse products to cover the entire range of market possibilities, advertising tidal waves to stimulate those markets, credit financing, cost accounting, the sharp wedge of the business mentality—which Henry Ford just didn't have—driven carefully under the concept of basic transportation. Phase I spoke directly to the consumer: Here is something you've never had before, transportation that is both affordable and private. Phase II said nothing to the public; rather, it tried to listen to the million voices, to divine a mythical consensus, and then to rig that consensus for profit. Phase III, as we will see, belongs entirely to the federal government, but that is another story.)

The key principle in this second phase is that no single element, no tiny fissure in the available market, can be left unplumbed. Car-makers would go to what seemed unimag-

28

inable lengths to pick up a mere percentage point in market share. A percentage point in an 8-million-car year is 80,000 units. At an average gross profit of six hundred dollars, that's $48 million. Suddenly it's all a little more imaginable.[2]

In 1955, horsepower was regarded as a sure bet for market percentage points. Acceleration was the newest automotive fad, somehow the only measurement that seemed to mean anything to the public. (Who talked about miles per gallon any more? We talked acceleration, and we called it—at first —"pick-up.") Acceleration is directly a function of horsepower. The horsepower race was a mixed blessing to Detroit from the beginning, giving sales forces something to talk about when very little else about the domestic automobile would support a conversation, but also bringing down the first chill glint of federal attention onto the product, stirring up critics to gales of wrath over the performance image and its impact on safety. After a period of brazen exploitation of rising horsepower, Detroit pulled in its horns and began soft-pedaling the performance image for awhile, going so far as to organize its own manufacturers' ban against participating in racing in 1957. General Motors—most visible target for an antitrust suit by the Justice Department—has never re-scinded the ban, but its competitors were heavily back into racing in the early sixties. The size and power of engines continued to grow, at General Motors and everywhere else in the domestic industry, and the trend has not quite been halted by the pollution crisis and resulting renewed government interest. But in 1955, the bigger engines were *necessary* to power the accessory-laden, ever longer-lower-wider-heavier new cars that America *wanted* so badly.

Within the parameters of the Detroit view of the market, nobody needed a new engine worse than Chevrolet did in 1955. For more than twenty years the company had struggled along with the hoary "Hot-Water Six," a dead-reliable, easy-to-repair, parsimoniously economical design (both in manufacture and in consumer operation) that performance enthusiasts insisted was far better suited for use as a boat anchor than as the engine of a modern passenger car. Even the Southern California hot-rodders, who seemed to be capable of drawing horsepower out of anything vaguely metallic, had given up on it. The performance of Chevrolet products was positively mournful by comparison with V-8-powered Fords, and more horsepower was needed for competition in the sales race. Ford was gaining. (In 1953, Chevrolet outsold Ford by more than 300,000 cars; in 1954 the margin was cut to 17,013.)[3]

The response of the Chevrolet Motor Division of General Motors to this marketing gap was a brilliant one, in execution if not in concept. The replacement engine (a supplement, really—the antique 6-cylinder struggled on as "standard equipment" for several more years, primarily so the manufacturer could keep the base price down) was the justly famous 265-cubic-inch V-8, the new cornerstone on which fifteen years of uninterrupted business success would be laid. It is undoubtedly among the half-dozen most successful industrial designs of the twentieth century.

The new engine was remarkably light in weight compared with its competition, reasonably inexpensive to produce on a long-term basis, and outstandingly reliable from the beginning. More important, it was efficient—a high revving, free-breathing mother lode of power. With a touch of engineering attention it might well have become the most economical V-8 in history. But in the domestic car industry the engineers take orders from the sales department, and another kind of touch was sought: power. In its second year of production, the V-8 was bored out to 283 cubic inches of displacement, and engineers managed to extract 283 horsepower from it in a production version. One horsepower per cubic inch of engine displacement was an output previously restricted to finely tuned and woefully fragile racing engines. Before long, Chevrolet engineers would find ways to get 325 HP from those same 283 cubic inches, in a limited production version. The basic engine design, in progressively larger and larger versions, has had a production life of well over fifteen years, and more than 20 million examples of it have been built and sold. At last count the little "265" was at 400 cubic inches—and growing.

It is doubly fitting to appoint the Chevrolet V-8 engine as symbol of the golden age of the automobile industry. Not only was it a magnificently engineered success, it stood alone as just about the only piece of landmark automotive development in the hundred million vehicles to be built in the fifteen years after its introduction. Ford came along a few years later with an even lighter and more powerful engine, in a 289-cubic-inch size (in highly modified form the engine was eventually to win the Indianapolis 500), but the principles were already established. Various other "monster" engines were produced, catching the enthusiasm of the hard-core car nuts, and a very few of them had even mild success powering ordinary passenger cars—although the thrust of their development came primarily from that highly suspect activity, racing. There were other technical successes in the period from 1955 to 1970, and one of them—disc brakes, imported from Europe more than a decade after a desperate need for them had been established—could even be described as socially redeeming. But none of the technological accouterments of the golden age was particularly noteworthy. It was the golden age of the automobile *industry,* not of the automobile.

The shift in emphasis is subtle from the outside, but revolutionary internally. It is no less a shift than from *product* engineering to *production* engineering. No longer do technicians sift the technology for ways to make a better product;

engineers and scientists now search for better (more efficient; cheaper) ways to do the *making*. Cost accounting *uber alles:* cut two cents from a part or a process, and multiply the savings by 8 million. Add a dollar's worth of quality (or safety) and get crucified by stockholders at dividend time.

Thus the Chevrolet V-8, a mechanical masterpiece in its own time, a foundation stone in the General Motors temple of profits, becomes in a peculiarly arch and poetic way a symbol also of what went wrong with automobiles. A good engine in a bad machine. And worse: a wrong-headed push toward making a bad machine worse.

(What arrogant nonsense, my fellow car buffs—and the car-makers—would say. Can you imagine the congestion with those hundred million cars so underpowered they couldn't get out of their own way? We *had* to have bigger engines, more power. We were building three-, four-, five-thousand-pound cars, equipped with air conditioning, power steering, power brakes, tons of accessories. Automatic transmissions—we needed big V-8's just for the automatic transmissions alone! Yes indeed.

Down the Yellow Brick Road to PRNDL

"They are, for the most part, steel boxes hung between four wheels and powered by reciprocating fossil fuel engines. Sure, refinements like automatic transmissions, unit construction, better manufacturing techniques, etc., have arrived, along with such esoterica as disappearing windshield wipers, stereo, power windows, etc., but the basic front-engine, rear-drive *thing* Detroit markets today is about as contemporary as the Twentieth Century Limited," said automotive writer Brock Yates, puzzling over the sour downturn at the end of the golden decade-and-a-half.[4]

The Age of Accessories

It never occurred to *Fortune* to wonder. In an article bristling with military terminology and totting up scientific scores like a box on the sports page, writer Lawrence Lessing tells us of the massive technological breakthroughs provided us by World War II: antibiotics, atomic power, cryogenics, computers, jet planes, rocket vehicles, radar, transistors, masers, lasers, and "other products that became the new industrial face of the mid-century." [5] That new industrial face does not include automobiles, however; with the possible exception of computers as a design and production aid, all those postwar breakthroughs have, in effect, gone right over the car industry's head. (Chrysler Corporation did begin offering electronic ignition—transistors in place of old-fashioned condenser and ignition points—in 1972, just about ten years after accessory-makers put add-on kits on the market.)

The lack of development hasn't gone unnoticed even by the car-makers themselves. Ralph Nader quotes Ford Vice-President Donald N. Frey in 1964: "I believe that the amount of product innovation successfully introduced in the automobile is smaller than in previous times and still falling. The automatic transmission was the last major innovation of the industry." [6] (The statement was made before widespread adoption of disc brakes.)

The automatic transmission is indeed something of a high-water mark in American automotive technology; it and the large displacement high-compression overhead-valve V-8 are perhaps the only significant domestic contributions to the modern automobile. Automatic transmissions were in use on London buses in 1926, but it was only in this country that the device was brought to a stage of development which allowed mass-production application. [7] Oldsmobile began putting automatics on some of its cars before World War II; by 1970, 91 percent of the domestic cars sold in the U.S. were equipped with the device.

The Car

Before the automatic transmission, drivers were faced with the onerous responsibility of changing gears for themselves. You may remember the drill (although if you were taught to drive in a public-school driver-education program or by a commercial driving school, it is quite likely that you have never been exposed to a manual transmission). You depress the clutch, move the gear lever, release the clutch; coordinate release of the clutch and depression of the gas pedal, the only part that is a bit tricky at first; repeat the whole operation at every start and stop and upon marked changes of speed. Because the manual transmission provided positive linkage between engine and drive wheels, it helped the moderately skilled driver to maintain precise control of engine speed. The unskilled driver might, however, find himself in the wrong gear at the wrong time, which made for stalled engines or bucking, lurching progress. The manual transmission took some getting used to—not much, but some. It made learning to drive a bit more complex than being told the names and functions of the controls, and then being set loose to learn to aim the machine. It was also possible with a nonautomatic transmission to do physical harm to a car engine or transmission, through various kinds of mechanical idiocy. That's a little more difficult to do with an automatic. (It is easily possible to build in protection of engine and transmission without abandoning the manual, of course, but the industry chose another route. Protection was the least of its worries.)

The automatic transmission proved difficult to get "right," from a design and consumer-use standpoint. Early versions were balky, temperamental, plagued with service problems. Notoriously inefficient in the early years, the automatic reduced gasoline mileage by as much as 40 percent, particularly in short-trip, stop-and-go situations. The Department of Transportation says that the average U.S. automobile trip is

34

for nine miles, over half of them are for less than five miles, and that an automatic transmission currently adds approximately seven cents per gallon to owner cost over the life of the automobile—three cents for the hardware and four cents in loss of gas mileage.[8] Automatics also sap enough horsepower to reduce performance noticeably (a characteristic which still handicaps most imported-car versions of the automatic, since the imports have not unanimously succumbed to the horsepower race and thus feel quite underpowered when fitted with an automatic). If performance falls off, what do you do? More horsepower, of course, which further reduces operating economy.

Mechanical failure of early automatic transmissions was frequent enough to support the establishment of nationwide chains of repair shops specializing in automatic transmission work, including one chain that was indicted by the City of New York in 1962 for a refined form of consumer swindle. Swindles were to be expected. While the manual transmission is a relatively straightforward mechanical device which announces its internal ailments in no uncertain terms, the early automatics were vague and unnerving devices, slipping over into the black-box mysticism of American mechanical consciousness. Cars fitted with them tended to proceed in sloppy, moaning fluidity; engines roared, transmissions slowly gathered themselves into action and then grabbed when the workings inside were ready to move, rather than the driver. The driver rarely knew much about his progress through the internally programmed, self-directing management of his gear ratios and engine speed. Millions of development dollars were spent defeating "creep," the tendency of the automatic to want to make the car go at times when the driver wanted to make it sit still—usually at stoplights, when the combination of a fast idle (product of another misbehaving automatic control, this time on the choke) and a "creepy" transmission would attempt to pull the car forward into the stream of cross traffic. Whatever the malfunction, the mechanic's litany was, "I think your bands are slipping, mister." Who could argue with him?

This singular major innovation in automotive technology could, however, eventually be domesticated. It could be smoothed. It was predicated on waste, substituting either fluid or friction slippage for direct mechanical linkage, which meant that if it got somewhere within the general ball park of its design task, the car would function. Then, there was a small benefit to the driver. The automatic cancelled the shock of transition from unmoving to moving. An inept driver could make a car that was equipped with an automatic *go* more smoothly. The rough edges of sensation were smoothed, the pulsations from the power source damped out. The driver was further insulated from precise information about his progress. Moving was more like not-moving, which was, to some drivers, reassuring.

Detroit giveth and Detroit taketh away. The automatic transmission removed us, as operators, from the category of engineers and mechanics, boosted us to that social class which doesn't have to know about things like gears and clutches. We no longer had to accrue any skills in order to manage our own private transportation. The driver no longer had to do all that tedious "work" of moving levers and operating pedals. Less bother. And there was even a safety argument: by simplifying the task, reducing the number of operations, the automatic diminished the distractions from the essential task of pointing the car down the road, of not hitting anything.

There is a profound and as yet unplumbed enigma to thinking about automotive safety. Since the safety crisis first began to make Detroit nervous, the industry has explained to us that driver education was the key to reducing the slaughter—"the nut behind the wheel," and all that. Yet domestic automotive design philosophy since World War II has been almost wholly directed at reducing driver involvement. The machine has been designed to supply everything needed to a barely flickering consciousness behind the wheel. Further innovations—air conditioning, power steering, power brakes, tinted glass, automatic speed controls—have heightened the insulation. Living-room interiors—the phrase comes from the car ads—complete with stereo tape decks and plush carpets; there is no need to acknowledge the difference between hearth and highway. We must sharpen the attention, hone fine the skills of our automobile drivers, say the manufacturers—giving us products calculated to drive human minds and bodies into a state of soporific doze.

None of this quasi-philosophical level of consideration had anything to do, however, with the development of the automatic transmission. Oldsmobile put the thing on some of its cars in 1939, it gave people something to talk about—people who bought 1940 Oldsmobiles *did* give their neighbors rides around the block. And Oldsmobile threatened to pick up some percentage points of market share. Go catch Oldsmobile. The cost of developing the automatic transmission to its present "satisfactory" state is uncountable. The average cost to the consumer is approximately $175 over list price. The industry sold us 7.6 million automatic transmissions in 1971. That's $1.3 *billion* extra gross, over standard equipment.

And in 1966, a new technological marvel was unveiled. In 1966, for a little extra money over what you paid extra for an automatic transmission, you could get a special *new* automatic transmission. With it, if you wanted to, whenever the notion struck, you could still shift by hand, through the gears, just like a manual.

A Machine to Steer the Machine

In the race to see what device could pamper the customer most, the successor to the automatic transmission was power steering. Most of the car ads of the mid-fifties, when power steering was first coming into popularity, carried an inset showing a dainty, gloved feminine hand, a diamond bracelet perhaps dangling from the wrist, index finger extended to rest lightly on the steering wheel, indicating that no matter how debilitatingly feminine the prospective owner's heritage might be (cars are a man's world, see?), she would be able to twirl her four-thousand-pound pleasure craft about as idly and imperiously as she might dial a telephone. Poor-little-rich-girl women drivers would now have a machine to help them steer the machine.

Power steering was an abomination in its earlier forms for feminist and masculinist alike. It insulated the operator not from his power source, as did the automatic transmission, but from the very sense of where, precisely, the machine was headed. The introduction of artificial hydraulic boost between driver and road was disorienting to drivers who had learned with non-power-steering cars, who had learned to rely on their sense of touch for a great deal of information about things such as skids, changes in pavement texture, surface variations, even the condition of the front tires. An experienced driver's first introduction to power steering was almost invariably one of dismay: there was this wall of *fluid* between him and the information he'd come to rely on. Not a few drivers destroyed a front tire completely by driving on it grossly underinflated, simply because the information generated by the malfunction couldn't get through the machinery to the driver's fingertips. There is no estimating how many drivers went off roads because they could no longer feel the delicate sensory transition from a condition of steering control to that of front-wheel skid.

But power steering sold. One must assume it was purchased in the early days by the infirm, the elderly, the debilitated, but also by the gadget-hungry, more interested in being *au courant* than in knowing what was going on at the front wheels of the car. Undoubtedly a great many power steering units were sold to the unwary and the uninformed. But interestingly enough, there was one other group of buyers, at the other end of the consumer spectrum. The car nuts, the enthusiasts, detested the insulatory capacity of power steering, but they bought it anyway, because there was no other way to get "quick" steering on an American car.

It is interesting that while Detroit has offered more and more horsepower, quickening the accelerative capacity of its products in quantum leaps over three decades, the manufacturers steadfastly refused for most of the same period to quicken the other controls of the car. Acceleration, yes, ever faster, and if that acceleration happens to be *into* danger, that's your own affair, driver responsibility. But provide the means to steer more quickly out of danger, or stop before it? No, that is dangerous. Americans are used to leisurely steering, a gradual transition from the straight ahead to the turning mode. Anything else, in the industry view, would make more danger rather than less. It might make us nervous. (Any driver who has ever experienced the quicker steering of the standard European car knows that it may take a block or two before one becomes accustomed to the faster response—and after that the fast action is extremely reassuring. But no domestic manufacturer wants to risk that a first impression of his product might be colored by that initial unsureness.)

The more practical reason for not providing faster steering

in domestic cars was, of course, the weight. With four thousand pounds of gross weight, well over half of it pressing directly on the two small patches of front-tire rubber, considerable force was required to steer the wheels at all. By providing slow manual steering with a high mechanical advantage, the amount of force required at the steering wheel rim could be kept—marginally—within reason.

Power steering provided the force that allowed faster steering ratios, finally, and the enthusiasts were willing to give up road feel for quicker reaction. (It seems likely that in line with other trends during the fifties toward insulating options, power steering was chosen specifically by many buyers because they *preferred* a lack of road feel. It is that kind of consumer response which has made the technological approach to automotive safety so difficult and confusing.) Like the automatic transmission, power steering has gotten progressively better through the years, and the most modern versions give fairly accurate control, a measure—simulated— of road feel, and almost none of the dithering wobble that characterized early units. The best of the modern systems even have variable power boost: less assistance in the sensitive narrow arc required for highway speeds, and more artificial muscle for slow-speed, gross corrections, as in parking. Power steering could, in the end, be made to work, if enough time and money were poured into it. Nobody ever said American engineers couldn't cope. As it happened, the industry was driven to that "perfection." By 1970, rapidly rising car weights put non-power-assisted steering out of the question for all but the most muscular of us, and power steering became standard equipment on most full-sized American cars. The device captured 81 percent of the market in 1970.

Fade-out Time

Power-assisted brakes have also become standard equipment on most big American cars since the turn of the decade, for most of the same reasons as power steering plus one fortunate additional reason. Disc brakes have now become common on the domestic automobile, and discs need power assistance. (Unlike drum brakes, discs have no self-servo effect—no self-energizing capacity—and thus need more operating pressure.* A few of the lighter new small cars with disc brakes need no power assistance—yet—but for large cars, power is almost a necessity.) The domestic industry coolly resisted the adoption of disc brakes long after such resistance passed the bounds of moral propriety. Chrysler attempted to introduce the feature in the early fifties, without much success. It was left to Studebaker, in its dying year of automobile production, to embarrass the other manufacturers into getting serious about discs. That was in 1964, and problems of manufacturing capacity held up general availability of discs for several more years.

For most of the golden era Detroit preferred to ignore the technological end, the braking systems themselves where actual gains could be made in the stopping capacity of the cars. Instead, the manufacturers concentrated on the consumer end, on what one could almost refer to as a sensory cosmetic: reducing brake-pedal pressure, so the frailest dam-

---

* Self-servo" is a bit misleading. When you apply the brakes in a conventional drum-brake arrangement, the *forward* motion of the car helps pull the brake shoe into contact with the drum, by mechanical means—giving you in effect additional mechanical assistance, and helping reduce brake-pedal pressure. Unfortunately, the same thing isn't true in reverse—which is why parking brakes often don't work so well when the car is parked so it can roll backwards down an incline.

osel could easily completely lock up all four wheels on her overweight chariot. She might not be able to *stop* it—might very well find herself, after locking the brakes, struggling for control of a skidding monster—but she could with very little physical effort jam the wheels to prevent them from turning. You can't ask for much more braking than that, can you? The capacity to lock the wheels, that's total braking, isn't it?

That argument has driven car critics into rages of frustration. The critics for years have rated the braking capacity of the domestic automobile from marginal all the way down to criminal, but the marginality is difficult to prove, requiring among other things a violation of habitual American driving patterns. In reasonable working order, any standard set of hydraulically actuated drum brakes—as universally supplied by 1955—would lock all four wheels if applied hard enough. Would do it once, in a panic-stop situation. Would, if given a chance to cool and recoup, even accomplish the same thing a second time. The rare, perfectly balanced and adjusted set might even do it a third time.

But locking up a wheel so that it skids cancels most of the tire's grip on the pavement, increasing stopping distances by as much as 40 or 50 percent—and in the case of the front wheels, also wiping out steering capacity, since a skidding wheel has lost the grip on the road it needs to steer the car. Given the capability of locking the wheels as the merest starting point, braking effectiveness can then be improved by a raft of changes to the tried-and-true domestic format, changes not beyond the capability of Detroit but apparently simply outside the industry's interest. Those changes involve such things as revised vehicle balance, more sophisticated suspension geometry, shock-absorber modification away from the pillowy ride and toward the capability of keeping tires in contact with the pavement. Such changes can be made within what reasonable men would agree are acceptable ride levels, as various European cars have proved. When it comes to "ride," however, Detroit is far from reasonable.

The problem of locked wheels reducing braking effectiveness could be remedied immediately with lockproof or "antiskid" braking systems. Large aircraft have been fitted with such devices for decades; the British successfully applied one to a racing car in the early sixties. Ford Motor Company finally brought out a rudimentary skidproof braking system in 1969—and made it available only on the luxury Thunderbird and Continental Mark III. As optional equipment, antiskid devices now cost about two hundred dollars. Mercedes-Benz is currently tooling up for production of a superbly effective antiskid system, and has offered open access to the system to other interested manufacturers. An official of Mercedes-Benz, commenting on that firm's hopes to have the unit as standard equipment by the fall of 1973, inadvertently pointed up the difference in attitudes toward safety equipment between his firm and Detroit: "How can we sell some cars that are safer than others, even by option?" [9] It seems likely that a federal requirement for antiskid systems as standard equipment on all American cars might produce a more significant level of social gain than low-speed impactproof bumpers—which seem to be aimed principally at lowering repair costs, post accident—and at a lower cost on a mass-production basis. Such an accessory is so far required only on the federal safety-car research projects, which are a long way from the nation's highways for the near future.

Power-assisted brakes dissociate the driver from the physical reality of what's going on between car and road surface much as power steering does. They cancel out a great deal of the sensory feedback that tells you how effectively your tires are gripping the road in a braking situation. They also cancel out any information that you might have gotten about how well the brake system itself is working. That isn't as important now, with the stopping power and reliability of disc brakes, as it was during those fifteen years of heavily merchandised power-plus-drums. During that time, the industry chose to ignore almost totally the problem of brake "fade."

Brake fade is easy to demonstrate. I once experienced a stuck throttle on a fully loaded, power-brake-equipped (drum brakes, of course) Oldsmobile station wagon, vintage early sixties. The first time the car continued to accelerate when I lifted my foot from the gas, I made the mistake of trying to stop the car with the brake. After three lengthy and progressively harder applications of the brake—with no change in speed—I woke up to the problem, gave up on the brakes, and freed the accelerator pedal by hand. At that point the brakes were simply gone, completely faded, and I literally could not bring the car to a halt until I had driven on for a few miles to give the brakes time to cool.

That's brake fade. It happens regularly when a non-disc-brake-equipped car is pushed to the limit of its braking capability—although brake fade is more familiarly evinced by sporadic or alternate locking of different wheels on the car, causing the vehicle to slew sideways, sometimes uncontrollably. Most car testers would prefer to use a multistop test to measure braking reliability. Five or six hard, fast stops from, say, 60 MPH, at intervals only long enough to allow acceleration back up to 60 MPH again. Most golden-era cars will not pass such a test (even with front disc brakes). Domestic driving habits seldom punish a set of brakes that severely. If we did, our already disastrous accident rate would undoubtedly go even higher. (Less genteel driving habits—as common in Europe—have forced their brake development to outstrip our own.)

Brake fade occurs on drum brakes when hard usage generates enough heat to warp the shoes away from total contact with the drum. (Precisely the same characteristic that makes overheated drum brakes ineffective is commonly used in bimetallic thermostats, to make and break electrical contacts. The drum brake attempts to ignore physics.) Disc brakes, by contrast, use spot linings mounted on clamping calipers; there is no way the disc can warp away from the enveloping lining. Disc brakes are exposed to the cooling air stream, are self-cleaning from a combination of centrifugal force and the wiping action of the pads, and can be relined by a repairman (or owner) in three to five minutes. The first disc brake was put on an automobile in 1902. Detroit chose to develop drums; pedal pressures were less.

Morality. We try to regulate traffic patterns with morality also. Most folks don't drive all that fast, and don't need to make panic stops very often. One panic stop, okay, anybody can get in a jam. But anybody who needs to make a second panic stop before his brakes have cooled from the first is just asking for it, isn't he? So we'll have brakes good enough to stop the wheels from turning, lock 'em up, one time. (If I'd hit the brakes *hard,* initially, in that Oldsmobile, they'd have worked well enough to lock the wheels—and I'd have been in a skid. By applying them gradually, I heated them up and faded them out before I called on their full stopping powers—and therefore they were all gone by the time I discovered the problem.)

There is another side to the morality question, of course. It may seem self-evident to you and me that the first faint blush of social responsibility would make certain that cars be given the very best braking systems that engineers can design—good enough, for example, at least to overcome the power of the engine, since from a safety viewpoint stopping can be a lot more important than going. What is self-evident to you and me is not necessarily self-evident to Detroit. Ford didn't even abandon mechanical brakes for hydraulic ones until late in the thirties, long after everyone else had given up on the lack of reliability and impossibly high pedal pressures of the mechanical linkage. Dual hydraulic systems for brakes were not introduced until 1962, and then by Rambler, with only 6 percent of the market. Discs were common in Europe in the fifties, were introduced into the U.S. market in 1964, and as of this writing (post-1972 models) are still not standard across the board on domestic cars. Nonskid braking is yet off in the misty future for all but the very affluent. How *can* we sell some cars that are safer than others, even by option?

The age of accessories: engines, transmissions, steering, brakes. A certain tendency manifests itself, a predilection for overpowering the problem. When technological intelligence fails, pile more power on top, in hopes the oversupply will trickle down to absorb the jangling harshnesses of inadequate engineering. In hopes that the customers' wide-eyed wonder at ever another machine to insert between man and function will preclude examination of either machine *or* function. Putting toys on toys; including toys to help you play with your toy. *Big* engines to power the toys (our symbolic Chevy V-8 was smaller than any V-8 now offered in American cars). Automatic transmissions, power steering; already there is talk of machines (computers, of course) to take over those functions also. Power boost for drum brakes, an artificial barrier to prevent knowing how badly the function is being performed. Enough in these accessories to make a bad machine, in and of themselves? Perhaps not quite. To try to pick the single symbol of the decline of the automobile is to stagger in bewilderment among the dazzling array of appropriate choices. But perhaps it is not a gadget at all that finally betrayed the car. Perhaps it is the vision behind the machine, the philosophy that generates such waste. That philosophy created the automobile's brief fifteen-year golden era, created both a product and an industrial structure doomed by their inability to respond or be modified to suit the changing demands of a rapidly fragmenting society. It is a philosophy that larded every single element of its own universe with excess. It is impossible to say now whether the historians will decide, post automobile, that the society fled the automobile or that the automobile collapsed of its own weight. But in either case, weight—as we will see next—was a singularly important characteristic.

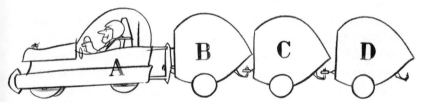

CHAPTER 2

En Route to a Bad Machine

Technological Obesity

"3860 LBS. OF SOLID COMFORT," said the headline on a Chevrolet Impala ad for 1965. By the end of the golden era the natural evolution of that car had added approximately 140 pounds of miscellaneous sheet metal and mechanical complexity. Car manufacturing being the process that it is, one can only assume that the Impala was held to the four-thousand-pound figure by a strict program of weight *reduction,* but if that was the case, the fellows at the ad agency would have been the last to hear of it. (I speak from experience—I was one of the fellows at the ad agency at the time of the 1965 ad quoted above.) Old myths die hard. Although the process of writing ads about full-sized American cars does involve a lot of energetic burrowing through the specification pages, in the attempt to find some little feature on which it is safe to hang an ad, this was not the case in the Impala weight ad mentioned above. In this case, the agency *believed.* Chevrolet's Sales Department had long ago decided that what the American public really wanted— if it couldn't afford a Cadillac—was "a big, heavy car," one that would "hold the road." Far be it from the ad agency to question the gospel according to Chevrolet Sales.

Now weight is a valuable characteristic in bridges, office buildings, dams, and other large structures whose functionality is enhanced by a certain permanence of location. Weight is not an asset, however, in physical objects intended to be moved. Cars are intended to be moved. This principle is somewhat simplistic, but easy to lose sight of when reflecting on the domestic automobile.

Weight is what must be put into motion from rest, kept in motion while motion is desired, arrested from motion when that need arises; the more weight that is involved, the harder each of these is to accomplish. Heavy cars need more gasoline to move, and more braking power (and tire rubber) to stop. Weight increases wear on engines, tires, suspension systems, shock absorbers, brakes, on *all* mechanical parts, as surely as a fat man wears out his shoes more rapidly than a thin man. Make a car heavier and you must then beef up all those parts which wear, which means you make the car heavier yet, which means you must beef up still further, in a never-ending Möbius strip of design patchwork. And, of course, as weight goes up, engine power must be increased to keep performance levels the same. Increasing engine power almost invariably adds weight.

Is the weight worth the price? As it happens, the peculiar advantage of the familiar sales pitch—"it'll hold the road better"—is best obtained by reducing weight, rather than adding to it. A heavy car does *not* hold the road better, unless that road is a mirror-smooth perfect straight line. Put in a ripple, a bump, a deflection, a turn of any kind, and a heavy car must fight its own groaning inertia to respond. More force is necessary to get a 4000-pound car around a curve than to get a 3000-pound car around the same curve. The turning force must come from the front tires which steer, and therefore from effort applied at the rim of the steering wheel. Effort of course being inimical to Detroit's concept of saleable cars, the solution is power steering, which doesn't reduce the load on the components of the car, but which does reduce the effort supplied by the driver. Power steering adds more weight to the car. So it goes.

The engineers who each year must fulfill in metal the fantasies of the sales and accounting departments are perfectly well aware of the detrimental effect of weight addition. They sweat blood over every component, shaving ounces wherever they can to keep the final product capable of at least some kind of stately motion. Their motives are not purely oriented to product superiority; bluntly put, metal costs money, and a pound per car on a million new Chevrolets is five hundred tons of steel. Juggling the unacceptable alternatives is the name of the game. (The styling of new cars took a pendulum swing between 1955 and 1970, for example, toward more glass area—sold to us in the name of better visibility, and therefore a demonstrable and perfectly sincere benefit—and then back again to *less* glass area—sold to us as fashionable new privacy. What happened was that the public good got too expensive: steel prices have risen more slowly than glass prices. Look for more privacy in the next few years from Detroit.)

I once tried to convince some fellow copywriters at Campbell-Ewald, Chevrolet's ad agency, of the basic illogic of trumpeting a car's gross weight as a virtue. If weight equals goodness, I pointed out, the engineers could bloody well pour the passenger compartment floor out of concrete, and pick up a cheap ton or so of goodness, not to mention gaining quite a bit of sound insulation in the bargain. Pennies for concrete instead of dollars for steel. To continue to make bold of the fact that our products were tip-toeing toward four thousand pounds was, in effect, to let the public know that Chevrolet had absolutely lost control of any kind of rationality in car design. We went right ahead advertising weight. It turned out that the chairman of the board of the agency liked a big, heavy car. You know, one that holds the road.

In 1963 Ford developed a new thin-wall casting technique that resulted in a better engine at a savings of about a hundred pounds. A hundred pounds removed from a modern V-8 is no mean feat; shave it off the engine, and you can lighten every other component in the car, right down the line. I asked a Ford engineer if the new casting technique would result in lighter Fords. "I doubt it," he said. "You can't do everything at once, and we have to amortize costs over the long run. Sure, we could probably cut a lot of weight off the front suspension right now, but we redesigned the front suspension last year, and we've got a fantastic investment in tooling for the new design we've got. The way it works out is that we'll maybe get ten pounds off the drive train next year, and something off the rear axle the year after that. That way maybe in ten years we can go through the whole car, cutting what weight we can.

"But you have to remember that the engine guys will be working those ten years too. Next year they're going to be asked to get more power out of the unit, and the year after that maybe add some accessories. If they pick up ten pounds per year, in ten years there's that one hundred pounds back on the engine—and so we can't reduce weight everywhere else after all."

There is a single aspect of a car's performance in which total weight is, by default, a benefit: "ride." Ride is something of a nebulous, subjective area, a little like star quality in an actress or charisma in a politician. It has to do with things like vibration damping and harmonic frequencies of spring rates and the sensitivity of the passenger's middle ear. During our golden era, the manufacturers began using computers quite heavily to juggle the multitude of variables influencing ride, to track down and isolate tiny vibrations and the like.

All other things being equal, if you keep constant the weight of tires, wheels, brakes, axles—those parts which don't have springs between them and the road—and increase the weight of the rest of the car, the ride will be improved. So will the handling or roadability, the car's ability to keep its wheels in contact with the pavement. The alternative to increasing the weight of the "sprung" portion of the car, while keeping the unsprung weight constant, is of course to keep the sprung weight constant and shave pounds off the wheels, axles, brakes, etc. This alternative is the method used to improve road-holding of racing cars, and incidentally results in a level of "ride" that compares favorably, on the more sophisticated racing cars, with anything ever produced by Cadillac or Rolls Royce. But in the mass-produced automobile, technological obesity—read "amortization costs"—precludes such sophistication. So the cars get fatter.

There is nothing immoral about amortizing tooling costs over long runs—it's a technique that has enabled Detroit to keep the costs as low as they have while they've lost control of the tonnage of their products. Because of amortization, we buy all that steel at a remarkably cheap price, all things considered. Nor are the engineers irresponsible, in this saga of ballooning avoirdupois. They must live with the problems that growing weight causes, anyway. But when the crunch comes on an engineering problem, and the decision must be made between adding poundage by beefing up, or retooling to avoid the problem, the scales are, one might say, already weighted. Particularly when the rationale for adding weight is ready and waiting: "It'll help the ride."

For ride, anything goes. Modern suspension theory, grossly simplified, says that good ride and road-holding are best achieved by providing a rigid chassis mounted on soft suspension. One constructs a basic chassis structure with as close to total rigidity as possible, then hangs the wheels on its corners so they can comply with surface variations without causing gross deflections of the chassis attitude. (It's also important to keep the wheels in contact with maximum areas of the road surface. That's where suspension design starts getting complicated.)

In the early days of the automobile, the classic chassis was made of large, parallel girders—"frame rails"—with stiffening cross-members. Some additional stiffness was derived from the boxlike body which was fitted, in essence, on top of the frame rails. In search of additional stiffness (and for some other benefits), the "unit-body" was developed. A box is stiffer (that is, resists torsional strains better) than a ladder; the unit-body was a complex but effective solution in which the automobile body structure evolved into a load-bearing element in and of itself. The unit-body eliminated the frame rails, a lot of weight, and a lot of rattles. A unit-bodied car was more all of a piece; its loads were distributed over wider areas, much like the sheet-metal equivalent of the tubular chassis used in airplanes and much more highly stressed racing cars. There were problems from the unit-body—resonant body panels were difficult to quiet, and complex structures made annual model changes more expensive—but the direction of the evolution of the automobile seemed to be clear. The cost of the changeover was estimated at $80 million for Chrysler Corporation alone, but it seemed worth it. With considerable ingenuity, Detroit began ringing variations on the unit-body itself: unit substructures which could be revised more cheaply and which offered greater opportunities for noise control. The unit-body was a beautifully simple idea that became a bit complex in the realization, but it was clearly a giant step forward beyond the frame-rail chassis.

By the end of the golden era, the unit-body was a dead issue. It had been replaced by something called a perimeter frame, which means a smaller, weaker, and incredibly more complex version of the old frame rails; plus a larger, stretched-out, load-bearing exterior shell. In 1965 the domestic industry turned in its tracks, adopted this "new" idea almost wholesale, and began selling the public its revised version of a concept that was obsolete in 1930 as an "advance." The reason for this reversion to Model-T technology? Ride. The perimeter frame concept is easier to tune for quiet, for absorption of high-frequency vibrations, for that soporific silken ease that Detroit seems to believe the sensitive backside of the American public requires.

The perimeter frame is fiendishly complex, which means it has thousands more junctures to misalign themselves on the automated production lines, to come apart during the rigors of everyday use, to admit corrosion; but which also means thousands more places to stuff rubber wedges and strips and washers and doughnuts to prevent the realities of the road surface from impinging on the insulated sensibilities of the occupants. And that was worth the immense expense of the switch back from unit-bodies.[1]

Peculiarly enough, ride seems to sell. Road-holding doesn't. Economy of operation, reliability, repairability, safety, any of a half-dozen other obviously significant automotive attributes which a consumer might rationally demand from his purchase, have seemed to be absolute duds in the marketplace—at least in the consistent interpretation of the industry's merchandising wing, throughout the golden era. But ride—an ephemera almost as intangible as "styling"—is a substantial enough consideration for the largest auto-maker in the world to hang its every advertising pitch on. "Jet-Smooth Ride"—you saw it in every Chevrolet ad for fifteen years. Nobody ever figured out what it was supposed to mean, even at the ad agency that kept perpetrating it.

We didn't give a fig for safety in the golden era. For some reason we stopped worrying about massive and painful intrusions on our ponderous travel capsules. Instead, we wanted all the *little* intrusions removed, the jiggles and jounces that would inform us that we were, in fact, in motion. Ride. We wanted quiet, softness, encapsulation. All the sensory information except the visual damped out: the windshield turned into a giant TV screen. We wanted to move, but we wanted insulation from the world we moved through.

La Belle Epoque

If Detroit's technological energies were poured into such inconsequentialities as ride, its creative fires were totally absorbed by "styling." What started with the decision to give the perfectly vertical and perfectly serviceable windshield a bit of a rakish slant to the rear in the late twenties grew into an obsession that has long since dominated the industry. Detroit was happy to admit it. GM stylist Harley Earl invented a name for it, thinly euphemistic though it was: dynamic obsolescence. It was supposed to sound vaguely patriotic. Earl claimed that product improvements would make for early replacement, fueling the economy; in practice it became the abandonment of quality for novelty. Not only did they no longer make 'em the way they used to, but now they were bragging about it. Not long after mobility was displaced as the prime consideration in the conception of new automobiles, integrity was similarly discarded.

It has long been an article of faith in the industry that the public can't tell an independent suspension from a hood ornament. Stylist Charles Jordan put it this way: "For economic reasons, the mechanical assemblies couldn't be frequently changed, since no sales appeal lay in changing them when the result had no dramatic effect on performance. This evolutionary engineering of the car's functional parts tended to promote near-sameness in the products of all major competitors. This, in turn, opened the eyes and ears of company management to the arguments of the men who could provide visible change under these conditions—the stylists." [2]

Thus the golden age of the industry became the age of the stylists. First indications of this came in the late fifties, when some radical experimentation was going on in wheel and tire sizes. Although wheel and tire dimensions are crucial to suspension design and tuning, braking capacity, and ride control, it turns out that the new specifications were being handed down by the stylists. If they wanted to lower the car an inch for the next year, and the only place an inch could be gotten off was at the wheel, then presto, that was it, and it was up to engineering to cope, to try to put back whatever capabilities had been taken away by the reduction. It was the styling department, not the engineers, who were responsible for such absurdities of the past as four-thousand-pound cars on thirteen-inch wheels.

It wasn't long before the stylists were designing whole cars. "The product planning committee, working closely with the stylists, had chosen the prototype and had approved the basic sheet metal and two body styles—*before* it informed the development engineers at Ford. Sheet metal, glass, bumpers and moldings of the vehicle were new, while the chassis, engine, suspension and drive-line components were copies of Ford's Falcon and the Fairlane models." [3] The commentator is the dread Nader; the car, of course, the Mustang, the ultimate pheenom of the golden age. Nobody ever pretended it was anything more than a warmed-over and reshaped Falcon, except the ad agency; no new car ever sold better in its introductory year. Something magic had been done with the sheet metal which was wrapped around the tired old Falcon. Detroit's convictions were confirmed once again; success didn't have anything to do with building better cars.

When "difference" sells cars, and there is no difference to be had among the multitudes, then the illusion of difference must be staged. A whole new set of similar differences every year. Sock it to 'em with styling. The stylists wrought. Hardtops: the illusion of convertibility, at the expense of the structural integrity of the sedan. Wraparound windshields: the illusion of increased visibility, when in fact vision was severely distorted by the device. The wraparound windshield introduced a breakthrough in styling and sales promotion. After a model year or two, when public enthusiasm for visual distortion began to wane, the stylists came up with another service for humanity. They would eliminate the "dog-leg" notch in the front door and the corresponding protruding corner of windshield molding on which we were continually smashing our knees as we got in and out of our cars. This meant they were taking credit for taking away the wraparound windshield that they'd taken credit for giving us in the first place. The tactic became an important new technique of the idea-starved promotion forces, saddled with the virtually impossible task of coming up with new descriptive superlatives every year for the zig in the fender that took the place of last year's zag. The Academy Award for scriptwriting in this field goes to the headlight boys, who somehow went from single to dual headlights, arranged the duals horizontally, then vertically, even diagonally, then horizontally again, put them inside mechanical eyelids, brought them back out again, and finally went back to single headlights—"classic simplicity"—and made every single step of the progression into a consumer benefit.

Styling. Bumper bombs, hood ornaments, tail fins, little eyebrows over lights and windows. Portholes, chrome spears, stripes, louvers, wings. "Sculptured metal," which meant that last year's protrusion would be this year's recess, and vice versa. ("Sculptured metal" also means, "maybe we can go to a lighter gauge of metal in that panel if we put a groove down it to work as a stiffener.") Parking and taillights that veer back and forth, from year to year, from round to square and back again, sometimes taking entire styling "themes" with them. Bumpers that float and bumpers that don't, that wrap pool-table-sized expanses of sheet metal in swaddling chrome, that pander to sexual fetish, that indicate that the car is a luxury speedboat or a jet fighter in disguise; but that do not, God forbid, do any bumping. Jukebox instrument panels which steadily lost their capacity to inform as they grew more ornate, whose very instruments were taken away as ribs and swaths and panels and decor were added—imitation Carpathian burled elm was the last I recall hearing about. Styling even of tires: thick whitewalls and then thin ones, then dual stripes, triple, *red* "whitewalls," or most recently, blackwalls with raised "bold" (thick) colored lettering proclaiming brand names and trademarks, so that the tires become billboards—for themselves.

And grilles. Water-cooled cars used to need a hole in the front of the body to admit air to the radiator; later some kind of grillwork was put over that hole to catch the large stones and other missiles which might damage that radiator. The grillwork became a design element. Classic marques used a distinctive shape as a badge of identification (Rolls Royce, Mercedes-Benz, Bugatti, Packard), in an early wave of car worship. Since 1955 no American stylist has been able to keep his hands off a grille long enough to allow its shape to do more than flicker across the public consciousness. (Possible exception: the ill-fated Edsel, the grille of which gave it what wags called "the vaginal look.") Instead, every conceivable shape into which cheap chrome-plated pot metal could be cast or extruded was explored; a lot of them have been ridiculous, none of them has been sublime, and the domestic car hasn't needed one of them for better than fifteen years.*

Styling cycles give a clear indication of the substitution of production engineering for product engineering. At the beginning of the modern era, three full years were required between drawing board and showroom floor, for engineering, testing, tooling, corporate approval, production, etc., with the main portion of the period going to retooling delays. By 1970 the industry had poured enough research and development into its own methods, and had streamlined its operations sufficiently (particularly with the aid of computer controls), that significant model changes could be effected in midyear. That means that a new model could be gotten into the showroom, public reaction to it judged (or errors that need correction discovered), and the modification that was called for could be put into production by the midpoint of the model year. Of course when the federal government began asking for modifications—the ones that might aid pollu-

---

* Okay, cars still need holes to allow cooling air to the radiators, and some protection for the radiator (when fitted—there is none on air-cooled cars). They're unlikely to get that protection from grilles of the past fifteen years. As evidence that the grille is more symbolic than functional, one must consider what removal of this symbol does to the public consciousness. At least two grilleless rear-engined cars—the Corvair and the Karmann-Ghia Volkswagen—have looked so strange to the public that accessory manufacturers have marketed dummy grilles for them, falsies to fake the necessary hole-in-the-front that a car just somehow *needs*.

tion control or enhance the safety of the products, but which did not add to their saleability—the old three-year lead time was resurrected as an alibi. (Chevrolet built a working pollution control valve in 1924.)

Finally, the hysteria generated by styling domination of the industry was to become unbearable. The pace was too hectic, too expensive; there were even hints that it was becoming counterproductive in generating sales. John Burby, at one time assistant to Secretary of Transportation Alan S. Boyd, describes the end of the stylists' era. Pointing out that General Motors, Ford, and Chrysler build 97 percent of the cars made in this country, Burby said:

> Operating with that degree of market control, the automobile industry has been able, and obviously delighted, to concentrate its creative energies on bucket seats, hidden windshield wipers, peekaboo headlights, exotic shades of blue serge, Coke bottle styling, and the noise car doors make when they slam. The industry's leaders were designers and salesmen, not engineers. With the market relatively fixed at eight million cars a year, the only way to make a profit on its investment was to produce bigger and more expensive automobiles. The styling concept of dynamic obsolescence, designed to make Americans feel ashamed of a car that was more than a year old, died in 1969, less by choice probably than by chance. With money getting tighter and competition from abroad eating into its market, Detroit simply decided to forego the $200 per car which the manufacturers said it cost them for new styling. The cost had once been estimated as high as $700 a car in a study by Professors Franklin M. Fisher of MIT, Zvi Griliches of the University of Chicago and Carl Kaysen of Harvard. They also found that, because of the increase in horsepower during the 1950's, the average motorist paid $40 a year more for his gasoline. But while it was boosting horsepower, Detroit left the initiative to others to improve safety, to devise pollution controls, to preserve the lives of pedestrians and of historic monuments which got in the way of the car.[4]

En Route to a Bad Machine

Mr. Burby's rhetoric is effective, but his dismissal of the annual styling change was a bit premature. In 1971, General Motors completely redesigned all of its big-car bodies—Chevrolet, Pontiac, Oldsmobile, Buick, and Cadillac—in what the corporation proudly claimed was the most expensive styling change in the history of the automobile.

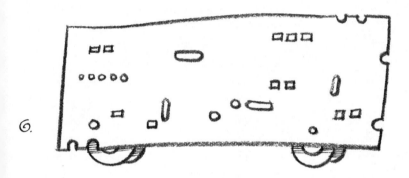

CHAPTER 3

The Fruition of the Golden Era

The Beast Entire

If we would fully understand what the golden era has meant to the individual consumer, we must examine the total automobile, the beast entire. To consider properly the total automobile, we must go to the apogee, the ultimate dreamboat, the highest statement of the domestic, mass-production car-maker's art and method. It is not, perhaps surprisingly, the Cadillac, which is admittedly a kind of metal-worker's Platonic ideal of excess, but which, freed from the strictures of really *mass* mass production, can be allowed to bloom with the Detroit version of "quality" as it balloons in price. (Half the thrill of Cadillac-buying must be in contemplating the price; few purchasers seem to care what it costs, so long as it is Cadillac, the most expensive American car.)

Neither is our industrial high-water mark the long-dead Model T Ford, the most successful car in history, with fifteen million vehicles built in nineteen production years. Nor can we consider what at this writing is the second-best seller in history, the Volkswagen, with thirteen million cars in thirty war-interrupted years. Both of these cars were created from philosophies so different from the principles that guided the golden era that they almost seem to represent solutions, rather than contributions, to the car problem. But instead, for a truly representative total automobile, we go to the 1970 Impala, the number one car from the number one division of the number one corporation in the entire world. The standard of the golden age.

(You don't know what an Impala is? Well, that's a problem. Everyone knows what a Cadillac is, everyone knew the Model T. Nobody has been able to *avoid* knowing what a Volkswagen is. But in the modern proliferation of nameplates, the flood of Monacos and Cutlasses and Novas, Torinos, Satellites, Furies, Camaros, Electras and Toronados, what, indeed, is an Impala? Who knows what a Ford *is,* or a Chevrolet? Ford and Chevrolet have overcome this identity crisis, obviously, depending on saturation and high-pressure merchandising, and a rare degree of customer sophistication, but the problem still exists. It's getting worse. People just don't seem to *care* any more about what the difference is between a Matador and a Monterey.)

Chevrolet introduced the Impala as a "new" car (meaning, in this period of merchandising, "Impala" is the name we're giving the most expensive model this year) in 1958, as the period of wide-ranging customer-ordered optional accessories began to flower. Before thirteen years of production life had passed, the Impala had sold more than ten million units. In 1965 well over a million Impalas were sold, comprising 11 percent of the market for a single model, exclusive of other Chevrolet products. That year—as most years—the Impala outsold all its direct competitors—Ford Galaxie, Plymouth Fury, Dodge Coronet, Pontiac Catalina—*combined*.[1]

In the heydey of the golden era the "big" cars made up about 80 percent of the market; that share has since slipped to 20 percent and is still dwindling. The term "big" cars is confusing; by "big" I mean the full-sized standard-bearers for the manufacturer—the above direct competitors for the Impala and their equivalents in more expensive price classes from other car companies. The confusion gets worse. In 1965, when the Impala was securing 11 percent of the market, Chevrolet Motor Division also produced the Caprice ("above"—more expensive than—the Impala in the model line-up; one critic described it as "a forty-five-hundred-dollar crypto-Caddie for the proles" [2]); three versions of the Impala series (Impala, Bel Air, Biscayne—all three, with the Caprice, sharing a single body shell and mechanical parts); three versions of the Chevelle series (the "intermediate" size of the day, probably destined soon to become the big car in the line); three versions of the Chevy II series (smaller yet); the Corvair (a rear-engined specialty car hanging grimly on against Ralph Nader's onslaughts), and the Corvette (a limited production sports car—about twenty-five thousand per year). Add the wagons in two series; a few convertibles still sprinkled through the line; two-door, four-door, hardtop and sedan models across the board (and two- and four-door wagons); three, four, maybe six engine options for each size category, plus three separate transmissions.

Consider that while Chevrolet is generally conceded to have the broadest spread of model availability, the competitors over at Ford and Chrysler—and, to a lesser extent perhaps, at American Motors and even at Pontiac Division of GM—all had remarkably similar line-ups, competing almost car for car. The industry's oft-repeated hosannahs of self-congratulation about the wealth of diversity and choice begin to sound positively modest.

64

The Fruition of the Golden Era

Yet if you wanted anything other than front-engine/rear-drive—that *"thing . . .* as contemporary as the Twentieth Century Limited"—for the first ten years of the golden era, you bought a foreign car or, later, an economy compact, the Corvair. Out of somewhere between ninety and three hundred nameplates (varying from year to year), a choice of one. Even that was dropped; at present the front-wheel-drive Oldsmobile Toronado and Cadillac Eldorado—both of them decidedly in the luxury class, both of them also products of General Motors—represent the only variations on the conventional format among well over two hundred nameplates.

It is important to lay to rest the myth of choice. In a section entitled "Design-a-Mustang" in *Future Shock,* Alvin Toffler expounds at length on how "super-industrialism" will move us "not toward a further extension of material standardization, but toward its dialectical negation." Thus in the late fifties, Detroit found customers wanting "custom-like cars that would give them an illusion of having one-of-a-kind. To provide that illusion would have been impossible with the old technology; the new computerized assembly systems, however, make possible not merely an illusion, but even—before long—the reality." Toffler quotes a dream sample of Detroit's capability of creating the illusion of one-of-a-kind.

Thus the beautiful and spectacularly successful Mustang is promoted by Ford as "the one you design yourself," because, as critic Reyner Banham explains, there "isn't a dung-regular Mustang any more, just a stockpile of options to meld in combinations of 3 (bodies) × 4 (engines) × 3 (transmissions) × 4 (basic sets of high-performance engine modifications)—1 (rock-bottom six cylinder car to which these modifications don't apply) + 2 (Shelby grand-touring and racing set-ups applying to only one body shell and not all engine/transmission combinations)." This does not even take into account the possible variations in color, upholstery and optional equipment.

Both car buyers and auto salesman are increasingly disconcerted by the sheer multiplicity of options. The buyer's problem of choice has become far more complicated, the addition of each option creating the need for more information, more decisions and subdecisions. Thus, anyone who has attempted to buy a car lately, as I have, soon finds that the task of learning about the various brands, lines, models and options (even within a fixed price range) requires days of shopping and reading. In short, the auto industry may soon reach the point at which its technology can economically produce more diversity than the consumer needs or wants.[3]

Or as another writer put it, "Last year [1965] a Yale University physicist calculated that since Chevy offered 46 models, 32 engines, 20 transmissions, 21 colors (plus nine two-tone combinations), and more than 400 accessories and options, the number of different cars that a Chevrolet customer conceivably could order was greater than the number of atoms in the universe. This seemingly put General Motors one notch higher than God in the chain of command. This year, even though the standard Chevrolet never accounts for less than two-thirds of Chevy's sales, Chevy is offering still more models (a total of 50) and options, indicating that while they may not be increasing their lead over Ford, they are pulling away from God." [4]

Marshall McLuhan, not renowned for the conservative nature of his pronouncements, estimated the possible different versions of a single model at only 25 million. Which in the end means 25 million different versions of the "front-engine, rear-drive *thing*," the differences coming more often from relocations of strips of chrome trim than from differences in technological approach or variations in engineering accomplishment. Biscayne and Caprice are four models and about a thousand dollars apart in the Chevrolet line-up, but they share everything except decor and level of sound and ride insulation. The consumer view, down the mile-long option

66

lists, is of diversity; yet the manufacturing aim is the antithesis, a frantic scramble toward just the kind of "rationalization" that is implied in the name "mass" production.

For example, Buick LeSabre, Oldsmobile Delta, Pontiac Catalina, and Chevrolet Impala—four competing nameplates spread, in the public consciousness, across most of the American automotive economic spectrum—share the same body, the General Motors "B-Series" body shell. The same floor pan, inner body panels, roof cap, and windshield have been used on *all* the intermediates from GM (as wide-ranging a selection of cars as Olds Cutlass, Buick Special, Pontiac Grand Prix, and Chevrolet Chevelle) since 1964, with rear quarter panel metal and rear window varied to make the cars look different.

This means more than a reminiscent aesthetic impact across the General Motors family of cars. (The various divisions are in fact more highly skilled at disguising this family resemblance, through the cosmetic decor of their styling departments, than they are at providing any engineering variation underneath those identical body shells.) It means that the single body-shell design must accommodate all the mechanical components that four different engineering staffs might want to hang on it or install within it. And because the same kind of rationalization that means production economies in body design also produces economies in mechanical component design—and because Buick, Oldsmobile, Pontiac, and Chevrolet are, after all, under a single corporate control —the technological evolution is obviously toward single solutions to the divisions' various mechanical requirements. GM has been able to cut its spare parts list from 318,000 items to 272,000 items in the past three years. There is a substantial rumor that the corporation will be able to cut the total number of different engines produced by its divisions to the round number of two—a small V-8 and a big V-8—in the next two years (excluding the radical Wankel, of course—see Chapter 9).

Nor is there marked variation even among directly competing corporations. In 1965 Pontiac was purchasing a 3-speed manual transmission from Ford and installing it in Pontiacs as just one more component stamped with the General Motors' Mark of Excellence. It was a rare occurrence, when one manufacturer actually achieved some small degree of product superiority, but GM had nothing to match the Ford transmission at the time, and Ford had the production capacity to supply Pontiac. General Motors, of course, had a comparable transmission in production soon thereafter.

The result of this production rationalization is a dreary uniformity in those 7 or 8 or 9 million cars sold in this country every year. The depressing resemblance is demonstrated by the rental car industry, the major members of which switched car allegiances round-robin a few years back, to the total unconcern of their customers. Rental fleets are composed almost entirely of full-sized Chevrolets, Fords, Pontiacs, Dodges, and Plymouths. All are equipped with small V-8's, automatic transmissions, power steering, and power brakes. The drive-yourself customer is unable to discern any appreciable difference between the makes outside of the lettering on the nameplates.

The rental car is the realized version of the Platonic ideal in the American golden-era market. Averaging full-size car figures for 1970, we come up with a kind of parameter car, the golden era's golden mean, against which to compare the Chevrolet Impala. That car will be about eighteen feet long, six and a half feet wide, four and a half feet tall; to be precise, 216.8 inches long, 79.4 inches wide, and 54.9 high, with 122.0 inches of wheelbase. The 1970 Impala is three inches shorter in wheelbase (119.0—representing a growth of 6.5

inches since 1955), but almost spot on the mean in its other dimensions: .8 inches shorter in length, .9 inches taller, .4 inches wider. (The full-size Chevrolet has grown a foot and a half in overall length and six inches in width since the golden era began—and about a thousand pounds in weight.) Our parameter car will be powered by a V-8, of course. (Although six-cylinder engines are still offered for sale in 1970, they found their way into just 14 percent of the cars Americans bought that year.) America spews out V-8 engines in a demonic fury, as if somewhere, in some magic combination of piston and crankshaft, the perfect engine will be born. In 1970 approximately forty "different" V-8's were offered by the various manufacturers, spanning a range of from 200 to 435 horsepower, virtually in 5-HP increments.

Horsepower is interesting. Every country measures it differently, and until very recently the American method—optimum conditions, no power-robbing accessories, bare engine on a test bench—was the most generous of all. (Equivalent testing methods would give German ratings an estimated 10 to 15 percent increase.) [5] Acceleration is governed primarily by the ratio of horsepower to gross weight; top speed is a function of horsepower and frontal area. Top speed is governed, legally, by speed limits (in every state but Nevada); no cars are offered for sale in this country which cannot break all its speed laws. Acceleration is useful for safety purposes in passing on two-lane roads, in merging into heavy freeway traffic, and—conceivably, to be generous—for the rare spurt *out* of danger (although the natural reaction is seldom to use it thus, but to brake instead). Otherwise, the function of acceleration is almost entirely sensual. Acceleration is a thrill.

There are no minimum standards for acceleration, that is, no "performance" so poor that it is legally banned. Neither is there an upper limit by legal statute, although some physical laws having to do with things like traction do limit the upper capability of a wheel-driven vehicle to accelerate. Volkswagen supplies, quite successfully, what one might assume to be the minimum acceptable performance capability for American highway conditions, with, in 1970, an under-two-thousand-pound car powered by a 57-horsepower engine. (Volkswagen sold half a million cars a year for years with a 36-horsepower engine, but that was before 1970; the horsepower race came, inevitably, even to the lowly Beetle.)

The lowest horsepower rating you could purchase in an American car in 1970 was 115, in a six-cylinder engine. The average for the 86 percent of the cars sold with V-8 power was 269 horsepower, and the Impala's minimum version had 250 horsepower, from a 350-cubic-inch V-8. One horsepower is the amount of work force needed to raise 550 pounds one foot in one second. The average Impala weighed in at just about four thousand pounds with fuel, lubricants, and coolant. Thus the smallest V-8 offered in the car had, on paper, the capacity to raise the car approximately thirty-four feet in one second. Straight up. Fortunately, something is lost between paper figures and showroom reality, and it is doubtful that you could duplicate that kind of performance in actuality. But then if you wanted to go the whole route you could have ordered a theoretical 52 vertical feet per second, with the 390-horsepower engine.

In addition to a "small" V-8, our parameter car will be fitted with a three-speed automatic transmission, power disc brakes in the front (drum in the rear), power steering, the "small" radio (i.e. not the most expensive version sold). It will also probably have air conditioning—61 percent of the cars sold in 1970 did. Even if it is not equipped to supply its own environment, it is unlikely that vent windows will be offered; instead, there will be a complicated and ornately wrought internal venting system designed to keep a positive air pressure within the car at all times, and thus keep harmful fumes from the engine away. Yet the moment you or I turn a window crank to open a window by the merest fraction of an inch, all that design work that went into the ventilation system is instantly negated.

The front suspension will be 100-percent-standard-across-the-board-on-all-American-cars unequal-length wishbones, with either coil or torsion-bar springing; at the rear will be a "live" (solid, unarticulated) rear axle with either coils or leaf springs. Whichever of the three springing methods—coil, torsion bar, or leaf—its maker will advertise it as a customer benefit, perhaps even a technological advance, in blatant disregard for the simple physical truth that a spring is a spring is a spring, no matter what shape you pound it into. On the Impala, it's coils front and rear.[6]

Power steering on the Impala gives, along with a reduction in steering effort by the driver, a reduction in the number of turns of the steering wheel to go from full left to full right. With manual steering—if you can get it—the number of revolutions of the wheel is more than five; with power, it is less than three. With either system, the minimum turning circle for the car is a stately forty-two feet. The 1970 Volkswagen, a make notorious among imports for its unwieldy large turning radius, can turn six feet inside the Chevrolet's smallest possible circle. Part of the advantage is because of the VW's shorter wheelbase, of course, but that's little consolation when you're trying to jockey an Impala into a parking space.

Only one model—the Custom Coupe—of the Impala includes power front disc brakes as standard equipment.[7] If Mercedes-Benz asks itself how it can sell some cars which are safer than others, Chevrolet doesn't admit the existence of the question. A bewildering complexity of brake options awaits the prospective Chevrolet buyer. Front discs with power assist were also standard equipment on two versions of the 1970 Caprice; elsewhere in the Impala-size line, discs were extra cost. Discs were not standard, for example, on the wagons, which with five hundred pounds more weight needed them more.

That's just the start of the confusion, however. In an effort to overcome some of the problems of drum brakes, Chevrolet developed—or borrowed from Buick, who borrowed from European practice—a finned drum for conventional brakes. The fins help stiffen the drum to reduce distortion under heat, and provide more surface area for faster cooling. Finned drums, in 1970, are standard on both front and rear for the Chevelle and the smaller wagons (which need them, but not as badly as the big cars do), and at the front only (Nova) and the rear only (Monte Carlo) of two other smaller cars which also don't need them as badly as the full-sized cars do. On the big cars, you pay extra.

Later, Detroit was to make the front disc brakes standard on several of the new small cars, without power assist—the smaller, lighter cars didn't require power brakes or power steering. It seems safe to predict, however, on the basis of the industry's history, that the small cars will grow fatter, that horsepower increments and optional extras will be used as sales tools, that the power-assists will come to the little cars too. That's what happened to Detroit's last desultory essay at rationality, the "compacts" of the early sixties.[8]

The Drive to Undersimplification

The Chevrolet Sales Album for 1970 refutes my cynical dismissal of the 1970 Impala as a stagnant monstrosity, of course. It lists no fewer than thirteen new Chevrolet features, plus some twenty-nine "safety and security features." The "new" features are interesting ones: new front-end sheet metal, new rear bumper, new side marker lights (required by federal law), color-accented wheel covers, new interior trim styling, new interior trim colors—these are the kinds of engineering breakthrough that had all America panting to trade in its obsolete 1969 Impalas. Plus such advances as a new transmission-controlled spark advance, devised in desperation to help meet emission regulations, and new "slim-line" spark plugs, whatever that means. (Spark-plug styling? What'll they think of next?)

"Features." The sales manual becomes a guided tour to technological absurdity. Curved glass for side windows is a "feature," adding a couple of inches of shoulder room in a car that is already cavernously wide on the interior, with more shoulder room than can possibly be used with the legal maximum of three in the front seat, but that in nearly nineteen feet of total length still cramps the knees of rear-seat passengers. Curved glass is the kind of detail the styling guys go crazy for. It boosts insurance replacement costs, severely overcomplicates sealing problems against wind, rain, and noise, and makes window-winding mechanisms a nightmare, but it's a "feature." "Full-door-glass styling" is also a feature; it means you no longer have a vent window, and if your "Astro Ventilation System" unaccountably leaves you feeling stuffy, you have to open a door-wide gap.

Also listed among the "features" are the following: silver-finish upper and lower grille; bright lower grille valance panel (on cheaper models it's called "body color lower grille valance panel," which means it is painted—still a "feature"); windshield molding; hood rear-edge molding; bright side-window moldings; bright roof-drip moldings; two kinds of body side moldings; body sill moldings; wheel-opening moldings; rear-window molding; color-accented (painted) deck lid molding; and black-accented roof rear-quarter belt moldings. In that list, "bright" means C-H-R-O-M-E, in effect if not in substance; a "molding" is a strip of metal that hides a joint that can't otherwise be camouflaged. Eleven different

73

moldings per car gives an idea of the patchwork nature of modern car assembly.

Not all of the features on the 1970 Impala were unnecessary complications or protective coloration for desperate last-minute fixes. The twenty-nine safety and security features evolved directly from the National Traffic and Motor Vehicle Safety Act of 1966, but in their production versions, Chevrolet has improved on the legal minimums. A great deal of attention has been given to such things as corrosion control, sound and vibration insulation, and weather protection. One might be justified in assuming that a sound, solid, nonrusting, quiet, weatherproof basic car is only the starting point in thirty-six-hundred-dollar automobiles. It happens that there were significant failures to provide those basics in the domestic product during the fifties and sixties, but the industry isn't about to call attention to new fixes for what shouldn't have been failures in the first place. Rustproofing doesn't sell cars.

Therefore sales attention is given to the gadgetry that Detroit assumes does sell cars; that it makes them virtually impossible to repair is just another price we pay for progress. You could get an instrument warning light for your 1970 Impala that flashed to warn you that your windshield washer fluid tank needed refilling. You could get an electrically powered trunk opener, an electrically powered automatic seat-back latch, an electric door-lock system, and a system that automatically left the headlights on for two minutes after you shut them off, "for extra security when leaving a parked car" (grim vision of the Impala-buyer's fear of crime in the streets). Included in that last gadget was a warning buzzer that sounded automatically when the driver's door was opened with the headlights or parking lights on. That's *in addition* to the warning buzzer when you open a door with the ignition key still in the lock.

How much technical and electronic complication is engendered by these fripperies, only the increasingly puzzled serviceman knows for sure. In 1970 Chevrolet's inventiveness reached some kind of new record high with RPO CD3, the New Fingertip Windshield Wiper Control, the operation and control of which (but not the repair tactics for) compare with Stanley Kubrick's instructions for operation of zero-gravity toilets, in the film *2001:*

> A miniature cowl-mounted computer programs the type of operation signaled by the driver. Cycles range from a single dry wipe to continuous high speed wash and wipe action. For a single sweep of the blades and return to the "park" position, the button [mounted on the end of the turn-signal control wand] is depressed to the first position and then released (increased spring pressure indicates first position). Button is fully depressed and released for a full "wash and wipe" cycle. Continuous "wash and wipe" action is obtained by holding the button in a fully depressed position. Whenever the button is released, the wiper blades automatically return to the "park" position. *When continuous wiper action is desired, the standard instrument panel-mounted switch is used."* (Emphasis supplied; from the 1970 *Chevrolet Sales Album.*)

This somewhat fetishist concern with the minutiae of windshield-wiping begins to appear justified when one considers just where that peculiarly simple little accessory has led the industry. Model year 1972 would be considered by Chevrolet to be almost a total write-off, since there was almost no restyling done to the 1971 models, and hence no way of differentiating between the two. How could a fellow be induced to turn in his old model when the new one looked just like it, so the neighbors couldn't tell the difference? An extensive styling change had been planned for 1972, but there was no time, energy, or money to spare for pretty new sheet-metal wrinkles. All that had gone into the massive effort required to meet increasingly rigorous federal standards for bumper protection. Windshield wipers caused the whole bloody fiasco.

It seems that in 1967 Pontiac Motor Division became embarrassed that the intimacies of its windshield-wiping mechanisms were exposed to public view. A body was therefore designed with a neat little trough below the windshield where the wipers could tuck out of sight when not in use. To hide the trough, a gentle, sensuous curve upward was put into the trailing edge of the sheet metal of the hood.

In the first year of the modification owners discovered that the wipers were inclined to freeze solid in the ice and snow that collected in the trough. Or, if the wipers were inadvertently left out of the "park" position, the trough collected the the ice anyway, preventing the wipers from being returned to their hiding place. Never mind. It was a "feature," and it could be sold; besides, it looked sexy, all that big broad smooth expanse of uncluttered cowl. So all GM cars had to have them. Your 1970 Impala came with "Hide-A-Way" wipers as standard equipment. Didn't cost you a penny extra.

Unless you hit something. Unfortunately, the sexy upward curve in the rear of the hood meant that in a very slight front-end collision, the hood was shoved back into the windshield, rather than into steel. Smashing the windshield in a 3-MPH parking nudge thus added about a hundred dollars to the repair bill over sheet-metal damage alone, and was the straw that broke the back of congressional indifference to Detroit's styling whims. As Morton Mintz and Jerry S. Cohen put it in *America, Inc.,* "Inexorably, the cost of insurance rises, even for owners of cars with naked wipers. Thus GM has exercised a private power to tax. Suppose the accident is severe. The hood or fender then is rammed through the windshield into the passenger compartment. GM may also have exercised a private power to imperil life." [9]

Former Federal Highway Safety Director Dr. William Haddon, speaking as President of the Insurance Institute for Highway Safety in 1969, told a congressional committee that the average damage claim resulting from a 5-MPH crash was

$200, for a 10-MPH collision over $650. Congress reacted, telling the car-makers to produce products that would withstand a 5-MPH crash without damage by 1973. As usual, when the desperate full-bore lobbying efforts to defeat the legislation were all over with, Detroit went home and laid on a show of engineering expertise, just to prove they were able. Many of the new 1972 models had the 5-MPH bumpers when they reached the showrooms in the fall of 1971. The bumpers added approximately sixty pounds to the weight of the car. The windshield wipers were still hidden.

Their Finest Hour

And thus, car fans, you have the 1970 Impala: the modern American full-sized car. As descriptions go, Brock Yates's "front-engine, rear-drive *thing*" doesn't say it by half. It is an oversized, overweight, overpowered, underbraked, undertired, dangerously fast (but ponderously slow to respond to any control other than the accelerator), hideously complex, overdecorated, underengineered, resolutely ordinary, badly assembled, twenty-foot, four thousand-pound, front-engine, rear-drive thing. It is very American.

Model year 1971 was to be no better. In fact the principal change to the 1971 Impala would be "total" restyling, despite John Burby's prediction about annual styling changes. The '71 was virtually indistinguishable from the '72 to all but the car-fixated; the increased complexity served to jack up the cost of repairs for a 5-MPH front-end collision from $196 in 1970 to $376 in 1971, a development which further inflamed federal wrath.[10] For 1972 the styling exercises were postponed in favor of bumpers that would bump, and the full-sized car continued to plummet in the marketplace. Meanwhile the domestic small cars were introduced and did well,

77

but failed to turn back the imports, whose market share continued to climb despite the financial juggling of Nixonomics which imposed a 10-percent surcharge on them for nearly a full quarter of the year.

Calendar 1971 turned out to be the biggest sales year in history for the car industry, but the conventional full-sized American car was a dead issue in a banner year, as dead as the Supercar that preceded it. And the pressure on the industry continued to mount, despite the last-minute economic rescue act from Washington. Ivory-tower analysts such as Charles A. Reich and Philip E. Slater diagnosed the source of the pressure—on all of America's hitherto inviolable institutions—as no less than a revolution in social consciousness. More conventional molders of public opinion, seconded by industrialists of every stripe, pooh-poohed the vision, but the forces continued to grow. A swelling national distaste for imperialism, for expansionism, for bigness of every sort, underlay the change. The issues floated up out of the sixties. Civil rights. Warmaking. Pollution. Consumerism. Congestion. Urban decay. The population explosion. Dislocation, rootlessness, psychic disaffection. Reform—of education, the judiciary, the political processes, welfare, medicine, police powers, of the corporate state—was in the air. General Motors was the biggest, most visible enemy of them all. Time after time, in issue after issue, the public *angst* was tied to the kind of arrogance in the wielding of economic power that most eloquently characterized the automakers during their golden age. The automobile industry became symbolic of the old, discredited way. The 1970 model was its finest product.

CHAPTER 4

The Makers

Production vs. the Product

There is a rare breed of automobiles produced in various parts of the western world, cars almost as distinctly different from each other as they are, as a class, from the rest of the world's motor vehicles. Perhaps their single shared characteristic is what seems to be a wholly unrealistic price: they each cost approximately the same as a three-bedroom, bath-and-a-half, brick veneer tract house. They are the super-exotics—Ferrari, Maserati, Lamborghini from Italy, the upper ranges of Mercedes-Benz from Germany, Rolls Royce (less exotic but more expensive) from England. Their ranks are drastically reduced now. The Bugatti, the Isotta-Fraschini, the American Duesenberg are no longer built. In their time they represented the apex of product engineering in automobiles; the remaining examples still do.

In the high-performance grand touring examples, the cars sparkle with technological sophistication. In the purely luxury versions, the cars represent fanatical attention to detail, selection of construction materials, and engineering workmanship. (One car, the "Grand" Mercedes-Benz 600, which in limousine version sells for thirty thousand dollars and up, represents both technological wizardry and watchmaking precision of manufacture. It is probably the "best" car in the world. It seems to be sold mostly to heads of state of small, oil rich Middle Eastern nations, although two have reportedly been exported to mainland China.) These cars consistently push back the boundaries of automotive capability, in performance, in comfort, in the gilding of the lily of pure mobility. Car nuts worship them; some even purchase them. To the American industry, they are simply irrelevant.

The European industry chooses to absorb and apply the technological lessons learned in the superexotics. The bizarrely expensive luxury cars serve as models, and the features that make them exclusive are carefully scrutinized for possible adaptation to broader automotive use. As a result, European economy cars regularly feature such technological advantages as all-independent suspension, disc brakes, economical high-output (relative to size) engines, variations in engine and transmission location for superior handling and traction, clever power/drive-train unitization for efficiency and increased safety. The facts of European economic life put a larger emphasis on economy and efficiency, of course, and different European tastes demand vastly different sorts of cars from our own. (It is interesting, for example, that sports-crazy and car-crazy America, during the fifteen years 1955 to 1970, produced only a single true sports car— Corvette—by a major manufacturer, while the much smaller total industry of Europe produced dozens.) Whatever the results—no matter how presumably distasteful the standard European car may be to the bulk of American car buyers— the lineal descent in the European automotive world is from the adventurous engineering of the luxury segment of the market downward to the proletarian application in cheap cars. The motivation is rational: cars are for mobility, and better cars are for superior mobility. Product engineering comes first.

American automotive design, by contrast, has been frozen so long that lines of derivation recede in the mists. Basic format is hewed to as if based on divine revelation. Some few innovative accessories have been introduced on the American equivalent of luxury cars, have proved beneficial and cheap to mass-produce, and have gradually filtered their way down to the transportation of the proles. But the thrust of the evolution is clearly in the other direction, to "upgrade," i.e. make larger and more expensive the minimum level of available automobile—a distinctly antisocial but thrillingly profitable course. Innovations to the low-priced lines have usually been limited to developments which are marginally advantageous for the product, but which achieve sizable production cost reductions, such as bonded brake linings (introduced by Chevrolet in 1948). When innovation is accomplished in the American industry, it is strictly on a production-engineering basis: how does it cost out? [1]

Yet we are reared—media-fed—on technological wonders, and so our frustration is doubled when no wonders appear in our local dealership showrooms. In the seventies, the popular chorus often takes as its refrain the single question, "If we can put men (not to mention an automobile) on the moon, why can't we . . ." (Get commuters home on time, design a nonpolluting automobile engine, lick the highway death toll, find a parking space?) The domestic automotive engineer is perhaps justified if in answer, he merely shrugs his shoulders and points either to the Ferrari or the Lunar Rover. Both represent apogees of cost-no-object product engineering. Neither, however, represents the faintest kind of engineering triumph in Detroit's terms. Given enough budget, man can no longer devise a mechanical task for which he can't also supply the technology to accomplish it.

To devise a three-thousand-dollar Chevrolet, however, is another kind of battle. It requires engineering of a high, if specialized, order. It requires alert, relentless, aggressive penetration of the forefronts of manufacturing technology. It requires the most exhaustively planned and precisely timed logistical backing, in the supply of everything from raw iron ore to investment capital. It requires the construction of an elaborately wrought megamachine involving factories, systems, labor pools, communication networks. If one is capable of positive emotion for such intricacies, as the men who build them undoubtedly are, it is very likely possible to look on such a labyrinth of interlocking purposes with something akin to love. It is not, however, easy to love the Chevrolets it produces.

In fact, of all the things that the megamachine does require, it does not require much interest in its own product. There seems to be very little time, amidst concerns about how to achieve production of X-million units at X-thousand dollars apiece, to ponder how to make a good car. Perhaps that is why so few of the men who run the automobile industry are "car men." Perhaps there isn't time.

One can project the course of involvement, imagine the heady thrills, back when the automobile was beginning to happen. The contemporaries of Henry Ford, young men swept up in the romance of creating a fledgling technology. Solving the problems, building, with scrap and raw ingenuity, cars that would run, that would accomplish tasks, that would set records. Can we *go* that fast, can we make it of this, can we get there from here? A thousand briefly flickering nameplates, each signifying a thousand sweaty solutions —some brilliant, some idiotic. Survival of the soundest; nuts-and-bolts Darwinism. The cars getting more and more dependable, serviceable, the solutions working. Ideas into machinery: the assembly line and mass production blessing the multitudes with the hard-won solutions of the yeasty time when men were making something new.

Inevitably, business arrived, with business solutions. Profitability superseded the demands of utility, mobility, quality, safety. There was a moment, in the early years, when designers considered steam and internal combustion to be equally sensible solutions to the problem of propulsive force. In the transition from product engineering to production engineering, the cost accountants looked at both and declared the internal-combustion engine the direction of the future: in mass production, it looked to be slightly cheaper to manufacture. Sixty years later, with 82 million tons of pollutants per year being hung over our heads and in our lungs, the sins of production engineering come home to roost. With hundreds of millions of dollars tied up in capital investment in producing internal-combustion engines, the immense weight of amortization costs stifles the first whisper of experimentation. Gradually, as government ire focuses on the irresponsibility of the auto-makers, the voices of response turn from arrogant dismissal to snappish irritability. The pressure builds from all sides. Not only is the car industry threatened; it drags along with it—risks dragging down as it had once dragged up—the immensely wealthy oil industry, still sitting on untapped billions in kingdoms in Kuwait, in the gurgling mother lode of Alaska, all that wealth lying up there waiting to be ripped open. Pollution threatens all of that. Pollution created by the flick of the cost accountant's pencil, sending the industry plunging after internal combustion rather than steam. A penny-oriented decision for production engineering in the 1900's, upon which the economy—and the very health—of the nation hangs, at the end of the golden era.

The Car

It is a high-risk business. Lawrence J. White has performed an extensive analysis of the problems of entry into the automobile industry and of profitability once there. Along with a careful debunking of many Galbraithean estimates of economies of scale, White came up with the minimum ticket for any mogul contemplating competition with the existing industry: a fat, round $2 billion. Put up that sum (intelligently), and then achieve 800,000 sales per year, White says, and you can hope to survive in the automobile business. (Selling fewer than 800,000 cars in 1970: American Motors Corporation, and, separately, Plymouth, Dodge, Chrysler, Imperial, Mercury, Lincoln, Pontiac, Oldsmobile, Buick, Cadillac, and Checker. Of course the corporations owning all of these divisions—except Checker—were well over the 800,000-mark in total sales.)

"The risks in automobile production are high," White explains. "Autos have to be designed well in advance of actual confrontation with the consumer. A three-year—or even a two-year—design cycle means that a manufacturer can be stuck uncomfortably long with a badly designed car. Consumer tastes do and have changed, and what looks like a good design now could turn out to be a disaster two and one-half years later. Further, as a consumer durable item, automobiles are especially sensitive to levels of personal income. . . . As national economic fortunes wax and wane, automobile sales expand and contract. Consumer choices among types of cars (for example, expensive or inexpensive) appear to be equally sensitive to income levels." [2]

Brock Yates updates White: "The result [of computerized model diversity] is that manufacturers are compelled to constantly fiddle with their line-up of cars simply to maintain their position in the market. Stagnate and they are dead; misjudge the market and they are dead; produce a sales success and they merely stand still—that is the present plight of the automakers." Yates goes on to quote a Ford executive: "We've had three sales bonanzas since 1960. First came the Falcon, then the Fairlane and the Mustang. When we started, we had a 23 percent share of the market, and now, after all the hoopla, we've got 20 percent. So what the hell did we prove?"[3]

The industry's response to the riskiness is manic oscillation between excruciatingly wrought production economies—such minutiae are pursued, for example, as the thinning of seat-cushion materials—and . . . more production. More models, more names, more variations. At the end of the golden era, the forces for production economy were winning again. Strolling through a Chevrolet engineering laboratory in 1971, I got a guided tour of computerization from a resident engineer/public relations man. Bay after bay of engine dynamometers surrounded us, set up for computer programming through the complex "drive-cycle" that the new federal pollution regulations required. A new $5-million building was just being completed across the street, equipped with second-generation pollution-control analysis machinery. My guide was in his early forties. "We had quite a battle in the beginning," he told me, "getting the senior people to accept computerization and computer predictions about performance of new components. But once a few of them proved out—once we got results in the field that matched computer predictions—they stopped resisting. Of course, we have been fortunate lately. Several of the older, more conservative senior people have retired. It seems like all of a sudden we've got a whole new generation of younger engineering minds operating the show. The resistance has lessened considerably."

(Do not expect the greening of General Motors, just because the industry has finally reached retirement age.)

I was talking to a "wizard," although I didn't know it at the time. Two factions had developed at General Motors in the late sixties. There was a kind of seat-of-the-pants, cut-and-try school—old fogeys, if you will—whose method of approach to an engineering problem was to build samples of every conceivable variation on a solution and then to put them into the field for real-life testing. Then there were "the wizards," who fed all the variables into computers and let the computers tell them—in a single answer—what to build. The seat-of-the-pants men number among their membership the remaining "car people" in the industry. The "wizards," of course, are winning out. Development is cheaper their way. The wizards win just as the cost accountants will always win. The goal is not good machinery, but maximized profits. Let us not delve into Norman Mailerish mysteries of computer vs. soul, of sensory vibrations and the nausea-inducing vaguenesses of the inner ear, smell-magic, fallible synapses vs. the electronic right angles of printed circuitry. The computer will describe perfection (in terms of cost-benefits); don't confuse the issue with poetry.

The car men haven't done all that much in the way of breaking design stasis anyway; there is little enough soul to forfeit to the computer, in the hundred-millions of cars we see fit to produce. Cost accountancy triumphant. The new chairman of General Motors is Richard Gerstenberg, who once referred to himself in Senate subcommittee testimony as "Ol' Dick, the bookkeeper"; he is a finance man, as have been the three preceding chairmen—financiers or sales geniuses. The current president, Edward N. Cole, is something of a car man, but he created the Corvair, created with it endless trouble for the corporation, and his rise, his effective direction of overall corporate fortunes, is over. Before him, Semon "Bunkie" Knudsen, car man and son of a car man (his father headed the corporation during the period when it successfully responded to the challenge of Henry Ford's Model T) struggled his way close to the top, was passed over for a financier, and quit. He went to Ford, and lost a power struggle there to another salesman, Lee Iacocca. The car men represent a dead issue: product engineering.

Woodward

To say that Detroit is the most American of cities is to be both mordantly accurate and balefully pessimistic about the future of cities in this country. Detroit is where the awful ugliness of urban life first began to be visible. From labor strife to racial disaster to polluted unlivability, Detroit has been the honor guard, its industry the entering wedge, its industrialists the advance men, setting up the territory, for the urban crisis.

Detroit is buried in a flat sump of American midlands, just above the grossly polluted Lake Erie (polluted primarily by Detroit, with a little help from Toledo, Cleveland, and Akron). It sprawls for uncounted miles and yet is almost impossibly congested. It is ringed, gouged, sectioned by freeways, most of them sunken in greasy, claustrophobia-inducing moats—freeways which despite frantic construction programs seem to hang ten years behind the mass of traffic volume. The city's murder rate has zoomed off-scale in recent years, its drug problems rival New York's, its police still maintain that car theft—in the Motor City—is the most significant crime. Two of the most severe and destructive racial uprisings in the U.S. in the twentieth century took place in Detroit, and racial ghettos—black impaction—now absorb most of the city proper. To the south the city is bordered by the Detroit River and somnolent Canada. On the east is Lake St. Clair and the enclave of the Old Money, the foundation fortunes in the Detroit industrial empire, Grosse

Point. On the west is Ford's-town, Dearborn, symbol to the rest of the unreconstructed U.S. of militant antiblack bigotry, best personified by its colorful perennial mayor, Orville Hubbard.

It is to the north—"out Woodward"—that Detroit limns the shape of the American sixties. Woodward Avenue begins at the river, in downtown Detroit, amidst broad plazas and shiny office buildings constructed two decades ago in a downtown urban renewal scheme. If the downtown area seems airy and well ordered, it is closely ringed by ghetto and crumbling freeway; if it seems limited, somehow too small for a city of nearly two million, it is because little of Detroit's reason for being—GM, Ford, Chrysler, and American Motors—is located there.

Woodward Avenue points . . . out. String-straight to the northwest, it penetrates the ring of urban renewal within a few blocks of the deepest heart of the city, and immediately enters territory still marred by the warlike ruins of the 1967 racial rebellion. Woodward splits the campus of Wayne State University, which, like so many urban universities, is also tightly surrounded by ghetto. The Avenue connects downtown Detroit with the General Motors Building and its ancillary office complex, a strange collection of 1930's-style buildings more than three miles from Detroit's "city." The GM complex is also encircled by ghetto, very close to the center of the 1967 riot's white-hot violence. Three of four miles of ghetto-strip line the broad expanse of Woodward beyond the GM complex; then, with meat-cleaver abruptness, the American Dream begins.

Parks. Golf courses. Churches. Eighteen miles of intermittent commercial strip, interspersed with woodsy suburb and public parks. The architecture, the decor of the commercial strip, rapidly escalate in both expense and garishness to the north, from filling station to fast-food franchise house to sporting-goods store. Carpet shops and tire-recappers, soft-ice-cream stands and pizza parlors. Used-car lot after used-car lot. And to the sides, beyond the borders of the thundering commuter traffic of Woodward, lies suburban Detroit, in rapidly rising economic brackets. The flatland countryside was early divided, in the Midwestern tradition, into neat squares; thus Eight Mile Road, Twelve Mile Road—numerical demarcation lines of the class of the neighborhood—butt up against the northwest arrow that is Woodward. The suburbs line up: Ferndale, Oak Park, Pleasant Ridge, Huntington Woods, Berkley, Royal Oak, and finally, Birmingham and Bloomfield Hills. Management country.

(Woodward goes on. As U.S. Route 10 it splits Pontiac, Flint, Saginaw, up the lower peninsula, toward the big Hemingway woods, Another Country. Big trout, clear streams, lakes, misty coniferous forest, half-breeds and subsistence loggers. A long way from Detroit, physically as well as psychically. There is aching symbolism in the way Woodward points toward all that, another kind of life.)

Birmingham, Bloomfield Hills, and Grosse Point—in rising order of exclusiveness—are the suburbs where automobile industry management resides. Birmingham is an imitation New England village, spotless white wood façades on expensive small shops, a couple of substantial modern department stores. Surrounding the village are concentric rings of progressively more expensive suburban homes, three-car garages and carefully protected maple trees, winding streets. The contours of the terrain have been religiously preserved, to relieve the rigid block-organization of more citified suburbs. It is affluent, snobbish, resolutely white. As Birmingham melts into Bloomfield Hills to the north, all pretense of town or village disappears, along with any democratic notions about inconspicuousness in the act of consumption: Bloomfield Hills is *rich*. It is countryside, one hundred-acre estates, the horsy set, country clubs and finishing schools. Tone. Memberships in upstate gun clubs, ski trips to Europe. Very carefully constructed to be as un-Detroitish as physically possible, a soft, rich antidote to the pain of the city.

Grosse Point is richer. The automobile industry rewards its captains very well. (The position of chairman of General Motors is carefully maintained as the highest-paid salaried job in the U.S. In a normal golden-era year, with bonuses, its occupant would gross well over half a million dollars. In 1969 James Roche received $655,000.) Grosse Point is where the supercaptains live, men who no longer run automobile companies but who run the economy instead, whose principal occupation could perhaps best be described as moving their money about, in order that it might grow. Women here, too —mostly widows of men who formed, founded, managed, inflated and deflated, and often simply sold out the car companies. A musty rich town of stone mansions and walled estates, fortunes seventy-five and one hundred years old—as compared with fifteen and twenty-five years in the other two managerial suburbs. Birmingham and Bloomfield Hills are relatively new, and thus are substantially buffered by other, cheaper middle-class white suburbs which have grown out from Detroit. Grosse Point is old enough that the city has grown around it with the squalor of the explosive urban Detroit ghetto.

The females who reside at this level of purest capitalistic entrepreneurship are exceptions rather than rules, attaining their positions through longevity rather than business careers. Below that level the society of the auto-makers is exclusively male. (The closest a woman ever got to a position in industry management was when Mary Wells's advertising agency, Wells, Rich, Greene, took over the American Motors account.) The males of the administrative-managerial class inhabit these three suburbs; their wives and children live their lives there, but the men inhabit. They put in legendarily long hours, choosing to compete not just with other corporations, not just within the palace intrigues of their own corporate politics, but even over such minutiae as who will be first at his desk in the morning, last to leave. It is an industry custom freighted with significance. (Might as well come early and leave late; the traffic jams made possible by the bounty of their production make standard commuting hours impossible for industry leaders anyway.)

Come early, go late, whisk through the city as quickly as possible. Duck home with relief to the splendidly affluent, total insulation of the suburbs. These men often fight their way into the industry from external purviews—the industry record for tight-family, father-son successions is not good, Semon Knudsens and Henry Fords to the contrary—but once inside, it is the industry life. They work, play, lunch, vacation in the industry. They belong to the same country clubs, hunt clubs, garden clubs, luncheon clubs. They attend Detroit's society affairs in each other's company, frequently sharing automobiles (which are often chauffeur driven). They meet in sterile but plush executive dining rooms for lunch, in the various administrative office buildings of the major manufacturers—or, if they want alcohol in a strangely puritan industry, they meet at the Detroit Club, the Athletic Club, the London Chop House. (To eat with the same faces, in the same places, year after year. . . .) When they travel, they fly—and are met at airports by regional managers delivering the most carefully prepared, sparkling new examples of their own product. They tunnel through the masses on the freeways, to work and home, insulated. Spinning up broad Woodward Avenue, they traverse a serial representation of the American *angst:* squalid ghetto, tawdry commercial-strip jungle, splintered campus, fire-bombed whitey furniture stores and glittering drive-in teen-age hangouts in that same eighteen-mile stretch. What must these men think about America while they pass through it? Soot-blackened, smoke-billowing public-transit buses competing for commuting space with chrome-plated supercars, art nouveau hot rods, sports cars, motorcycles, hitchhiking hippies, as well as executive limousines. The whole arteriosclerotic urban sprawl and its commuter tangle, twice a day, and the men who make it insulated from it, air-conditioned out of contact, dreaming of sales campaigns for ever quieter, ever more insulative dreamboats, at whatever cost.

The public stance of the industry becomes automatic, built in. It comes with the territory. It sees Vietnam as defense contracts for its distant corporate divisions, as draft calls that squelch the Youth Market. It sees racial unrest as a demarcating force that cordons off sections of the city no longer safe to travel, as a vague terror that somehow enervates governance of the city, as irritating pressure from do-gooders such as the Fair Employment Practices Commission to force expensive, wasteful, risky new hiring policies.[4] It sees the crisis of the cities as short-sighted failure on the part of government to build enough new streets and roads. It sees ecological disaster first as a scare campaign to play on the fears of the weakhearted; later as another uncomfortable pressure from the federal government intended to crimp free enterprise; still later, finally, as a whole new bonanza market, endless profitability to be gained, albeit at the distasteful cost of learning new technologies. (Profit on the waste-making, and then profit on the waste-removal; and the government is even doing the selling!) It sees automobile safety as the exclusive responsibility of its customers—and the police. It sees poverty as laziness, youth rebellion as slack discipline, the erosion of institutions as encroaching communism. It looks at these eruptions on the fair epidermis of society only in search of places to insert the lance of profit. Prick them just right, and they might somehow yield up another fraction of a percentage point of market share.

The Smugness of Abundance, and Vice Versa

There are men in Detroit whose sensibilities are not blunted to the anguish of the country, men sensitive enough to recognize the reasons for their own insularity and humble enough to seek external, non-automobile-industry assistance in understanding the public who buy their cars. The very best help is sought: psychologists, motivational researchers, men whose scientifically sound research methods yield computer-quantifiable results, as well as men to whom public accolade gives credit for certifiable wisdom. The purpose of the seeking is additional profit, of course, and no great amount of money is spent on these pundits—nothing like the sums invested in a new rear-fender shape, for instance. But wisdom is sometimes sought. Even the advertising agencies—high-priced agglomerations of professionals trained to gauge public taste—are consulted. The industry gets a lot of advice, not all of it worthless. That it chooses so consistently to ignore the advice it purchases is not, in view of recent history, entirely surprising. It sought the advice that led to the creation of the Edsel. It sought the advice that generated the compacts, in 1960—but it misunderstood the advice it got (it often does), and turned an intelligent marketing gambit into a short-lived defensive reaction. Somewhere the industry must have gotten the advice that it could ignore pollution and safety for a long, long time.

A great deal of the industry's imperviousness to advice undoubtedly comes from the sales figures. Against the insubstantialities of external market advice, the industry can point to the reality of 7 million passenger cars sold, on average, every year since 1955. If we are so insulated and unresponsive to public needs, the industry seems justified in saying, why are we so rich?

Given the traditional public faith in the sovereignty of the free market, the argument is tough to refute. We bought 'em, we must love 'em. Perhaps Detroit *does* give the people what they want, as the industry is so fond of saying. If the numbers are to be believed. One might even go so far as to assume, as Detroit has assumed, that the industry has some kind of magic taste-indicator—the stylists claim to live five years ahead of the desires of the great unwashed—and can therefore unerringly fashion machinery and sheet metal to match that taste.

A number of counterindications, however, undercut the industry's self-proclaimed position as ultimate arbiter of public taste. The infallibility of that taste produced "up" years—upward rising scales curves—in only a little more than half of the model years of the golden era. Of course sales successes are always triumphs of judgment and perspicacity, but slippages are the result of "the economy"—or strikes. That 7-million-car average hides wild fluctuations of sales totals—a drop of 47 percent between 1955 and 1958, of more than 25 percent between 1968 and 1970—despite the best efforts of the industry's planners to gear for consistent production figures. The sales charts *do* mirror the major economic indicators, although no one seems quite willing to say whether car sales push or are pulled by those indicators.[5] At any rate, if the economy is responsible for the plunges of the sales curve, it seems quite likely that the sales peaks are also a result of national economic health, rather than the product of specific design responses by the industry to the public's ineffable aesthetic needs.

Imported car sales also seem pegged to more stable indices.

The imports began to come into this country in statistically significant numbers before the beginning of the golden era; Detroit said it would begin to worry about the imports in the, heh heh, unlikely event the little bugs ("shitboxes" is the almost universal familiar term among Detroit's forward thinkers) ever got 3 percent of the market. The little bugs did. Detroit revised its worry point upwards to 6 percent; the imports surpassed it. By 1959 the foreign cars were getting 10 percent of the market while Detroit sales were sagging badly. Detroit counterpunched in 1960 with the compacts (in the works since about 1957) and scored, and foreign-car dealerships throughout the land began closing their doors. But with two or three years out for retrenchment (and for some makes, badly needed redesign to fit American driving habits), the little cars began slowly and steadily chomping off those percentage points again. In 1971 import sales peaked out at just below 20 percent of the market; Nixonomics thereupon scrambled the picture so badly that the future of imported cars sales in this country is virtually unreadable, but no less a seer than Henry Ford II has estimated that the imports will hold a steady 15 percent for the foreseeable future.

The imports are, by and large, "rational" cars, predicated on economy, functionality, simplicity (sports cars excepted, of course). Their manufacturers have not engaged in styling wars, attempting to anticipate in sheet metal the fickleness of American tastes. In fact the import manufacturers haven't worried much about "giving the public what it wants"; they've simply produced as many cars as they could, to their own standards, and in the case of the more successful makes in which a high level of quality is clearly present—Volkswagen, Volvo, Mercedes-Benz—they've sold all the cars they could spare for the American market. Meanwhile the domestic small cars—counterpunch number two against the Old

95

Country menace—seem to be succeeding primarily in taking percentage points of market share away from their own big brothers.

The compacts eventually died because they were not profitable enough as "economy" cars, and so Detroit loaded them with extras and let them balloon in size. The new domestic small cars are clearly less profitable than the old compacts, and their chief function so far seems to be to reduce the sales for domestic big cars. It is little wonder that the moguls are crying poor about profitability these days. It is little wonder also that the industry looks askance at the outside advice; everyone told them they had to stem the foreign invasion, but nobody told them how to do it and continue to make money.

In the final analysis there is, as ex-Department of Transportation aide John Burby has pointed out, a market for about 8 million new cars a year in the U.S., come what may. The figure will expand gradually with population growth until the detrimental aspects of car ownership outweigh the service it provides. "Market" isn't precisely the term—"rate of consumption" might be more accurate. That "market" is virtually captive. Our motorized miles per year mean that 86 percent of our travelers use private cars, for 79 percent of the trips (by number) that are taken. Commercial airlines absorb another 13 percent of the trips, leaving a full 8 percent for all of the other transportation systems in the U.S. to grow rich over—and expand to the point that they can relieve us of the necessity of pouring our personal wealth into private automobiles. No less than 82 percent of our commuting workers use automobiles to go to and from work; the same percentage of our families now own automobiles. Sixty percent of our *poverty-level* Americans "own" cars, as do 25 percent of the under-$1000-per-year population (the figure must include a lot of teen-agers). The statistics roll on and on; they are the Automobile Manufacturers Association's own, published annually in a paperback horror story of overconcentration of an industry.[6]

It is pointless to try to convince ourselves otherwise: we have a single transportation system in this country, pure and simple, with a couple of curious small-time competitors in the form of airplanes and railroads. We have a population pushing 210 million, and we throw away more than 7 million cars a year. The manufacturers—those fellows who defend every tasteless and wasteful gimcrack tagged onto the cars in the effort to stimulate sagging public enthusiasms with the justification that they are giving the public what it wants, nay, demands—know their market so well that in 1970, 25 percent of it slipped away they know not where, and their miniaturized competitors from across the seas stole away almost 20 percent of what was left.

We can, perhaps, be thankful. If the industry really *did* know how to give the public what it wants—rather than simply grinding out units of production to stuff into the gaping hole of otherwise unfilled transportation needs—our nation might be even more desperately unbalanced in its transportation network, its economic centricity, its misplaced social priorities, than it already is.

The Desperate Men

It is not that these men don't like the cars they build; they simply are not particularly interested in them. Cars are not, to them, engineering or even styling achievements; they are units of inventory. It is not that these men don't understand their market. They perhaps understand it too well, to the extent its vagaries and whimsicalities can be known. They understand the bulk nature of the need, the base upon which they can rely, and, dimissing that, they focus in compulsively on the manipulable fringe, the margin where reputations are made and lost. In so doing they come to know as much as can be known about the market, and nothing of the people, of the nation that makes it up. It is not that these are evil men. They are aggressive, achievement-oriented, enormously competitive. And they are, in a pressure-ridden industry, desperate.

The desperation is endemic, fixed, irreducible; it flows naturally out of the multi-million-dollar fractions of percentage points, out of billions of capital investment risking idleness at the slightest waver in the economic construct. An ore train is an hour late to the mill, and 6000 workers go idle 700 miles away, at $4.50 an hour (and up) per man. A day's wildcat strike and $60 million a day in gross receipts is irrevocably—in the eyes of the industry—lost.

The desperation surfaced early in the industry; it is well-documented in such curiosities as the celebrated exchange between Alfred P. Sloan, Jr., President of General Motors, and Lammot du Pont, President of E. I. du Pont de Nemours & Company, in 1929, on the subject of safety glass. The invention was established, proven, making its way into American car windshields. Du Pont produced it, and was pushing its adoption from the comfortable position of making a profit on a demonstrably humanitarian product. He wanted GM to adopt the new glass immediately.

No, said Sloan, not yet; although "non-shatterable glass is bound to come," GM was not to lead the way in making driving safer. To do so would "materially offset our profits." General Motors leadership in the area would pull the competition into the same expense: "Our gain would be a purely temporary one and the net result would be that both competition and ourselves would have reduced the return on our capital and *the public would have obtained still more value per dollar expended.*" [7] (Emphasis supplied.)

98

Although the correspondence in question didn't surface until 1952, other exposures and embarrassments kept the industry leaders blushing. From Charles F. "Boss" Kettering's "It isn't that we build such bad cars, it's that they are such lousy customers," to "Engine Charlie" Wilson's infamous misquote, "What's good for GM is good for the country," * the leaders of the industry have demonstrated a consistent inability to conceal the industry's own greed.

The accepted public stance of the industry is one of lip service to social responsibility. Internally, however, the mood is compounded of private agony at the business' uncertainties, and vituperation at any interference with the ongoing profitability of the enterprise. Pressure builds; the manufacturers ricochet between the disasters of business downturns and the heady but nervous triumphs of the years of maximum production and matching sales. The captains who guide the industry are drawn wire-thin by the pressure. Slips are made; private intent becomes public outrage.

The most recent, most eloquent example is the case of James M. Roche. Roche was elevated to the presidency of General Motors in 1962, and ascended to the chairmanship in 1967. He led the corporation through more than half of the golden decade-and-a-half, presiding over the largest corporation in the world during the most profitable years in that corporation's history. It is a bit difficult to grasp the size of General Motors and the size of its profits:

> Its annual revenue is greater than that of any foreign government except the United Kingdom and the Union of Soviet Socialist Republics, and greater, as well, than the gross national product of Brazil or Sweden. In 1965 GM's sales of $20.7 billion "exceeded the *combined* general revenues of the state and local governments of New York, New Jersey, Pennsyl-

---

* What Wilson actually said was, "For years I have thought that what was good for the country was good for General Motors, and vice versa." The press leaped on the "vice versa," and there was no Spiro Agnew around to defend GM's good name at the time.

vania, Ohio, Delaware, and the six New England states." This figures out to $2.3 million per hour, 24 hours a day, 365 days a year (by 1969 it was $2.8 million). On the same hourly basis, its profit after taxes was $242,649.[8]

Although a corporation presidency may be the most limited sort of monarchy, it was to a kind of kingship that Roche was named in 1962. His position in automotive history is secure, but not for his leadership. His reign will not be remembered for the size of its profits, nor for any of the products with which it flooded the American scene. James Roche will go down in the history of the industry as the man who was at the helm when the corporation hired private detectives to look for scandal in the private life of Ralph Nader. Roche was the man who was asked for, and made a public apology to Nader and to the U.S. Senate.

And if there was a man-of-the-decade in the car business, a single figure who symbolizes the significance of the automotive sixties, it was Roche's nemesis, Nader. No creative financier, no imaginative salesman, certainly no brilliant automotive designer emerged as the central figure of the automobile's most prolific decade. The most important figure was not a member of the industry at all, but its most persistent critic. Ralph Nader discovered, with his book and its response—and with his subsequent leadership as the guiding intelligence behind the rise of consumer advocacy—a broad vein of public rage against the automobile industry and all it stood for. Nader forecast accurately, if perhaps inadvertently, the death of the automobile. He and he alone breached the insulation of Detroit.[9]

PART II

Some Ancillary Disasters

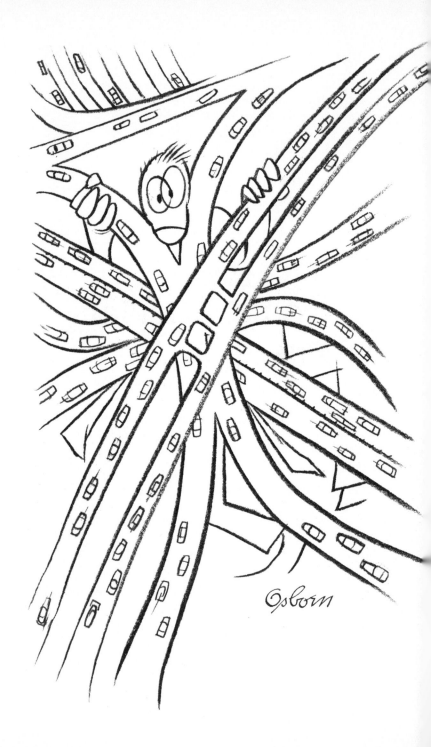

CHAPTER 5

The Road

A New Parkinson's Law

All roads led to Rome; the Appian Way was a miracle of modern engineering before the Interstate System was a gleam in Dwight Eisenhower's eye. Man has made a virtual religion of road-making. The Tao means "the way," the path to enlightenment. The road is a common symbol for man's life. Sects mount pilgrimages in their religious fervor. It is animal instinct to make paths, to trace and retrace until the unknown becomes familiar. The road is a form of knowledge; it organizes and classifies, reveals, tames, civilizes. It is a form of communication, as clearly a medium of interchange as speech. The road symbolizes the light side of man's nature, his courage and optimism, as clearly as the wall symbolizes all that is dark, distrustful, resolutely ignorant. Poets have worn both symbols thin with overuse.

But nobody has ever been as road-possessed as the Americans. The Westward movement, the history of the nation, is woven of "Trails": Cumberland, Overland, Oregon, Santa Fe,

Some Ancillary Disasters

Chisolm—stringing together the gaps and notches and passes which allowed the movement of men, then conveyances, then goods across our vast distances. America is a road epic; we have even developed a body of road art, Huck Finn to *The Grapes of Wrath* to *Easy Rider*, cutting loose to pursue the dream. Gold rushes and land grabs. No El Dorado or Seven Cities of Cibola ever materialized, so we built our own out of the prosperity and progress that followed our manic compulsion to clear pathways, carve soil, lay paving. We "opened up" the country. Now we can flow.

Suddenly we have run out the string on our own ancient instincts. The rate of our road-building accelerated to the point of self-parody. With no place else worth opening up, we began building roads to get to roads, roads on top of roads. We ceased to build in service to the noble motivations of interchange and communication. We stopped building roads *to* places. We began building roads *for* automobiles.

It is no coincidence that the initiation of what the Bureau of Public Roads is fond of calling "the largest single public-works project in the history of the world" occurred just as the golden era of the automobile industry was getting under way. Despite decades of almost totally ineffectual planning (projections of our current traffic glut began bouncing off Congress as early as 1944), we seemed capable of coping by conventional methods prior to 1955. That year, however, nobody could misread the production figures emanating from Detroit. A whole new concept of road-building was proposed, and failed by a whisker in Congress that year, primarily because no adequate funding method could be conceived for so large an undertaking. In 1956—aided, no doubt, by the pressure from 10 million more vehicles—imaginations were a little more fertile. The Interstate Highway System was launched, backed to the hilt by a generous and clever device called the Highway Trust Fund, which decreed that all federal taxes collected on motor vehicles, gasoline, and ancillary equipment would go to build a varicose network of "superhighways," for now and forever, amen, or until completion of the System. Specifically, the Trust Fund bumped gasoline taxes from two to three cents per gallon—increased to four cents in 1960. At the present rate, that fund generates $5 to 6 billion a year for more paving.

Well it might. As originally conceived, the System would cost $27 billion and take thirteen years to complete. Fifteen years and $43 billion later, the System still not completed, the estimates have been revised to twenty-five years and $70 billion. Some high government officials doubt the System will ever be finished. But in 1956, it was well and truly begun —at nine federal dollars for every one dollar from the state.

Look on our works, ye mighty, and despair. How the press releases rolled! Four hundred square miles of pavement! One and a half million acres of new right of way! Excavations to bury Connecticut knee deep. Sand, gravel, and stone to build a wall around the world fifty feet wide and nine feet high. Concrete enough for six sidewalks to the moon. Lumber from four hundred square miles of forest, 30 million tons of iron ore, 18 million tons of coal, and 6.5 million tons of limestone to refine the steel required. Culvert and drainpipe enough for both water and sewer systems for six cities the size of Chicago. Inspired by the *autobahnen* built by Hitler in Germany, 32,000 miles of Interstate were built by 1971; the system was then already twenty-five times as long as the total source of inspiration. It had already absorbed 2.2 billion man-hours of labor.

Also, by 1971, local lawsuits or local government action had halted the construction of Interstate projects in fifteen major American cities: Boston, Chicago, Hartford, Providence, Philadelphia, New York, Baltimore, Washington, Memphis, Nashville, Shreveport, Cleveland, San Antonio, San

Francisco, and Seattle.[1] It had become virtually impossible to gain acceptance for a new Interstate in any major urban area, and many rural segments of the plan—particularly those aimed like concrete daggers at the heart of any scenic or historical spot in the nation—were in trouble. For the same concerns which were inexorably bringing about the death of the automobile were similarly arrayed against the road-building empire. New accountings of new costs were here, too, applied. The sea change in the American mood is precisely characterized by the Bureau of Public Roads' press releases. When the Interstate was initiated, consumption of a million and a half acres of right of way or four hundred square miles of forest was fit material for boasting; now it has become a shameful admission.

Meanwhile, the new sorcerers of the American economic scene had appeared: the planners. The *new* planners, whose principal initial contribution was to demonstrate how perfectly incompetent, how diametrically wrong, the old planners had been. The old planners had told us that we must build more, wider, longer roads to ease traffic congestion, and so we plunged into the building as if possessed by furies. Joke: the new planners have discovered that more, wider, longer roads *make* congestion, manufacture it as systematically as Detroit manufactures the cars of which the congestion is composed. The old planners had told us that roads connected; the roads we built for that purpose have more effectively divided. The old planners told us that roads would make us free; the roads we built have become instruments in our own repression.

Freeways make congestion. It is a difficult premise to accept during those rare and beautiful moments when you burst free of two-lane congestion onto recently constructed, open freeway, accelerating as if at the start of the Indianapolis 500. Go whistling through the heart of any city at an off-hour (or rather, *above* the heart of the city, on concrete-stilted freeway), and you won't believe that freeways cause congestion—forgetting that the local streets of the city itself are often uncongested at off-hours. Why *don't* more and better highways reduce traffic congestion? Do they suspend the law of supply and demand?

If supply and demand operate at all in the only vaguely understood world of traffic management, then freeways represent an element of demand, rather than supply. Simply enough, we build too many cars too fast. (President Nixon, appealing to Congress for mass transit funds in 1969: "We cannot build roads fast enough to keep pace with the production of automobiles.") Worse, our automotive productive capacity is accelerating as fast as capital expansion can push it, while our highway-building capacity is not. Even if our appetite for new highways were to continue unabated, we are approaching limits in available space in the areas where we "need" freeways most. Automotive production, absorbed by fifteen years of relatively steady economic growth, by urban and suburban sprawl which have come about almost specifically to provide storage and operational space for that production, suffers no such constraint.

Add the sure knowledge, never adequately weighed in early freeway planning, that freeways simply generate their own traffic. Helen Leavitt calls this "a variation on Parkinson's Law that expenditures rise to meet income . . . congestion rises to meet highway capacity." [2] Freeways attract cars like magnets, pulling traffic off the secondary roads and local streets. Freeways funnel local traffic, in search of convenience, into the streams of long-haul through traffic for which the freeways were originally planned. Cars that feed onto a freeway must, eventually, get off. It's a simple enough notion, but one on which superhighway project after superhighway project turns from glorious freeway to dangerous

Some Ancillary Disasters

bottleneck. Freeways are built *to* something; they are intended as connecting devices; they are target oriented. Although traffic may come onto them sporadically, in well-dispersed entry points, all too often that traffic is, in the end, simply dumped, at whatever destination inspired the building of the highway in the first place. Six lanes into two, the bottleneck sending waves of congestion rippling back out the freeway to close off the very freeness for which it was created. Heavily patronized exits, even if they don't mark the terminal point of the freeway, cause several times more stoppage and congestion than do entrances.

Nothing works. The most elaborate and carefully wrought plans, when converted into concrete, suddenly bulge with overloads in wrong places, sucking cars seemingly out of thin air and giving them nowhere to go. Attempting to reduce congestion simply by spreading cars out over more roadway is like attempting to avoid drowning by brushing back the sea.

Planners work from maps. People don't live on maps. To look at a map is automatically to visualize connecting lines, here to there; that's what maps are for, to establish symbolic relationships of distance and direction. But to move from home to store, one does not trace lines; one moves through terrain, neighborhoods, living locales. Roads provide *borders;* life stacks up along the edges. What is only a symbolic interconnection on the map is in reality a living interface, a method of organization in the real world. The road is not so much interconnection as division.

Man's fortunate adaptability has allowed him gradually to become able to tolerate the movement and disruption along the dividing lines. The bordering traffic has accelerated not only in density but also in speed—3 miles per hour, 10, 30, 50. As speeds pick up the dividing widths necessarily grow larger, physically and psychically. The attendant resculpturing of the earth grows more dramatic. The division gets more massive as the mobility through it grows swifter. Finally, the division must be protected from man himself; one finds the ultimate absurdity of the stilted, concrete-encased, landscaped, fenced-off freeway, a total barrier. Built *for* the automobile, not for any human purpose; allow any human intrusion and the precious *flow* will be stopped. No access; one must go under or over, which multiplies the astronomical cost astronomically. To save costs cross-flow is dispersed to wider and wider points, reinforcing the barrier.

We do not place our barriers lightly, in this society. In practice we use them to separate the pleasant from the unpleasant, the safe from the dangerous, the bearable from the unbearable. For unpleasant, dangerous, unbearable, read "ghetto." Only the rising effectiveness of the civil-rights movement has slowed our comfortable tradition of using road construction to wall off the under classes, as an instrument of repression.[3]

The Interstate System isn't the only road-building concept in America that has gone awry (it consumes only $5 to 6 billion out of a total annual expenditure on roads of about $21 billion). But it is the most visible, and generates the most criticism. As the biggest, most expensive, most disruptive, and undoubtedly the most graft-ridden roadway project in history, this fifteen-year exercise in conspicuous tax consumption is as eloquently symbolic of what went wrong with road-building as the 1970 Impala is symbolic of what went wrong with car-building. The Interstate provides a kind of rueful guide to changing national priorities *in absentia,* and the effect of those changes on the best efforts of the beleaguered planning profession.

It was in overlooking the crisis of the cities that loomed in the sixties that the planners erred most tragically, and it was in the urban end of the Interstate System that a great portion of the trouble with that system lay. The original plan had been to skirt the cities entirely, and when President Eisenhower discovered that subsequent modifications had the Interstate piercing most of the major American cities, he kicked the plan back for further study—a study that was completed during John F. Kennedy's first year in office, at about the same time the Highway Trust Fund was jumped from three cents per gallon to four. Nobody expected an equitable distribution of urban and rural Interstate mileage or funds. The estimated differential between urban and rural land acquisition and construction costs led to a planned urban-rural split of the original $27 billion funding on a 55-45 percent basis. Even this was less than fair, as 80 percent of the mileage, and consequently the tax money, would be generated by users of the urban portions of the system. Restriction of tax benefits strictly to the specific payer of the tax is always a difficult scheme to apply, but in the case of the Interstate, its legislative architects felt that something approaching an equitable version of such a scheme had in fact been devised. The people who buy gasoline pay for the highways on which to burn that gasoline; what could be fairer than that?

As Helen Leavitt has pointed out, in practice the Highway Trust Fund has become a little like using a drinking-alcohol tax to expand the liquor industry. So far, however, the Trust Fund has been relatively unassailable. It ought to be—it's got enough people looking out for it.

Power Is as Power Does

The first principles of the Interstate were laid down, and some of the route selections made, in the late thirties—indication of a degree of foresight without precedent in the halls of Washington bureaucracy. The plan was approved in 1956, to meet traffic projections for 1975. The projections were undoubtedly exceeded within ten years; no stretch of urban freeway in the Eastern or Western megalopic corridors has been completed since 1955 that hasn't exceeded within three years the projected maximum traffic volume for which it was planned, not just for the next decade or so but for its useful lifetime.

And highways do last a long time, nailing down patterns of movement and organizational relationships in ways that are extremely difficult to change. According to John Burby, 70 percent of the nation's highway bridges were built before 1935; by extension the bridges built today will be in service well past the year 2000.[4] How wide does that mean they have to be? (The trucking interests are even now clamoring for larger gross widths and weights.) How much can we afford to spend on them? Planners considered 1971's $21-billion road expenditure inadequate. That was *in* 1971, not *by* 1971. It was equal to a tenth of the federal budget. There is no end in sight.

The automobile and highway interests are given to painting rosy pictures of what by any other standards than their own is a dreary future indeed for this country. There were 109 million cars, trucks, and buses using the nation's roads in 1971, and the car-and-road people project that this figure will double in thirty years. On the face of it, that means doubling the 3.7 million miles of roadway we've already built, repairing what wears out, and finding space somewhere for twice as much parking as is now—now and then—available, just to maintain the nation at its present state of congestion.

On the basis of those figures, the announced goals of the American Association of State Highway Officials—one of the visible tips of the highway-lobby iceberg—sound modest:

Some Ancillary Disasters

$80 billion of federal funding for 360,000 miles of new roads, 53,000 of them to be expressways. Department of Transportation officials estimate that the $80-billion figure will rise to $200 billion by 1985, if the inflationary rate for costs for the first fifteen years of the Interstate System is a workable guideline. Pork-barrel legislation by various congressmen pending at the end of the 1970 session of Congress called for another 30,000 miles of highway construction. Extensive experience with the highway lobby has made the DOT leery of just about anyone else's figures. Perhaps a more accurate estimate of the road people's plans for the nation is given by the acerbic Burby: $320 billion in new roads by 1985, and "a level of spending on highways after 1985 which . . . would, by the turn of the century, reach the staggering total of $100 billion a year." [5]

The car-and-road people are immensely powerful. Early in Secretary of Transportation John Volpe's period of office, he told *The New York Times:*

> I don't know who the "highway lobby" could be except the 205 million Americans who want to travel more efficiently than they do today. The average American spends 13 percent of his working day behind the wheel of a car, getting to and from work. He wants an improvement, and that's what highways can provide. [6]

In the unlikely event that Mr. Volpe—a former president of the Associated General Contractors, a powerful lobbying body in itself—is still unclear as to the composition of the group in question, specific identification is not difficult. One might start with the fact that six of the ten largest U.S. corporations in *Fortune*'s "First 500" are directly connected with automotive transportation (car manufacturers and oil companies). Add steel, and twenty-two out of the largest fifty are in automobiles and highways for the bulk of their income.

But the corporations most directly involved are only the

most visible. The scurry work, the wheedling and coercion, the swapping of favors and collection of political debts, is done by a large and complexly interwoven network of associations and pressure groups. More or less overt lobbyists. The American Association of State Highway Officials (AASHO—seldom pronounced acronymically) is just one of them—an association of state government representatives whose bureaucratic empires depend on more highway construction. Another, the American Road Builders Association, indicates in its own literature the pervasive reach of highway interests; it is made up of "highway contractors, manufacturers, and distributors of highway construction equipment, materials producers and suppliers, faculty members and students of engineering colleges and universities, engineers, investment bankers, state and federal highway officials, and members of Congress." Half the membership consists of contractors. Helen Leavitt points out, "The association is located, appropriately, in a new building side-by-side with the Donohue Building which houses the Federal Highway Administration in Washington's southwest renewal area."[7]

Add half a dozen other specific lobbying groups in Washington, including the civilian-sounding Highway Users Federation for Safety and Mobility, a group formed out of the old National Highway Users Conference, the Automotive Safety Foundation, and the Auto Industry Safety Committee. The new organization's first piece of creativity indicated the level of commitment to mobility, if not to safety: "Act Now!" the organization warned its huge mailing list. "The Highway Trust Fund should be continued on a permanent basis for highways—with none of its money diverted. Now is the time to say, loud and clear, 'I want the money I pay for highways used for highways.'"[8]

Add tire manufacturers, building trade and teamster unions, truckers, concrete, paint, and asphalt manufacturers (and the distributors, retailers, haulers, and their service industries for these commodities). Add such associations as the U.S. Chamber of Commerce, for generalities, and for specifics, the American Public Works Association, the National Automobile Dealers Association, the Rubber Manufacturers Association, the National Crushed Stone Association, the National Limestone Institute, the National Asphalt Pavement Association, the National Ready Mixed Concrete Association, the American Concrete Paving Association, the Asphalt Institute, the American Petroleum Institute, the National Association of Motor Bus Owners, the Private Truck Council (or better, the American Trucking Associations, the organizing body for sixty-four separate state trucking associations, plus the District of Columbia and thirteen other "conferences"), the Truck-Trailer Manufacturers Association, and even such benign and superficially public-spirited organizations as the National Safety Council and AAA, both of them captives of the car-and-road legions. Add the tourist industry, the motel and hotel operators, the travel agents. Add the various affiliated and disaffiliated automotive "aftermarket" industries.

Add you and me. Just to make Mr. Volpe happy. We want better highways, or if we don't most of our fellow citizens do. We sweat and curse in the commuter traffic jams, dodge the potholes, wander fruitlessly in search of the parking spaces. We demand representation in city, state, and federal governments to cure those ills, and in so doing we construct other, more powerful lobbies, closer to the funds. About 70 percent of the capital expenditures of the individual states goes for the building and maintenance of roads. From the other 30 percent comes schools, public buildings, offices, hospitals, parks, and anything else the state might want to build.

My state, New Hampshire, has no income or sales taxes, no obtrusive government at any level. Ice and snow removal is a tremendous problem in winter, repair of the winter's ravages a major budget item in summer. The only way a state legislator can show the folks at home he is doing *anything* is by securing good road service for them. The only political hold, therefore, that a pressure group can apply to the legislator is through the highway department. The highway department is the political powerhouse in state government, the one function that a governor meddles with only at grave risk to his political future.

Good roads are right in there with motherhood and apple pie as political issues in the U.S.—*vide* that $21 billion in 1971. It is hard to imagine a more comfortable seat than that of a lobbyist who has the voters on the side of his client, in his attempts to arm-twist the government. The car-and-road forces, however, weren't satisfied with the weight of that power base; for the Interstate program they also pulled the Pentagon into the act. The bill was sold as an essential aspect of national defense, despite the fact that in our last full-scale mobilization in World War II, the railroads carried 90 percent of the military freight and 97 percent of the military passenger traffic. In the campaign to sell the Interstate, add to motherhood and apple pie that other cornerstone of political stampede-making, the grand old flag. When the original bill was passed, there was a single vote against it in the U.S. Senate. That, folks, is big-league lobbying.

One might expect such a congruence of economic, political, military, and public support to provide sufficient momentum to pave the entire nation, and for a decade and a half there seemed little likelihood of any other fate. We *had* to pave, of course, for the *cars*. "I still have not found anybody who can tell me," said Robert Moses, New York City's premier of paving, "how you are going to keep on turning out all these cars without decent, first-class, modern highways for them to run on." [9] To the increasing consternation of the highwaymen, however, there is now possible a vision of the end of the road. There is political pressure building to stop the bulldozers. Golden ages have a way of coming to an end.

What If We Just Don't Build It?

Alfred E. Johnson, executive secretary of the AAHSO, describes the rise of the enemy viewpoint: "There's about three percent of our population that's at the creative level, the prima donnas, the critical ones. And right now, they're anti-highway. I always say you can afford to satisfy ninety-seven percent of the people, but if you try for one hundred percent, you break the banks." [10]

The prima donnas have been gathering ammunition. Burrowing through piles of statistics, gauging human reaction, measuring the cumulative effect of our fifteen-year orgy of Interstate-building, the prima donnas have been gaining recruits; judging by the fate of the Interstate program in our major cities, one would have to assume that 3 percent of Alf Johnson's estimate is a little low. One result has been the development of a politically potent work kit of antihighway ammunition. Perhaps that's one of the problems with creativity. As a kind of countermelody to the hymns of the highway builders, the resistance points to the following arguments.

• Highway projects systematically devastate ghettos, historical regions, and park. Cost-conscious engineers understandably go where land acquisition is least expensive. The ghetto combines this unhappy feature with the added attraction of endemic political powerlessness. It is classical repression to take from the Have-Nots to give—in this case, "luxury" highways—to Haves. The effect of highway programs on the ghetto is one of impaction, in the medical sense.

As cities develop in drift and dislocation, the movement is traditionally away from the older, hence historical sections. History has a low property value. Even in those instances where public acquisition of historical sites has taken place, the engineers are not necessarily stopped. Failing to obtain cheap private property, the highway program will then seek public land. In a dispute between tangible values (hospitals, administrative offices, city halls, bricks and mortar) and intangible ones (history, beauty, parks), the "soft" values always lose.

• Highways kill inner-city retail activity. Merchants have often been self-sold on better access to their wares via freeway, failing to realize that a convenient way in is more frequently used as a convenient way out. About 80 percent of inner-city freeway traffic is composed of commuters. Commuters don't shop; instead, they take up parking space from would-be shoppers. Inner-city department stores which have experienced the freeway phenomenon estimate the value of a convenient parking space for a single car at $10,000 per year in retail business. The lone U.S. city which has rejected freeways (and an accompanying $240 million in federal funds), San Francisco, has had an increase in inner-city retail business in the last decade. Otherwise the national trend is distinctly downward.

• Freeways have missed their market. They were envisioned by the planners of the forties and fifties as through routes for trucks, buses, and defense machinery, with a minimum of private cars; instead, they are instantly filled with commuters, living outside the city and working within. The automobile commuter is the specific disaster that is killing the cities. Freeways make him possible.

• Highways remove property from the tax rolls at the very time when the cities are starving for revenue. See commuters, above, who pay property taxes only outside the cities, but use the city services. In actuality, highway space merely stops generating property tax and starts generating gasoline taxes—which go directly into building more roads. We've paved about twenty five thousand square miles of the U.S. so far, an area roughly equal to West Virginia. That's a lot of property tax.

• Multilane, limited-access roads concentrate high-speed traffic at dangerous levels. Although safer on a nationwide statistical basis, freeways benefit statistically from the large percentage of rural, minimum-traffic miles. When something goes wrong in four lanes of 60-MPH traffic, it goes wrong in a big way—and the rash of chain collisions which the freeways have "created" as a new phenomenon of American life —such as the one hundred-car smash-up in California in 1969 —provide a counterinterpretation of the safety statistics.

• Highway programs tend to turn into a Big Casino for land speculators; 2000 percent profits are commonplace for astute—and often political—land investment. Watch the freeway go in, see the Big Rich get richer. Nine road-builders have accounted for more than $100 million in road work in the past six years; Holiday Inns has managed to get 545 motels onto Interstate interchanges, for a 1970 profit of $1.2 billion; the rental-car agencies have doubled their revenues in ten years, and attribute much of the growth to the Interstate System.[11] Profit fits comfortably into the American Dream, of course, but these are a little too clearly tax supported to be politically clean.

• Growing public demand for local control has no place in the road-making mechanism. Most projects are planned by highway engineers from the state, with no urban-planning experience, working against urban planners with no real concept of the requirements of "good" highway design. Despite the DOT's recent doubling of the public hearing schedule— over violent highway-lobby objections—no highway official is under any legal ruling to do more than listen to the complaints of the public.[12]

- Highways are planned on the basis of highway use, rather than as adjuncts to a community. The highwayman's concept of research is the "generation" of "desire lines"— traffic volume estimates obtained from roadside surveys of existing traffic. (With a fudge factor called "trip generation" —the capacity of a road to *create* use—thrown in.) When community research is done, as by Chicago's Crosstown Design Team (involving architects, urban designers, city planners, sociologists, urban geographers, economists, lawyers, and market analysts, as well as highway engineers— perhaps the most thorough job of highway planning yet done in the U.S.), the cost is invariably multiplied by 100 to 250 percent. See Mr. Johnson's prima donnas; even the Highway Trust Fund can't sustain the cost of doing highways right. If we're going to make the cities inhuman, there is a better, more efficient way to solve the problem at a fraction of the cost: mass transit.

- Roads make community designers out of land speculators. The speculator acquires some acreage in a convenient place, puts up a mass of housing, and the city must supply him with roads—it must rescue its citizens from entrapment out there where they've bought homes. Suddenly the city has grown in a new way, in a direction nobody, not even the speculator, had really planned on. There is no mechanism for preventing the speculator from taking the money and running from the responsibility, as most statute books are currently constituted. Protecting the citizenry with more careful planning and less ready dispersal of road-building funds would slow the sprawl.

- Roads, tend, at worst, to increase our population imbalance; at best, they freeze the imbalance at current marginally operable levels. Roads allow the suburbs to remain under-

119

populated, in community planners' terms, and sprawled to the point of absurdity—so that cars are necessary for all services, and roads are necessary for the cars, and so on. That's why—without even considering more serious questions such as racial balance—our children get thirty-mile school-bus runs.

• Road construction in the developed portion of the nation destroys housing (usually the low-cost variety, of course) at a time when there is a critical shortage of that commodity, a vitally more important basic requirement than mobility. Nobody knows how much housing has been destroyed in the past fifteen years; the original Interstate scheme called for the condemnation of 750,000 pieces of private property, and since that time the plan has been expanded by another twenty-five hundred miles, most of them urban.

• The Interstate System and similar long-haul roadways subsidize commercial users at the expense of private users. Trucking companies gain two dollars in operating efficiencies for every ninety cents they pay out in taxation for the Interstate. It's a notion that might well be recalled every time you see one of those lumbering monsters with a sign on its rear saying, "This vehicle pays $3200 in highway use taxes." Such a subsidy of one form of transportation comes at the expense of others, allowing an already badly skewed national transportation system to plunge further off balance.

• Road-building programs militate against development of workable public transit systems. Fully 25 percent of the population of the U.S. *must* use public transportation to travel at all—the young, the poor, the infirm, the elderly, the resolutely nonautomotive. Road-building taxes them to provide mobility for the rest of us. It also taxes them *and* us to subsidize the auto-makers, the road-makers, and the auto-users while they are destroying our environment.

• While at the urban end roads cause congestion, tax

depletion, urban flight, and a host of environmental disasters, at the rural end they simply cost too much. Elaborate cost justifications on the part of the highway lobby ("cost-benefits" in lobby parlese) invariably distort the figures: rural road costs compared with urban benefits, for example, or costs to the population as a whole compared with benefits to high-mileage users. Paid lobbyists are fond of elaborate accounting measures which reduce wildly incompatible categories of costs to simplistic benefits. Almost never do the lobbyists include postconstruction maintenance costs which the state and local community are stuck with. These run approximately 10 percent per year, according to *Earth Tool Kit*.[13] Suddenly the 90 percent federal money for Interstate mileage (50 percent for major national highways) begins shrinking, when the municipality realizes it will "pay back" the funds at such a maintenance rate.

• Highways increase congestion. Mass transit decreases congestion. A lane of highway filled with cars carries about thirty-six hundred passengers per hour. The same lane filled with buses will carry sixty thousand people per hour. A train, using the same amount of space, will carry forty-two thousand people an hour. Yet we subsidize highway construction and refuse to subsidize mass transit.

• Highways are aimed at providing convenient routes between more and more distant points, at reduced traffic levels. Linking more distant points with a single form of transportation increases the need for automobiles. More automobiles need more highways to rereduce traffic levels. The urban-suburban-exurban sprawl isn't just exacerbated by road-building, it was created by it.

• Besides, nobody knows how to make highways work. For automobiles, yes; for the nation, for the public that pays for them, that is dislocated by them, not yet. Very likely never.

The crucial year for the highway battle was to have been

Some Ancillary Disasters

1970, the year in which the Highway Trust Fund ran out with the Interstate System only three-fourths completed. Despite a series of major urban victories by the antihighway forces, stopping freeway construction in many cities, the pros—in every sense of the word—persevered. Representative George Fallon of Baltimore, the Democrat who invented the Trust Fund in the first place, lost his race for reelection. His Republican partner-in-paving, William C. Cramer, chose to run for the Senate in Florida and also lost. Presidents Johnson and Nixon occasionally withheld Trust Fund money from the program, keeping it frozen as a damping influence on inflation—and drawing political hailstorms from the state governors and the lobbying groups as a result. Nevertheless, 1970 accounted for more highway program gains than losses. The Trust Fund was extended for another five years, giving it time to gather and disburse another $30 billion for highways. Minor antihighway concessions will divert small sums for suburban parking lots and express bus lanes, to the chagrin of the lobbyists, and $150 million (3 percent of the year's total Interstate funding) will go into safety programs, but the bulk of the booty still goes to stringing out Interstate mileage.

The future for the bulldozers may not always be so bright. Perennial maverick Henry Ford II kicked off 1972 by finally breaking the monolithic unity of the car-and-road alignment. Mr. Ford actually recommended diverting Trust Fund revenues to the development of mass transit. He didn't specify a percentage, in fact insisted that the beginnings must be small, but he did suggest that a start must be made. A gloomy day ensued at AASHO, one must suppose.

Meanwhile, the planners are campaigning hard for a systems-analysis approach to traffic control and to the problems of the transportation system in general. Such an approach, they say, might allow us to reduce the highway portion of the cost by reducing the estimates, always headily inflated, of the future need. Which in turn might prevent the outright extinction of all forms of transportation in this country other than commercial aircraft and public and private motor vehicles. Lacking such a sense of proportion, the planners tell us, they are reduced to such retaliative measures as painting lines on the pavement to control traffic. ("Don't ever sell the paint can short," the late Traffic Commissioner Barnes of New York City was fond of saying. "You can do more with a gallon of paint than you can with ten traffic cops.")

The planners can also synchronize traffic lights. If you synchronize the traffic lights on a length of roadway, the capacity of that roadway is increased by between 10 and 30 percent, which is considerably cheaper than building an additional road. Then you have the road filled to capacity *with* synchronized traffic lights, and there you are again.

If one is toting up the scorecard for Bureau of Public Roads' statistics on square-miles-paved, highway-building seems to proceed quite rapidly. If you are fighting daily traffic on the homebound commute, watching in frustration as the bulldozers grind away at the adjacent unopened freeway, then road-building seems the most ponderous of processes. The road lobby plays on the latter impression. "We must build for the future," they are always telling us. "We must plan now to avoid the traffic jams of the next century." Positively geologic is the pace; one cannot avoid comparisons with the Ice Age, particularly since our own seems also best characterized by a sheet of inorganic devastation that sweeps all before it.

Yet we began building roads for automobiles only about seventy years ago, and for twenty-five of those years we've had serious congestion—while spending federal and state funds with what can only be described as grim abandon, in the fruitless effort to buy our way out of that congestion. Obviously we will have escalating congestion throughout the foreseeable future, as long as we are inextricably wedded to the automobile. If we could not solve the problem with 100 million vehicles, how can we hope to with 200 or 300 million? We are "attacking" the problem by giving in to it.

A more rational approach would have us think about transportation problems a little less apocalyptically. Twenty-five years of experience in living and coping with irreducible congestion would seem to remove the urgency from our road-building plans. It isn't going to get any better as long as we have automobiles as the sole basis of our transportation system, and twenty-five years of experience has pushed us to no cleverer solution than to build more roads to hold the more cars that we've built and bought. But twenty-five years have kept the pressure on; maybe with another twenty-five under our belts, we will begin to think of new ways to go. Or maybe we won't go at all. On examination, the latter course seems much more probable. The question seems to be whether we will choose that course or be forced into it.

CHAPTER 6

The Law

Flogging the Devil

It appears to be an inexorable rule that the laws with which we attempt to control our machines go wrong.

The fatal flaw that precludes a workable legal attitude toward the automobile was introduced in the beginning, by our own psychology—happening, one can surmise, in the second moment of automotive experience. There was that initial sensation—movement, speed, wind in the face, noise, excitement: this is *fun*. The second moment carried the countersensation: therefore it must be wrong. The carefully nurtured American sense of guilt triumphed. If it is fun, it is evil. It is very likely morally sapping, inimical to the common weal. Maddening, perhaps. The early mechano-wizard popping and sputtering across the back pasture didn't have to wait for the parson to thunder down from the pulpit that the horseless carriage was the devil's instrument. He already knew, from the sheer sensation of driving it.

We've been trying to exorcise that devil ever since. Actually, we do know better now, but superstition is stronger than science. In seventy years of experience with the machine, we have come up with no better central basis of its control than speed limits, surveillance, arrest, punishment. The other traffic control mechanisms are beside the point, almost automatic. They work. Speed control doesn't. It is the only one we keep juggling, jiggling, trying to make it function.

The scientists hand us other information, different tools. More than 85 percent of the traffic accidents that happen in this country are caused by factors other than speeding (so the other 15 percent confirm and reinforce our dark view of ourselves, "human nature"). If no one ever exceeded 50 MPH, at least 60 percent of the fatalities and an even larger portion of the injuries would still occur (but you can just *feel* the danger when you go too fast). Mile for mile, 65 MPH is a safer speed on a major rural highway than 35 MPH; a nationwide rural speed limit of 40 MPH would boost the fatality rate to nearly 100,000 per year. During World War II when a nationwide speed limit of 35 MPH was enforced, the accident rate on the Pennsylvania Turnpike—ordinarily 70 MPH, even for 1940 automobiles—reached a peak never since equaled. (But if there were no speed limits, why, the highways would just be chaos. There would be no *order*.)

We commute, fight traffic, stew in waiting lines and congestion. We learn the unconscious truth that escapes the lawmakers but informs the reality of those who live with traffic: we must move. Faster. Watch a traffic cop directing cars out of a lump of congestion. His driving impulse is *speed;* he snarls and whistles and frantically waves us on, faster, move it *out*. He knows that traffic is bad but stasis is worse, that traffic stops being traffic when it halts. Observe Manhattan traffic, where there is a legal statute assigning some meaningless number of miles per hour as a limit beyond which vehicles may not go, but where in fact the operable speed limit is how fast you *can* go. The reality, whether it is 4 MPH or 55: if there is space in front of you, fill it, move through it as quickly as possible. There is no time for obeisance to archaic notions about traffic; too many others want to move also. Speeding arrests on Manhattan Island? Perhaps rarely on the two outer parkways, almost never "inside." What policeman dares stop the flow long enough to write a citation?

Most Americans, quite simply, drive as fast as they safely can. We have a survival instinct; "safely" means in a manner safe not only from death but also from arrest. We trip along the line. We know all the tricks. We learn quickly, when we begin driving, which kinds of cars are likely to be patrol cars, where they are most apt to be located. We know how to recognize the bubble-topped silhouette, how to tell the hump of a taxi from the hump of a squad car. A driver friend once explained to me how she knew police were about: "When everyone else starts being supercautious, creeping along, you know right away someone has seen a cop. It's almost a vibration." We know how important it is to reduce our driving behavior to its most unobtrusive level when we feel we are being watched. And we do feel we are being watched.

They are looking for us. Most routine efforts to control crime are relatively passive; traffic enforcement is active. And we very likely have been breaking the law—it is almost impossible not to, with the pace of traffic and the ubiquitous complexity of the traffic codes—and we accept the guilt.

Motor-vehicle law in this country deals with three distinct segments of car use and ownership. At the base are a relative few, simple rules of form, devised to promote flow. One does, after all, keep to the right. Enforcement of the form is necessary; violators are truly antisocial. But violation of the form also implies such a catastrophe that our universal experience with the consequences—by media scare campaigns and the visual evidence of our junkyards, if not by the law of averages —that self-enforcement is effective.

The next level of motor vehicle law is the realm of the arbitrary. So many miles per hour for certain types of highway. Urban area limits of 25 MPH whether the urban area consists of twisting 25-foot two-lane or semideserted industrial park. Highways on which 70 MPH is "legal" in howling ice storms —in daylight—but which are restricted to 55 MPH on the softest and most clearly moonlit summer nights. No-passing zones laid down by rulebook rather than the rational requirements of the specific situation. Oscillating inconsistencies in the placement of stop signs and yield signs. Rapid sequences of speed-limit changes based on bureaucratic classification of highway types, rather than on experience with the roads in question. This arbitrariness invites violation by the public, which in turn invites a kind of arbitrary enforcement of the laws. It is this enforcement which has grown in importance until it has long ago overshadowed the purpose the enforcement was designed to achieve.

The third level of motor vehicle law is simple—no, never simple—bureaucracy: the explosion of functions pasted on after the fact, primarily in uncoping attempts to stop this gap or that in the network of custom and commerce surrounding the automobile and its use, that has proliferated almost as quickly as the automobile itself. The mad tangle of ponderous machinery entangling the municipality, the state, the owner, the buyer, the seller, the thief, and the threatened bystander: licensing, registration, insurance, inspection, sale and resale, notarization, taxation, driver qualification. The legal mare's nest.

Toppling the Block

The rules of form for traffic governance are perhaps best examined through the medium of our various attempts at driver education, an enterprise that so far in this country consists almost entirely of training in the first level of elementary coordinations of vehicle management. Driver education is a singular phenomenon, particularly in its public-school version. It serves to enlist our young in support of a single industry by offering them the twin bribes of an ordered and semiautomatic progression toward an operator's license (hallowed certificate of adulthood in our culture), and the economic reward of a lifetime of insurance rate discounts (a practice now being abandoned by insurance firms as unproductive).

That is perhaps too cynical a view. Since we are at present trapped into a single transportation system, a sure knowledge of how to operate within that system is almost as much a part of citizenship as franchisement. Furthermore, since our accident rate amounts to a major national health problem which strikes with particular viciousness at our younger drivers, any attempt to upgrade the driving skills of those young might be regarded as a patriotic and socially useful mechanism. Car dealers are perhaps to be congratulated for their public-spiritedness in loaning new cars to high-school driver's-ed programs (24,231 cars loaned in 1967). Never mind the get-'em-into-the-product-while-they're-young connotations of such programs.

Unfortunately most driver's-ed programs in the public schools are organized almost obsessively around the attraction of the cherished license, and while slight attention may be given to other aspects of the automobile and its safe operation, the focus of the student is on obtaining that ticket to freedom. Commercial driving schools are worse offenders: most of them in their promotional come-ons provide an ambiguously worded "guarantee" that the license will be obtained, and usually shepherd the student step by step to the license examiner's doorstep, then abandon him.

Although the operator's license is a part of the bureaucracy of automobile law, its focus is narrowly centered on the minimum rudiments of operation. The standard state requirements vary slightly, but usually include a brief written test on the basic laws, a rough check of visual acuity of the applicant, and a brief demonstration of his driving in the company of an examiner. In the last test, the driver must demonstrate smooth operation of the vehicle at low speeds on city streets, avoid for perhaps ten minutes the violation of any laws governing the movement of vehicles, and, usually, demonstrate one or another curious fringe skill of car management, such as parallel parking or back-and-fill U turns in a narrow street. Many states require a demonstration of a "panic stop"—the last of these I observed (from the driver's seat) required braking the car suddenly and severely enough to topple a small wooden block that the examiner had placed on the floor of the car. No consideration of judgment of distances was involved, no mention of clearing the immediate rear to avoid a tail-end collision, almost no demonstration of control of the car during the emergency test. If you topple the block of wood—and don't have an accident in the process —you pass. The virtue of such a test in the eyes of the examiners, and the state, is that it is objective; *any* license examiner can judge the results.

And so the driving schools teach the subject. One learns to check both ways before pulling away from the curb, to give hand signals, to beep before passing, to keep to the right, to stop for stop signs and yield rights of way when so bidden.

One does *not* learn to control a car in a skid, to judge limits of adhesion and thus when skids are about to commence, to know the parameters of car behavior, to take evasive action, to spot escape routes for emergencies, to stay awake on monotonous freeways at high *or* low speeds, to find routes or interpret confusing direction signs, to maintain a car in safe mechanical condition and to recognize incipient mechanical failure that might be dangerous, to cope with failed brakes, runaway throttles, jammed transmissions, or dead batteries. One doesn't usually learn anything about dealing with the quite different circumstances and problems of night driving. One New York City commercial driving school—eight dollars for each forty-five-minute lesson—requires that the student sign up for an additional course of instruction to learn "freeway driving." The assumption seems to be that the standard course of instruction teaches operation of the vehicle at speeds up to approximately 30 MPH—enough for the license—but for higher speeds, another course is necessary. Too bad the same distinctions aren't made in the licensing.

Thus, as former *Car and Driver* magazine editor Gordon Jennings pointed out, "There is nothing in any state driving test that would detect simple incompetence; detection is now left to direct exposure on the road." [1] One learns only to flow smoothly within the minimum requirements of the driving skill, as if everything was always going to go exactly right. Accidents don't happen when everything goes exactly right. Driving schools so far are incapable of setting up learning situations to give experience with failures of the system. (Exception: *racing* driving schools. Yes, such bizarre institutions do exist—see Chapter 8. Quite frequently they also serve to teach highway patrol officers high-speed and emergency car handling. Any motorist would benefit from at least a brief exposure to such a curriculum.) The standard driver-education courses pour more inexperienced fledgling drivers into traffic. Perfectly *legal* inexperienced fledgling drivers, of course. The effect isn't totally negative; the drivers would pour into traffic anyway, with or without training in the minimal skills.

Despite decades of lobbying by the automobile industry to insure that total responsibility for the formation and enforcement of our traffic system be dispersed among the states (rather than administered coherently on a nationwide basis by the federal government, thus opening the door to the dread specter of federal intervention into other automotive matters), the system works, albeit sometimes marginally. In all fairness, if the industry has fought against uniformity administered from above, it has labored—and invested—mightily to achieve uniformity from below, at the state and local levels. A licensed American driver can fly to any state, rent a car, and launch himself into traffic with confidence that he is not going to be befuddled by an exotic system. Most of this is the result of the labors of various industry-subsidized associations of code-writing and law-enforcing officials. A few rare exceptions to the uniformity do occur. State laws vary with regard to speed limits, school-bus rights of way, right turns on red lights, passing on the right, stopping for pedestrian crosswalks. But while the driver may be momentarily confused by such variance (if he even notices), he will by and large be able to drive without too much danger of running afoul of the law, or of initiating an accident by violation of the local system. So long as his fellow motorists also choose to stay within the rules. If everything goes right.

It is tempting to say that such a system of workable minimums is all we need in the way of regulation, despite the hue and cry of the more zealous protectors of the public safety. It probably isn't, however; we probably do need some kind of further regulation, on evidence of the accident rate alone. If we could get it. We can't. Minimal though it is, our basic rules of flow are the only part of the traffic system that works at all. It's when we begin to get clever—technologically, bureaucratically, sociologically, moralistically clever— that our automotive legal system begins to fall apart.

Slow Down and Die

The importance of flow as the ultimate goal of traffic planning (as opposed to control, as with arbitrary speed limits) can best be judged by examining the findings of the Bureau of Public Roads, in a massive study of six hundred miles of highway in eleven states. The study was authorized by the same law that created the Interstate System in 1956, submitted to Congress in 1959, and virtually ignored ever since. The Bureau interviewed 290,000 drivers, collected statistics on 3.7 billion miles of travel and on accidents involving ten thousand vehicles. The results indicate, among other things, that a motorist driving 65 MPH on a main rural highway stands to travel almost three times as far (22 million miles) before he becomes, statistically, an incipient fatality as a man going 35 MPH (8 million miles). It is not that more people are killed at 35 MPH because more are traveling at that speed; rather, 35 MPH is a less safe speed on a main rural highway. The safe speed is the one that acknowledges the pace which the majority of the other drivers want to achieve.[2] (When the 65-MPH driver does get killed, after his statistical 22 million miles, it is most apt to be the result of a tangle with the 35-MPH plodder.)

But the importance of control rather than flow-inducement is all pervasive in our traffic-management thinking. Brock Yates pulls together some random samples:

> In a small village a young boy stationed himself ahead of a police radar trap and tried to wave motorists down to the legal speed. He was immediately arrested for "obstructing

governmental administration," leaving one to ponder why it is illegal to attempt to prevent a law from being broken. What if the boy had talked a robber out of entering a bank staked out by the police? Suddenly the radar becomes unrelated to law or safety. It is an entity in itself—"governmental administration," if you will—and it justifies its being simply by its presence. It is, therefore it is relevant. . . . Elsewhere a seventy-year-old man took a leisurely trip with his wife. A few days later he received a mailed notice that his car had been clocked at 65 MPH in one of the villages he had passed through. He was advised to mail his $25 fine in order to avoid further inconveniences to himself. Unaware that his constitutional rights had been virtually suspended, he complied. Law by mail. In the interests of safety and order, of course. "Government administration knows best." . . . When a major city near the [New York] Thruway flared into riot several years ago, every available law officer was rushed to the scene except the roadway's radar patrols. After all, someone had to collect the revenue to pay for rebuilding the city.[3]

If the erection of elaborate governmental machineries for traffic control were simply ineffective, it would be a minor tragedy. Wasted time, money, energy, and emotion are far from unusual in city and state government. Effort would still be siphoned off from more effective efforts at reducing the traffic toll, and a sizable social cost would still be paid in the hindrance to flow that control seems to create. But the effect would be relatively small, within the parameters of inefficiency and congestion that we have come to accept from a foundering automotive system.

Unfortunately, however, traffic control is more than simply ineffective; it is a postive contributor to our traffic toll. A significant example is provided by the massive antispeeding campaign that Senator Abraham Ribicoff, then governor, conducted in Connecticut from 1956 to 1960. Ribicoff is not one to play safe political bets; he incurred the wrath of fifty thousand citizens who lost their operator's licenses for speeding convictions during the four-year campaign, but he balanced that wrath with the support of the general public whose opinion was amenable to the manipulation of scare tactics. It was, after all, a good cause—crack down on speeders to make the highways safe for the law-abiding common folk.

The joker in the campaign's deck appeared after two years of crackdown: injuries were going up. Between 1955 and 1958, Connecticut's highway toll went from 210 accidents per hundred million miles to 227 per hundred million. A driver's chances of being injured increased by 8 percent during the first two years of the all-out war on speeders. To the analysts, the campaign must have seemed jinxed by the same crazy irrationality that was later to characterize our involvement in Vietnam. The enemy was feeding off the efforts to destroy him, growing stronger. After four years the campaign was quietly abandoned. A similar total assault on speeders in Wisconsin produced virtually the same results.

Conventional wisdom about the highway toll would have it that three major causes—somewhat simple ones—are the offenders: speed, law violations, and lack of courtesy. A five-year study by the Harvard Medical School under a grant from the U.S. Public Health Service found that the three causes are, however, without significance in the national accident rate. Instead, as *Car and Driver*'s Gordon Jennings put it, 'Crashing follows with excruciating exactness the number of cars on the road. We crashed 1950 cars with 100 HP engines at the same rate we are now crashing 1970 cars with three times the power." [4] The hue and cry about the horsepower race may be justified by ecological concerns, but not for safety considerations. As far as the conventional wisdom is concerned, that was an unproductive twenty years (and deadly—enough people died in traffic smashes to equal the present population of Cleveland, Ohio).

Some Ancillary Disasters

Speed in particular seems unjustly accused. In test after test in which average speeds over a stretch of highway are measured without reference to arbitrarily established speed limits, it has been found that approximately 85 percent of the drivers will post figures in a narrow band that precisely establishes a safe, self-regulated standard for the particular highway. When speed limits reflect that figure, flow is maximized. When existing speed limits are too low, and are then adjusted to reflect the "illegal" driver-chosen rate, astonishing things happen to the traffic on the road. In Illinois, when limits were raised in forty-five low-speed-limit areas to match the 85 percentile figure, obedience to speed limits increased, as expected, by 119 percent. But average speeds also actually went down, from 42.6 to 42.4 MPH—and accidents *declined* by 36 percent. In Utah the speed limit of 40 MPH on one stretch of two-lane road was so low that 90 percent of the traffic on the road was in violation of the law; when the limit was raised to the 85 percentile mark of 60 MPH, the average speed went down and accidents were reduced from ten to three in the first year of the new speed limit. The Nebraska Highway Department raised the speed limits on a major highway as it went through twenty-nine Nebraska villages, and found the accident rate reduced by 34 percent as a result.

Yet the enthusiasm for traffic control continues to grow. City and state police budgets expand to underwrite more patrols, more surveillance, more technology. Automatic speed-control devices are used in all fifty states. Radar was the toy of the sixties. Radar operates efficiently only in clear, dry weather (rain, snow, and high winds affect its performance), on flat and open stretches of highway (the beam is about one thousand feet long), in relatively light traffic (selectivity is a problem in heavy traffic). Thus the conditions for effective use of radar are precisely the conditions for

136

the safest flow of traffic, and picking speeders out of those conditions has virtually nothing to do with promoting traffic safety. Instead, it is a kind of harassment best serving to point up the arbitrary aspect of speed limits, and to destroy public confidence in the body of traffic law.

Radar is now virtually obsolete. It is supplanted by VASCAR (Visual Average Speed Computer), which operates from a moving vehicle and tracks other vehicles coming or going. Third-generation control technology is represented by ORBIS, which is, according to its maker (LTV Aerospace), "a tireless traffic sentinel designed to regulate highway speeds effectively by letting the motorist know it's there and that it can detect unsafe speeds—automatically, around-the-clock, and in any type of weather." * ORBIS photographs car, driver, and license plate from an armor-plated box; it records location, time, date, posted speed limit, and the speed of the offending car. More advanced models are expected to be able to wirephoto the collected information instantaneously to a receiving unit at police headquarters.

In a demonstration by the maker, ORBIS gathered evidence of 276 speed violations in a three-hour period, operating on only one lane of a three-lane expressway. The maker seems to feel that this performance proves the effectiveness of ORBIS; a more objective observer might find that the demonstration only points to the gross inadequacy of the speed limit for the roadway in question. A rate of ninety-two crimes per hour against the laws of traffic control implies a vastly distorted system. Of course while ORBIS was nabbing those ninety-two offenders per hour, drunk drivers, fleeing criminals, hit-and-run dodgers, sideswipers, and cars with dragging tailpipes or bald tires—in fact any accidents of any

---

* Most freeway systems have posted minimum speeds as well as maximums. We'll know the revolution is here the day an ORBIS unit is set up to nail offenders who are going too slowly for the traffic flow.

kind which might have occurred within the surveillance area and time period—would have gone undetected, so long as the vehicles involved didn't exceed the magic number of miles per hour that would tickle the electronic sensors.

The escalation of this fruitless war against speeders is virtually automatic, and, given the conventional wisdom, irreversible. Lacking any other meaningful measures of accomplishment in the effort to "enforce" traffic safety, traffic departments invariably go to statistics. Rising curves on a graph paint a visual picture that any legislator or budget committeeman can grasp in an instant, without the necessity of any deep understanding of the nature of the problem or the complexity of its solution. The one statistic that the traffic agency can always obtain, and can always manipulate to show any total desired, is speeding convictions. Conviction rates for electronically obtained speeding citations run over 90 percent. A traffic department can even budget convictions: put enough men at roadside with electronic equipment for enough hours, and the desired total will be rung up. (New York Thruway patrols average seventy arrests per six-hour working day.[5])

The popular mythology errs also in its estimation of the more cynical aspects of rigid speed-limit enforcement. Administrative costs have risen so rapidly in recent years that revenue from fines only partially offsets the cost of processing citations. Yates estimates a loss, in the more populous states, of more than five dollars per conviction—borne by the taxpayers, of course. That makes that last speeding ticket you paid one of the state's better bargains, in these inflationary days. That's why governors are going to Washington in search of federal subsidies to support ever more widespread enforcement efforts. A lot of the money they are trying to obtain will go to electronic surveillance equipment —not wiretapping gadgetry, but for traffic enforcement. There's a reasonable argument to be made that bugging and

ORBIS represent the same grade of violation of civil rights.

A few years ago, driving out to Kennedy International Airport in New York on the Van Wyck Expressway, I spotted a radar unit ahead. I felt the familiar stab of panic, narrowly averted slamming on the brakes, realized I was at least close to the speed limit after all, and sailed through unnabbed. Coming back in the other lane an hour later, my passenger and I shook our heads in dismay at the traffic jam caused by the radar trap. Some unwitting motorist had seen the radar unit and *had* slammed on his brakes. He got smacked in the tail for his attempt to obey the law, and his smacker in turn became a smackee, in a three-car chain collision. Traffic was reduced to one lane past the debris, and the stack-up wound back upstream for a mile or so, into the center of Queens Boulevard. A couple of extra patrol cars had arrived on the scene to help untangle the wreckage and comfort the survivors. The radar unit was still set up beside the road, dutifully clocking, I imagine, the 3- and 4-MPH gawkers as they painfully worked their way past the smash-up.[6]

Okay, Mac, Let's See Your License and Registration

It is through their automobiles that most Americans have their first contact with the working face of the law. Indeed, it may be their only contact: weighty legal transactions such as the acquisition of real estate, joining of families, and disposal of mortal remains are often effectively insulated from the grubby realities of the law. Banks, churches, hospitals, mortuaries, and other lofty institutions function as agents to protect us from the machinery. Few such agencies exist in the ownership and operation of the automobile.

The law of averages gets most of us. During the experimentation and trial and error of youth, we begin days of recreation, nights of courtship, the extended automotive initiation into adulthood. As adults we still use the automobile heavily in our leisure time, and in the bulk of our recreation. On top of everything else, we are DOT Secretary Volpe's average men, who spend 13 percent of our working days in our automobiles. It is unavoidable: eventually we violate the complex web of code and statute, becoming momentarily, perhaps unconsciously, criminal. We deal with the police. Most of us are at least mildly frightened by the experience, although of course there is absolutely no reason to be. After all, it is in the interests of our own safety, isn't it?

The young people who went South during the activist days of the civil-rights struggle got a new and educational view of the law's concern for their safety. The activists quickly learned that the mildest variance with the local law would bring instant arrest. Arcane regional interpretations of standard driving custom were invoked; citations were commonly given for such vaguenesses as "improper turn" and "failure to yield."

In the end, even a high level of driving skill and utter knowledgeableness were not sufficient. The drill was to stop any car with out-of-state plates, any that contained black as well as white faces—or, failing that, any car driven by blacks. Stop the car, roust out the occupants, conduct an extensive—nay, exhaustive—"safety inspection." The slightest anomaly of equipment (quick, surreptitious snap of pistol butt against taillight lens, or a little underhood rearrangement of wiring) and the offender was hauled in. If the equipment check was not fruitful, the examination would proceed to the documentation of car and driver. A strikeover in the typing on the registration form would be sufficiently suspicious for detainment.

Thus did our nice white children learn what the blacks have always known, what the poor understand automatically. The hippies, the flower children, the unshaven and unwashed who chose The Road in the last half of the sixties learned it also. We use the law not only to control the flow of traffic; we also use it for strict social control. Poverty and the geographic impaction of the ghettos are not enough. We have established, maintained, elaborated a second line of defense against the possible escape of our disadvantaged: an unscalable mountain of bureaucracy, whimsically applied, to withhold legitimization. For the poor, the black, the "foreign," obtaining the legal right to move about in the transportation system can be as difficult and degrading an experience as attempting to register to vote in Selma, Alabama, when one is black. (The process is in fact quite similar.) Maintaining that right can be even more difficult. The civic authorities may shy away from crimping the business practices which would unload automobiles onto the disadvantaged, but after the sale is made there is little profit to the community to be had from allowing them to continue to move freely about.

I've owned twenty cars in five states, and I'm not sure I understand the process yet. There is the legal title to the car, and the registration of the car with the state. Some states do not require a title, and do heavy traffic in stolen cars as a result. In some states the title-registration-licensing function is virtually the same; in others quite separate. (Near my home the offices where registration and license-plate purchase take place are approximately thirty miles apart. A who-cuts-the-barber's-hair situation therefore exists about driving a new car from place to place in order to obtain the right to drive the car about. The transactions must take place in the proper order, and it is not unusual for the unwary, one vital piece of paper or another missing, to be forced to make two and three trips back and forth between the two offices.)

Some Ancillary Disasters

Some states require proof of insurance, others will accept proof of financial responsibility (a ten-thousand-dollar bond will do if you don't believe in—or can't afford—insurance). Although some states don't require proof of ownership for registration, some even require proof of competence, in the form of a valid operator's license. Although I doubt it is standard policy, there is even one recorded case of a state requiring proof of existence before issuing the operator's license: a New York magazine editor got in a beef with a state clerk a few years back, and was required to produce a birth certificate before his license would be renewed. (In a similar situation a Massachusetts attorney was originally denied an operator's license because he refused to divulge his social security number. He sued and won.)

The process of legitimization takes place, usually, in the sullen gray corridors, among the sullen gray people, of city hall. Civil Service. The congestion of the roads translates to congestion of the halls: long lines, empty waits, while the professional blank-fillers creep through the paperwork. It is a deadening and dehumanizing experience for the most fortunate; for the marginally franchised, driven by desperate needs, the process borders on the impossible. I fret at thirty-mile trips to the license bureau in my own rural setting; if I had to pursue that legal guff via subway, juggling dollar bills to squeeze over the interminable list of fees and taxes, turned away again and again for my lack of knowledge of the system, trying to solve the puzzles of code and statute from a street-language background, I would simply give up. I would, as surprising numbers of our citizens still do, ignore all that legal confusion. I'd go outlaw.

The bureaucratic portion of automobile law doesn't work either. Car theft is the largest single urban crime today, growing 700 percent in recent years. Efforts to ascertain, document, and locate automobile ownership—the bureaucracy's attempt to provide a deterrent to that common crime —are almost totally ineffective. Some 180 cars per day are stolen in New York City, the car-theft capital of the world, and fewer than 50 percent are recovered. (The industry's own efforts to inhibit car theft are similarly ineffective. The new steering-column locks delay a car thief for approximately eight seconds, by one professional's estimate. He works on the principle that if he can't be driving away within three minutes of approaching the car to be stolen, he looks for another target.) [7] Engines—and therefore engine serial numbers—are swapped, chassis identification replaced or altered, license plates swapped and reswapped, stolen and re-stolen. It is virtually impossible to ascertain that a used car is not a stolen one, with new paint and trim, swapped engine, altered chassis numbers, forged registration papers, and actual mileage three times more than the odometer indicates. There are, no doubt, honest and reputable used-car dealers. There are also used-car dealers whose lots carry only the cream of the haul from a car-theft ring, the lesser prizes dismantled for parts, shipped to South America, or cut up for salvage. If you find out how to tell these two kinds of used-car dealers apart, let me know.

Efforts to connect car with driver, to legitimize the driver as well, are similarly ineffective. A recent study in Los Angeles showed that 50 percent of the drivers whose licenses were temporarily suspended, and 75 percent of those whose licenses were revoked outright, went right ahead and drove anyway. (They had to—Los Angeles has perhaps the most severely inadequate public transportation system in the U.S.) Nobody knows how many people just never bother to get licensed in the first place, particularly in rural back-waters where all that license stuff is regarded as unnecessary expense and bother, just another one of the authorities' shucks.

Some Ancillary Disasters

(The middle-class respectables *must* have driver's licenses, however. It is the universal badge of identification for all those middle-class activities like cashing checks, establishing credit, renting cars. A driver's license will prove you exist when a birth certificate is insufficient; bureaucratic faith extends most readily to *recent* bureaucracy. A nondriving friend of mine carries his passport for driver's-license-type identification; he gets static. Thus the social security number on the driver's license application: another cross-linked form of identification, thrusting toward the day of the universal computerized Citizen's Number.)

For the solid citizen—stable, established, reachable with things like renewal notices, able to establish legal residence —the ongoing aspect of automotive legitimization is reasonably smooth. For the nomadic, the fringe level of society, every change may necessitate a repetition of the whole dreary business, another assault on the impervious walls of the bureaucracy. One aspect of the law is, however, a pain to established and transitory alike: vehicle inspection. Not all states yet require regular repeated inspections, and certainly not all states agree on vehicle standards that must be met. (Variance among state vehicle codes sometimes serves to inhibit what little technological advance Detroit attempts to make. In 1969, for example, Dodge wanted to equip certain cars in its model line-up with an improved head lamp as an optional extra. The courts denied the firm the right to market the improvement—which would have surpassed existing standards—in New York, Vermont, and New Hampshire, because it didn't fit the written specifications.) Inspection requirements vary widely from state to state, ranging from a cursory glance at lights, wipers, and tires to complex electronic testing of pollution-control devices and partial disassembly to check such things as brake wear. But inspection campaigns are, of course, a positive good, aimed primarily at driving unsafe junkers from the road.

Safety inspections also stimulate petty graft (many inspection stations sell repairs for the faults they allegedly find, just for starters), and provide a solid industry-supportive push toward the bright, shiny, expensive new cars we already have too many of. They verge on the administratively unmanageable, with rapidly changing technical standards (particularly in pollution control) and frequent inspection schedule shifts, which throw motorists into mass confusion about due dates. They lay yet another layer of bureaucracy on an already unwieldy body of civic authority. They become a tool in the politics of technology, removing us further from management (diagnosis, maintenance, repair) of our own appliances, driving us once more to pay up to the experts. They provide one more means of oppressing the poor and the disadvantaged, serving in effect to force the lower economic classes to live up to middle-class standards of material wealth (or to abandon their freedom to move, their access to ready mobility). But they do accomplish a lot of good. They are a force for safety. That's more than can be said for most of the rest of automobile law.

Hoist by Its Own Lobby

The purpose of this recitation of automotive legal woes is not to call for anarchy, nor to propose new automotive legal structures, unsatisfactory as the old ones may be. *Some* body of law seems to be necessary for our automotive society, to deal with the more oppressively antisocial if no one else. The accretion of new laws, particularly since the federal government has begun to take an interest in areas where the state and local governments have been most glaringly remiss, is proceeding all too rapidly anyway.

The case can even be made that, in the face of the astronomical rise in number of vehicles, in miles driven, and in horsepower and gross weight of those vehicles (without concomitant gains in braking and evasive capability of the vehicles, or in driver skill in the operators), the avoidance of a similarly astronomical rise in the highway death toll indicates a startlingly good performance rating for highway law. When systems begin to break down, the tendency is toward epidemic growth of failure. That the death toll has kept a close relationship with total vehicles represents a not-quite-Pyrrhic victory. Given a less explosive rate of growth of the automobile population than the law attempted to deal with during the 1955–1970 period, the existing legal structure might have made positive headway.

The body of law that we have is a massive social institution constructed after the fact, in piecemeal fashion, based on emotional hunches rather than measurable objective realities—indeed, often in direct contradiction to the previously measured realities. It emanates from a vastly more conservative consciousness than it serves. In these senses it is little different from most aspects of American civic law; perhaps equally flawed, rather less serviceable. It is accepted custom; portions of it work, occasionally, albeit painfully. It is hardly likely to ennoble the race.

To the extent, however, that automotive law represents the most rapidly growing aspect of the mentality of external control, it represents social danger. When it regulates for control rather than flow, it merely congeals the fluidity of our society; when it regulates for control rather than safety, it becomes a positive evil. The established bureaucracy which administers automobile law has already demonstrated considerable power of self-replication and self-expansion. As it increasingly expands its authority into nonautomotive applications, and thereby becomes an instrument of repression by the state, it contributes heavily to the public's growing revulsion for everything that the automobile has come to imply. It is not surprising that the automobile industry has long taken an active part, through its lobbying activities, in the creation, implementation, and application of automobile law. But here, also, the industry has failed; it has created yet another monster. Its motive was to assist in the formation of a body of law that would allow it freedom for unlimited expansion. In failing, it finds itself in the curious position of assisting in the creation of one more force that will help destroy it.

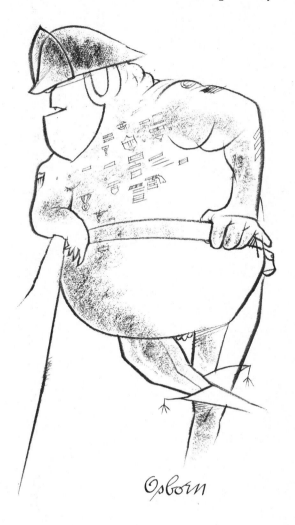

PART III

The Costs

He'll put you behind the eight ball

Osborn

CHAPTER 7

In the Manner to Which . . .

The Okie Charmer *

Monologist Mort Sahl used to have a routine about an airliner in trouble, in which the pilot advises the passengers that some of their number will have to be jettisoned to save weight. The passengers are to be thrown overboard in reverse order to their usefulness to society; immediately a raging argument breaks out between a disc jockey and a used-car salesman over who should go first.

It is perhaps unfair that used-car salesmen have acquired an almost-mythic reputation for unprincipled greed. In many cases they are towers of integrity by comparison with their new-car colleagues. The used-car market deals in something close to reality. The market does fluctuate severely, partially

---

* A mechanical calculator, usually a Friden, used by car salesmen to figure car deals backwards, i.e. starting with the customer's ability to pay and working back to determine the price of the car. I am indebted to Leon Mandel for the terminology, and for much of the information about retail car sales in this chapter.

as a result of the success or failure of new-car model years. There is no doubt a great deal of mechanical hanky-panky involved, only the first blush of which is the turning back of used-car odometers (illegal in most states, but still done). Used-car dealers do tend to prey very sharply on the economically disadvantaged. But the customer who ventures into used-car territory *knows* he is embarking on a horse trade (particularly if he is trading in his own old car, on which he may or may not have practiced his own hanky-panky). Swindles work both ways, in the used-car market. It is the new-car customer who is apt to get sandbagged.

Most people still regard the new-car dealer as a different class of businessman entirely, a cut above the used-car man. The enterprise is somehow more legitimate; perhaps it is the larger capital investment involved, and the sometimes luxurious trappings. The products, being new, are assumed to be uniform in their mechanical condition; they emanate from huge and reputable manufacturers; there are warranties and policies and fine print to protect the customer. All this serves to lull the customer into letting down his guard. Pity the poor customer. The System awaits.

My own first experience with the System came in early 1955—Year One of the golden era—when I bought a used car from a new-car dealer in Xenia, Ohio. Obviously, the fellow was having such a good year that he was practically giving away his used cars in order to make room for the flow. I made my choice near closing time, and wanted to drive it that evening, of course. (Not half so badly, I'm sure, as the salesman wanted me to drive it away.) In a glow of good fellowship I signed enough papers to be able to leave with my new purchase, to return the next day "when the secretaries would be back" to complete the paperwork. When I returned the penciled-in figures on the signed contract had escalated via typewriter by fourteen dollars a month. I raised hell, but I was a callow youth, easy to convince that a contract was a contract and that it had all been an honest mistake. I had been shuffled more effectively than the papers of the evening before. I made the payments: $336 extra over the next two years. I didn't find out about the cracked cylinder head until the "guarantee" on used cars had run out. I had been Systemed, albeit crudely, and on a used car at that.

(I've been Systemed many times since—I've bought more cars, haven't I?—but the details are too embarrassing to go into here.)

The System has infinite variations, refinements, complications, but its basis is succinct: customer cupidity. Leon Mandel, a former editor of *Car and Driver* and once manager of a foreign-car dealership into which the distributor introduced the System, describes his experience:

> . . . I came to understand that the System says three things. One, the buyer is essentially larcenous, and that's how you lure him through the door. Two, of the three elements in the sale of a car—the trade-in, the payments, and the cost of the new car—you can make sure the buyer loses track of at least one. Three, the house can put the buyer in the position of making *it* an offer, which results in a deal the house wants— because it has the ultimate choice of whether or not to sell the car. And the house is not about to take a loss.[1]

With these three clearly defined shells under which to hide the pea, the sales force is then set to shoot its cuffs and get creative. The creativity is bolstered by the fact that there are, of course, shells within shells. There is even a fourth shell: down payment, a misty figure indeed. The banks will tell you that it must amount to one third (or one fourth, or one fifth, depending on the economic mood of the moment, and, perhaps, your credit rating) of the new car's "price," in order for a bank loan to be issued for the car. Finance companies aren't so sticky about these details. In any event, the prospective car purchaser should not let the down payment worry his head; the salesman will see that the customer is somehow able to come up with the sum even if he has to go through the customer's pockets to do so.

Flexibility is the key to new-car sales methods, flexibility in spades. What better place to start the flexing than with the price of the new car? Unfortunately, thanks to the Automotive Information Disclosure Act of 1958, the dealer is required by law to display the price of the car right there on a window sticker. However, since the "sticker price" is pure fiction, the law has not put any unnecessary crimps in sales creativity. The only redeeming social significance contained in the literature pasted on the new-car window is that it prevents the salesman from starting out to sell two-thousand-dollar cars for four thousand dollars. He has to introduce the inflation later in the game. The sticker price only marks a rough beginning point for the bargaining, if the customer has the foreknowledge and the energy to attempt to bargain. Rest assured that the salesman will have the energy for his portion of the transaction.

The "list price" on the sticker is based on the "wholesale price" of the car. To arrive at a rough estimate of the wholesale price, as when strolling through a showroom, knock off something between a fifth and a quarter of the "base" price at the top of the sticker. To determine wholesale prices more precisely, you may require considerable skill in mathematics and the advice of an economic analyst. The dealer "margin" during most of the 1955–1970 period was 26 percent on the luxury cars (Cadillac, Imperial, and Lincoln), 25 percent on full-sized cars, 21 percent on compacts and intermediates, and 17 percent on the subcompacts. Imported-car dealers have traditionally struggled along with a 17 percent margin. The most recent industry trend has been an effort to push the margin back to an across-the-board 17 percent, a move begun in order to bring in the new sub-compacts at under two thousand dollars, and continued because the profit squeeze is on (when hasn't it been?) and the manufacturers just decided they'd get theirs first. Lower sticker prices make everyone feel better, except perhaps the dealer, who no longer has as much room to wheel and deal in the lower figures.[2]

The sticker price is a complex figure, unclearly itemized. It consists of the wholesale price plus dealer margin (the 17 percent figure is based on the total of these two amounts) plus excise tax (varying in golden-era years from 7 to 10 percent of the wholesale price, but at this writing suspended) plus preparation and delivery charges (usually forty-five to fifty dollars, whether or not the dealer chooses to do more than wash the road film off the newly delivered car). Scandals have attached themselves to each of these items in the history of the automobile industry, of course.[3]

A dealer margin of 17 to 26 percent would seem to offer considerable flexibility for bargaining, as long as one accepts the principle that cars, unlike all other American consumer items, do not *have* set prices, that one "makes a deal" for a car and that the cost of the car as it goes out the door can depend entirely on the dealer's whim. But an already complex price formula skitters off into worse confusion with the fact that the wholesale price, upon which all the other costs are figured, is also a fiction, a floating figure which the dealer himself may not be able to ascertain from month to month during the sales year.

Not that you'd ever know it. "List prices" are set, rather inflexibly, after some industry backing and filling in the fall of the year.[4] The list prices are based on wholesale prices established shortly before the first on-sale date for the new cars, wholesale prices to which the maker adheres strictly—for all public purposes—throughout the year. Yet the actual sales year amounts to an involved series of totally unpredictable rebates to the dealer—rebates which effectively allow the wholesale price to float throughout the year, and by means of which the manufacturer tries (quietly) to control sales.

The paper wholesale price is actually only in effect in October and November, when the clamoring new-car customers are snapping up the new models at something close to full list prices. As soon as that demand drops off, as it invariably does, the manufacturer begins manipulating wholesale prices by means of rebates, in hopes of stimulating sales by giving the dealer more finagling room. Not for the dignified manufacturer are the grubby price wars of the retail market—instead, the maker slips money back to the dealer, and lets him attempt to deal with public confidence as the only retail businessman in his community whose prices are completely flexible, who therefore is obviously doing business strictly on a what-the-traffic-will-bear basis.

Rebates on the wholesale prices usually involve shifting sales quotas for the dealer:

> Thus, for example, in August 1966, General Motors had in effect a rebate program on its full-sized cars (except Cadillac) that offered a rebate of $50 on every car sold from 0–50 percent of the dealer's quota, $75 for every car sold from 51–75 percent of the dealer's quota, and $100 for every car sold above 75 percent of the quota. . . . These rebate programs have sometimes started as early as December and are usually in full swing by March or April. Rebates of $200 by August are not unheard of. . . . Also, ever since the dealer relations reforms of the middle 1950's, the manufacturers have been offering their dealers an automatic 5 percent rebate on the list price for any old model still in the dealer's hands when the new model year cars are announced. . . . The manufacturers are adjusting their prices to the changing conditions of the market over the model year. To a large extent they are

acting as discriminating monopolists, segmenting their market over time and succeeding in this because the inelastic, high price segments are the initial buyers.[5]

The fictitious list price based on a fictitious wholesale price serves the maker very handily, of course. It provides the appearance of stability in a market situation that, primarily by virtue of the makers' own insistence on hanging major sales campaigns on the exotic neuroses and emotional hang-ups of the public, is about as stable as free oxygen in a blast furnace. It also provides an extremely serviceable veil of secrecy:

> The rebate programs can be granted and withdrawn quickly and quietly as the state of the market changes, without having to attract the attention of the press and of Washington by changes in list prices; price cuts can be achieved on particular models with no explanations to reporters about those models that have been selling poorly, thereby avoiding the impression that there is something wrong with those models and deterring other customers. Also, at the transition from one model year to the next, the increase in list prices, if any, will be less under the current system than if list prices floated down at the end of the model year along with actual prices. The companies simply look better if list prices remain stable or rise only slightly between September and October than if they rise 8–10 percent and the company has to explain how September's prices were really 8 percent below the previous October's prices. The wholesale rebate schemes make life easier for the companies.[6]

Thus car prices, beguiling fictions that they are, sow distrust in the American retail system. (The automobile industry accounts for twenty-five cents out of every retail sales dollar—and seventeen cents out of every wholesale dollar as well, according to the *Boston Globe*.) But let us assume a shrewd car purchaser, one who knows all this. Assume he knows that even if he buys at the precise dollar of wholesale cost to the dealer, the dealer will still probably make a profit on the sale. Assume he knows that while the dealer's margin on the basic car is between 17 and 26 percent (before rebates), that margin runs as high as 100 percent on the accessory items, and that in these days when the bulk of new-car sales result from specific orders to the factory (rather than walk-in purchases off the showroom floor) for "custom" assortments of accessories added to a chosen model, the options often add as much as 50 percent to the cost of a car. (The average new-car purchase in 1970 went out the door at about $3600, of which $500 to $1000 was for optional add-on items above the base price of the car.)

Assume, in fact, consumerism's dream, the superconsumer, who knows about the System and has no fears of the magic of the Okie Charmer. Who knows all the elements of the carnival con game of retail car salesmanship: the "spiff"—a special bonus for the salesman who succeeds in moving a previously unsaleable car. The "liner"—a greeter, with responsibility limited to showing you a car and making sure you are disposed to buy. The "closer"—the man with the virtuoso touch on the calculator, who can keep track of all the variables, can juggle the figures so that the appearance is the financial deal the customer has in mind but the reality is the profit the dealership wants. Assume our superconsumer knows about "the pack" and all its variations (top pack, plain pack, finance pack). This is an artificial sum of money introduced early into the negotiations for appearance's sake. It may take the form of an artificially inflated trade-in price for the customer's old car, or even a cash "gift" to the customer. ("We'll even give you a hundred dollars in cash for your pocket, so you can take a long weekend vacation with your new car.") The pack is always put into the dealing early, and pulled out again at the last moment; the $100 in cash, for example, is padded onto the final price for the new car, and the customer of course pays it back—plus interest, if he finances his car.

Assume Superconsumer also knows the "switch": luring him into the showroom with ads for nonexistent bargains which have "just been sold" as he arrives, but as long as he's there, wouldn't he like to see. . . . He's familiar with the "bush," an extremely low price quoted at the outset of negotiations, which somehow rises as rapidly as the customer's commitment to a specific new car grows. And he knows all about the high ball, the low ball, the blitz, the balloon, unhorsing, paper-trading, the sales contest, and the infinitely manipulable nature of credit ratings.

Superconsumer also recognizes the fact that a volume car dealer often makes more money in finance charges and insurance commissions (and finance charges *on* insurance premiums) than he does on the sale of cars. He knows too that the universal practice of computing car loan interest rates on a nondeclining balance commonly results in true interest rates of over 18 percent per annum, even from banks (which everybody "knows" are the cheapest source of car loan money). He knows that such interest rates often make it to the dealer's advantage to sell at a higher dollar figure but a lower profit. The dealer can offer $500 over the value of the trade-in, jack the new car price by a like amount, and have another $90 in interest, over a three-year car loan, to manipulate back into his price finagling. (Interest makes the various versions of "the pack" doubly juicy. Cities, states, even the federal government quietly approve of such practices, since taxes paid are on the basis of the inflated figures. The car-makers don't mind what numbers the dealer chooses to juggle about in the process of shoving cars out the dealership door. Customers, interested primarily in the simple difference between their trade-in allowance and the new car price, seldom care what the total dollar figures are, although they pay taxes on the sum. Dealers complain loudest, since they too pay taxes on inflated figures. But in the crunch between not moving cars—thus risking the franchise —and fudging figures to move cars, the dealer usually elects to shut up and keep fudging.)

In fact, Superconsumer knows that the dealer, like the manufacturer whose cars he sells, is unlikely to be a "car man," in the business through any deep knowledge or long-standing interest in or affection for automobiles. Like the manufacturers, the successful dealer is a money man, a financier, albeit a penny-ante one in Detroit terms. And he makes more money on his used-car operation than he does on new cars. And if his car sales operation is best characterized as tripping along the outer border of the institutional flim-flam, it is a better-than-even bet that his parts department and his service facilities are operated at approximately the same level of integrity.

Forewarned of all this, and thus stoutly forearmed, Superconsumer walks into the new-car showroom prepared to screw the dealer to the wall. He signs for his Impala at the exact dealer cost, leaving the dealer to rake a profit out of whatever rebate is applicable. He even has the effrontery to bargain over the cost of options, and wins, cutting the dealer's take from 50 percent to a more reasonable but still healthy 25 percent. He orders precisely what he wants on his new car, and does not sucker for this or that convenience-group or style-package, taking seven extra-cost items to get one that he really wants. He offers no trade-in at all, automatically preempting approximately one third of the System at the outset. Instead, he has already sold his old car himself, through a classified ad, and cleared approximately 25 percent more for the car than he would have if he'd thrown himself into the clutches of the System.

Furthermore, Superconsumer pays cash for his car, unlike

66 percent of his fellow consumers, and therefore adds nothing to the $35 billion in installment credit extended to car buyers in 1970. He has previously arranged for his car insurance—a sensible minimum—privately, and he has only to call his insurance man with the appropriate registration numbers to be able to drive away fully insured. In short, miracle of miracles, Superconsumer has purchased a three thousand dollar car for three thousand dollars; when it arrives from the factory, ever-cautious Superconsumer has only to inspect it to make certain that the delivery preparation has been done.

At that point our hero can get in and drive away, leaving the dealer, one must suppose, a beaten man. (The dealer won't actually lose money on such a transaction; he'll just be uncomfortably aware that an opportunity to *make* a great deal—if only some other sucker had come along—has just gone out the door.) We might even assume a certain amount of vindictiveness on the part of our hero, a product of System deals he has suffered through in the past. Perhaps his heart—or his adrenal gland—is swelling as he drives away. Revenge is sweet. It is also short. By the time Superconsumer arrives home with his new purchase, he will have lost about one thousand dollars. His new car is now used; depreciation has just gnawed about one third of his investment away.

The Money Machine

"Let's go in my car. We can split the gas money and it'll cost almost nothing." So ingrained is our notion that automotive transportation is somehow free transportation that we commonly refer to the car as "the second largest capital investment" in the American citizen's lifetime, as if the automobile were a one-time, fixed expenditure. Let's see, now,

The Costs

$20,000 for a modest house, $3600 for a nice new car, and gee, all the rest, in a lifetime of earning, can go for vacations, life-insurance premiums, and the kids' orthodontics. New-car buyers keep their new cars an average of not quite four years. (Some 20 percent trade off in the first two years, 40 percent within three years, 60 percent within four years, over 70 percent in five years; the remaining less-than-30-percent keep a car for over five years. The median is forty-three months.[7]) The Department of Transportation estimates that in the somewhat idealized hundred-thousand-mile lifetime of an automobile, it will generate $11,800 in costs, over ten years—$98-plus per month. The DOT figures seem to include everything: 3.2 cents per mile in depreciation; 1.9 cents for maintenance, parts, and tires; 1.9 for gas and oil; 1.8 cents for tolls and parking; 1.7 cents for insurance; and 1.4 cents per mile for taxes, for a total of 11.9 cents per mile.[8] That's where the 12 cents per mile for expense accounts and tax deductions comes from.*

The figures are wildly inaccurate for the first forty-three months of a car's life, however. Based on current used-car prices, the average $3600 car is worth approximately $600 to $700 at age 43 months. The $3000 in depreciation—using the DOT's average of ten thousand miles per year—yields a depreciation rate of more than *eight* cents per mile throughout the first owner's bill-paying period. Insurance rates are based at least partially on a car's dollar value, which means that the DOT insurance figure is skewed as severely as the depreciation rate. Taxes also tend to bulk around a car's earlier years, when its value is higher. Rationally, one might expect the cost of the "maintenance, parts, and tires" cate-

---

* Subsequent to this writing the DOT revised the expense estimates to a total of 13.7 cents per mile: 4.4 cents per mile for depreciation; 2.1 cents for maintenance, parts, and tires; 2.8 cents for gas and oil; 1.8 cents for tolls and parking; 1.3 cents for insurance; and 1.3 cents for taxes. The new figures are almost as far from reality as the old.

162

gory to provide some balance for the extra expense connected with a car's newness; as a car ages, obviously its mechanical components should begin to wear out, requiring more expenditure in the latter portion of a car's useful life. Yet with the recall rate for serious mechanical flaws in new vehicles approaching 40 percent (15 million vehicles recalled between 1966 and 1970, out of 38 million sales), the opposite situation seems to exist. Most major mechanical components are engineered for a useful life approaching a hundred thousand miles; given routine maintenance, failures result from material flaws or assembly mistakes. Such failures occur as regularly in the first ten thousand miles as the fifth or sixth, and the recall rates give reason to assume that four years may be a reasonable length of time to mellow a car into a rickety kind of mechanical dependability—meaning that all the material flaws and assembly mistakes have finally been run to ground and corrected.

Furthermore, new and late-model car owners are more concerned with keeping their cars "right." They see themselves as protecting their investment, as well as attempting to get their money's worth in pleasure out of a huge expenditure. When something small goes bad, the new-car owner gets it fixed. Older cars have lapsed into the "transportation special" category, and their owners worry primarily about keeping the old heap running. You don't deliver your eight-year-old second car into the hands of the servicemen if the dash clock starts losing time. While "necessary" maintenance and parts costs—that is, maintenance necessary to keep a car capable of daily service—may remain constant or go up as a car ages, the rate of expenditure for that maintenance tends also to bunch up near the car's earlier years.[9]

Even such apparently constant expenses as gas and oil, and tolls and parking, are less evenly distributed than the massive statistical picture from which DOT draws its figures would indicate. The American Automobile Association has found variation in gas mileage between similarly equipped, similarly tuned models of the same car to range as widely as 50 percent. (In a test of two identical Chevrolet Impalas in 1969, the AAA came up with operating costs of 9.2 and 14.5 cents per mile, respectively. All that standardization of precision engineering that assembly-line techniques are going to bring us seems to lie yet in the future.) And in the end, gas expenditures, as well as tolls and parking, depend on use—and nobody goes for pleasure drives in transportation specials. Annual mileage goes down sharply as a car passes out of the luxury-toy state and into the desperation-measure category. Expense goes down to match.

On second thought, maybe we ought to go in *your* car and split the gas bill. It is difficult to keep this kind of sliding scale in mind while slipping about the country traveling on credit cards. Most people who travel professionally feel a slight tinge of guilt when they sock it to the company or the IRS for that twelve cents a mile. Compared to the gas bills that come in, or the immediate filling-station-oriented cash outlay, the sum seems positively munificent. It is probably worth keeping in mind, to allay the guilt, that to break even on the twelve-cents-per-mile return, you have to keep your car ten years, drive it one hundred thousand miles, and keep in line with the national median in all car expenditures all the while.

(Actually, you have to stay well below the national median. The cost figures are based on a $3300 new cost for the car, but the DOT says it figures roughly eighty-nine cents a pound, which in our four thousand-pound Impala comes closer to $3600. Ninety-one percent of new cars sold in 1970 had automatic transmissions, and, as we have seen, an automatic adds the equivalent of seven cents a gallon of gas. Sixty-one percent of us now purchase air conditioning with our cars, which adds six cents per gallon. At a national average of 12.2 miles per gallon—down from 13.5 in the past twenty-five years—the two accessories add a penny a mile all by themselves. You also have to use regular gas to hope to meet the national cost figures; five years ago you could buy few V-8's tuned for regular—and the federal figure for reimbursement for automobile expenses was then only ten cents per mile.)

With these figures in mind, we might return to Superconsumer, who is not about to offer the use of his car even if we'll all kick in on the gas money. It's not that Superconsumer is stingy; he just knows that any kind of equitable sharing of expenses for the real cost of operation of his car would make him out some kind of rapacious bandit. Superconsumer is also not going to be suckered into any dreams of letting the company (or the IRS) "buy" him a car, by using his own car for a great deal of business travel and collecting so much money at twelve cents per mile that it almost feels like somebody else is paying for the car. He did the arithmetic once. For instance, if he travels twenty-five thousand miles in directly reimbursable mileage in one year, he "clears" the three thousand dollars he paid for the bargain car. But he will then have to pick up the rest of the expenses himself—maintenance, parts, tires, gas, oil, insurance, and taxes. Even by DOT figures, this comes to $1725 out of pocket—and he's put, by DOT standards, two and a half years of use on the car, which means that for the next nine years he must reduce mileage to 8333 per year to keep his operating costs close to the twelve cents per mile the IRS will allow. He's not sure his business travel is flexible enough to allow him to cut it by two thirds. For nine years.

No way. Superconsumer knows that he's much better off to rent a car for business travel and let Hertz and the IRS fight out the pennies (and the hundred-thousand-mile life of the car). He knows that use of his car costs him plenty, and that cutting down on that use is the only sensible solution. He may pause to reflect a bit on that paradox—that this "free" method of transportation on which he has spent three thousand dollars becomes a more intelligent investment the less he uses it—but if he's like most of us, he can't survive in America without a car anyway, so he grits his teeth and takes his financial lumps. And watches his mileage. If he uses the car a lot, he knows that something might break or wear out. Then he would have to put the car in for service. And that is a fate our Superconsumer avoids like the plague.

Flat-rate vs. Flat Out

Automobile statistics are similar to medical statistics: even though odds for success of a surgical procedure may be as favorable as 100 to 1, that's little comfort to the fellow who ends up being the 1. DOT and Bureau of Public Roads figures filter down a trillion miles a year, a hundred million cars from assembly line to scrap heap. The resulting boiled-down essence has little meaning to the citizen who just wants to keep a clean, dependable, late-model car operating.

Mechanical service for ailing automobiles has also been given the statistical treatment, with predictably expensive results to the consumer. It all started with the perfectly logical desire of the customer to get some kind of prediction of the cost of repairs at the outset of automotive surgery. Standardized cars suffer standardized ailments, requiring standardized repair routines, in theory, anyway. Long before computers began making that sort of thing a simple task, the allied segments of the repair industry arrived at flat rates for common jobs. The rates are expressed in hours: to reframmis your whozis takes 3.2 hours, but to get to the whozis requires removal of three blivets at .4 hours apiece, etc. To make a repair estimate the shop foreman diagnoses —perhaps roughly—your car's ailment, looks up the various repair steps in his flat-rate book and adds up the total hours, multiplies by the shop's flat rate in dollars per hour, adds in the cost of parts used to make the repair (also enumerated in the flat-rate book), and hands you the total. You, of course, faint. But you've gotten a fair estimate of the cost of the repairs by current standards. (The book is updated from time to time; new mechanical wrinkles from the manufacturers come equipped with new flat rates for their repair and replacement.)

The flat rate is a perfectly rational solution to the problem of estimating repair costs that opens up a Pandora's box of customer abuses. If every part of every car wore out or broke in exactly the same fashion, and if every mechanic had the same skill and intelligence (and available tools) as every other mechanic, the statistical treatment might insure fair costs paid for good work done, just as in the American Dream. As soon as individuality is introduced— even in chunks of metal—the odds against equitable charges and competent repair work go sky high.

For starters, the mechanic who works on your car gets a cut of the flat rate as a basis for his salary, usually a 50-50 split with the house. On a given job he can't get paid more than his share of the flat rate even if he goofs and has to spend more hours than the book allots to accomplish the work—although the shop will do what it can to cover for his goofs. He will, however, get his split of the flat rate if he can beat it. The premium then is automatically shifted from getting the car fixed properly to getting the car out the door. The shop is really only concerned about "come-backs" —repair work done so sloppily that the car is returned for more work under the original flat-rate estimate.

The Costs

It all amounts to the whipsaw effect of another System. With the premium on minimum work time, the pressure is on the shop to overdiagnose (advise repairs more extensive than are needed) and to underrepair. The flat-rate manuals are models of benevolent concern for the workingman; it is a ham-fisted mechanic indeed who cannot match the flat rate on most jobs, even if he does all the work specified, a practice as out of date as the celluloid collar in our automotive society. It is very much to the mechanic's advantage to extemporize, invent timesaving measures, determine early and quickly which steps he can overlook, omit, or camouflage.

Travelers to foreign lands (and to the distant rural backwaters of our own country) are continually coming back with amazing tales of car repairs effected under immense handicaps. In the standard travel story a malfunction will develop, a local mechanic will be located after diligent search. Upon first sight of his tools and working methods, the traveler will despair, considering the possibilities of permanent local lodging. Then the local will repair by hand, in painstaking, step-by-step fashion, the faulty part. He will either fashion new pieces out of abandoned Coke signs or will by-pass esoteric and hence fragile mechanisms, using hemp and chicken dung where only polymerized wondergoop went before. It will take endless hours, but upon completion, the car will function perfectly well all the way back to civilization. The labor-and-materials charge from the local will come to thirty-two cents; at least two hundred dollars will be required to put the car back into original condition at a civilized repair station.

The narrator can only dine on such stories because of our nearly universal familiarity with the backwoods mechanic's civilized counterpart, who pursues the black-box theory of car repair, i.e., throw the faulty part away and bolt on a new one. Voltage regulators, coils, water pumps, fuel pumps, generators, distributor assemblies, starters, and carburetors are commonly replaced rather than repaired (or even adjusted, in some cases); the vogue is spreading to engines and transmissions. Our automobile service facilities are less workshops than assembly stations, mini-Detroits in which parts storage is more important than work space.

Part of the responsibility for this working method lies with mass production, which has reduced some replacement unit costs considerably. (The shop makes 40 to 60 percent on parts sales.) The rest, however, is the flat-rate mentality, which no longer allows for such eccentricities as the careful overhaul of "minor" assemblies and subassemblies, doesn't even provide for training in such procedures. As a result, if something goes wrong with your car, you are better off if it *is* a black-box component. Repairs which require adjustments, alignments, careful fitting—rattles, noises, leaks, fine tuning—go begging for the quality of workmanship that can cope.

Some of the replaceables are now manufactured as sealed units, and can't be repaired anyway, even if there were time in the flat-rate scheme of things. That can add immeasurably to the initial despair twenty miles from the barefoot mechanic in Tamazunchale, and also add luster to the dinner-table conversation later: your barefoot friend will probably be able to find his way into the sealed unit, and dope out the trouble when he does. He spends his professional career coping, rather than whizzing cars through his repair bay. Automobile mechanical principles are not nuclear physics, and having no new sealed unit to bolt on is a wonderful stimulus to ingenuity.

Every car owner has his own horror stories about car repairs and repair bills. Routinized abuses such as automatic spark-plug replacement every time the hood is lifted are not so much the stuff of legends as the stuff that pays the rent and light bill. Spark plugs cost the car manufacturer less than a nickel, cost you and me about $1.25, cost the shop about 60 cents. A V-8 gobbles eight per change. Nobody *ever* changes just one. A new set should last about ten thousand miles, but if you complain about the way the engine is running, the place where the mechanic will start looking for a cure is with the plugs. The really unscrupulous—and stupid—mechanic may clean and replace your old ones (which makes your engine run like new for a while), and charge you for new ones. Most mechanics won't bother. It takes about five minutes to put new ones in, about twenty minutes to clean old ones properly and replace them so that you get the immediate sensation of new plugs. Better to go for the quick $5.20 than the slow $10.00—profit on new plugs instead of outright swindle.

Demanding proof of repair, such as examination of the worn-out parts which have been replaced, is about the only protection the nonengineer has, and that doesn't amount to a hell of a lot. (Experts aren't much better off, unless they stay to watch the work done.) As the car salesman says of the System, "I sell two or three hundred cars a year, and the customer buys one every two or three years. You're going to tell me he's going to come in here and beat me in a deal?" The same holds true of car repairs. You can ask to see the old parts for whose replacement you have just paid so dearly; any mechanic dumb enough to show you chunks of metal that aren't obviously beyond repair—even if they have to come off an abandoned school bus—probably won't have enough intelligence to fix the car anyway.

Being an automobile mechanic is not, by contemporary standards, a very nice job. It is hard labor under execrable conditions, even moderately dangerous. It is irremediably filthy. A good mechanic in a very good week can approach a two hundred dollar gross, but the rates are slow to change, and to improve his economic status the mechanic must either get faster or cheat harder. There are human limitations to increases in speed, and besides the other route is a lot less sweaty. The other way a mechanic can improve his lot in life is to move up to foreman or service manager. He will be promoted at that point in his career when he demonstrates his grasp of repair-shop economics more clearly than his coworkers.

One reason car service is so dependably rotten is a crucial shortage of good mechanics. It is the despair of car dealers everywhere, who regret not only the loss of income that a bustling service department can produce, but also the loss of repeat business from customers who get fed up with lousy service and search out a more satisfying dealership—perhaps even of a competing make—with which to do business. Okay, the car mechanic's lot is hard, dirty, dangerous work, not terribly well paid. But the pay isn't below the scale for other hard, dirty, dangerous jobs, and we are supposed to be a nation of car lovers, every man's son a backyard tinkerer, a home-built hot rod spending at least some driveway time with every American family. Our national image presumes mechanical aptitude as a birthright. We *love* cars, obviously; why don't more of us love making them work better?

Some of us do, or did. I have a theory about the mechanic shortage, one which involves a rather large dose of sweetness and light but at least stops short of the perfectability of mankind. I have a young friend who is an expert mechanic, who loves cars and aspires to little more, at least for the present, than to be allowed to be a full-time line mechanic. Unfortunately, he is possessed of a mild and cheerful but nonetheless resolute honesty. I've watched him migrate through five independent garages and dealerships in the past half-dozen years. He works well at his own quite respectable pace; he sticks with each job until the pressure from management begins to build. When the boss begins to lean on him to shove the work out faster, or when he sees about him more excesses against the customers' trust than he can stomach, he packs his tools. He quits amicably, and always gets good references from regretful bosses. He is protective of human dignity. Mechanic's jobs aren't.

Right here is as good a point as any for the insertion of the standard demurrers. There are, of course, honest shops and honest dealers, non-System houses, even non-flat-rate repair shops. There are car salesmen who are pillars of their communities, dealers who understand and appreciate not only cars but honest commercial relationships. Et cetera. You may fill in your own blanks. In two decades of car ownership, I've even run across a couple of honest men myself. Usually, when I go back for the next tune-up or the next car purchase, they're out of business—or "policies" have changed. (Thus the migration of my young friend is doubly frustrating: not only have I lost close contact with a nice guy, now that he's left the area, but I also no longer have a local mechanic I trust when my car needs work. The search goes on. . . .) I admire my friend a great deal, but I suspect he is going to have to find another line of work if he is going to hang onto his principles.

So much for sweetness and light. My theory isn't all that original anyway, as any reader of Paul Goodman or the current wave of apocalyptic thinkers will attest. A writer named Mark Kram identifies the problem as the quantifiers. In a piece in *Sports Illustrated* about the inspired athleticism of ballet dancer Edward Villela, Kram pondered the incongruity of so *rara* an *avis* as a male dancer emerging from the Queens boyhood that Kram and Villela had unknowingly shared. It was a neighborhood where "a badge of acceptance was a blue work shirt, and dented beer kettles were old school steins":

> . . . It was through sports that the people found expression, and they devoured the seasons like chunks of raw meat, insensitive to essences: the esthetics of movement, the myriad of delicate lines to each sport. It was the catch by Mays that counted, not the brilliance of his flight.
>
> Their minds belonged to the quantifiers. They were locked into a scoreboard attitude toward life, from the grim mathematics of factory production to the simplest of recreations. It was not how you did something, it was the result that mattered. . . . It was just a matter of time before it all would blend into the worst sort of cynicism—into craftily bungling plumbers, weight-manipulating butchers, gouging TV repairmen. It was, though, not their true spirit. Once they had been an inquisitive people with creative, rowdy style, with an infectious feel for life and the zest for making their lives count in some special way. But that was before they learned that nobody put any of this up on a scoreboard.[10]

The End of an Affair

I'm not sure what Superconsumer can do, in the face of all this. Inform himself, yes; approach car purchases with numbers noted and decimal points in place, the fine blandishments of the ad campaigns shrugged off, the pitfalls of trade-in, financing, insurance carefully mapped. A hint of relief is on the horizon, in proposed federal legislation to require considerably more, and more meaningful, information from the manufacturer and dealer with regard to car prices. Some new commercial ventures promise to help the prospective buyer secure the car of his or her choice (within certain limitations) at a flat rate of $125 over dealer cost.[11] The cost of the service to the customer is $5, to the participating dealer $25 per sale. The $125 figure seems to be above the manufacturer-established wholesale price (plus delivery and preparation charges, and excise tax if any). With the rebate system under which the industry operates, the service doesn't sound like a shockingly dangerous threat to free enterprise, but its progenitors have recently claimed that newspapers are refusing its advertising for fear of reprisal in reduced newspaper advertising from local dealers, so perhaps it's a more sinister threat to the profit motive than I realize.

A moderate revolution is also going on in car service, stimulated primarily by federal attention to the arrogance with which the manufacturers have traditionally ignored the abuses committed by their franchised dealers. All four major U.S. manufacturers are currently mounting expensive campaigns to convince the public that someone in Detroit is, after all, listening. It won't help the flat-rate banditry, but it will cure a lot of ills of the warranty system, which is closely related (in its faults) to the ills of the standard level of automobile service.

Consumer advocate Ralph Nader has written a large paperback manual with associates Lowell Dodge and Ralf Hotchkiss, pointing out dozens of avenues of recourse for the consumer afflicted with faulty warranty work or bad car service in general (post purchase). It's called *What to do with your bad car, "An Action Manual for Lemon Owners,"* [12] and the descriptive subtitle is apt. The book lists possible and probable flaws, their remedies, and most important, names and addresses of everybody—*everybody*—to whom the resourceless consumer can bitch. A sample carbon-copy list is supplied for a letter to a manufacturer complaining about a warranty problem. The book suggests you also send copies to:

> dealer
> zone office

your attorney
President's Committee on Consumer Interests
your U.S. senators and congressman
Federal Trade Commission
Center for Auto Safety (a consumer action group)
Consumers Union
Action Line
National Automobile Dealers Association
State or Local Dealer Licensing Authority

Superconsumer can do all that. He can make the phone ring off the service manager's wall, inundate the dealer in broadsides from Washington, drive the paranoia level at his local auto shop right off the upper end of the scale. Being Superconsumer, he just may do all that. He'll likely get more courteous treatment on one level, for a time or two, but eventually he will turn his relationship with the people who sold him his car into guerrilla warfare. It is only fair, he may reason, since they have been warring on him and his pocketbook for lo these many seasons. Tit for tat. It won't cut the actual costs of owning and operating an automobile, but it may help reduce the extracurricular swindles that aren't purchasing even a ponderous, limited, and expensive "free" mobility.

It won't be pleasant. Procuring car service by shouting match is not conducive to good digestion and a benign view of the world. It could even be considered another cost; gastric turmoil and tension headaches are not included in the DOT's twelve cents per mile either. It may even be worth it. The doormat approach is not conducive to peace of mind *or* to lowered costs.

Superconsumer can also do it himself, which a surprisingly large number of Americans already do. The knowledge is available, and not impossibly arcane, although the recent evolution of the American automobile is toward increasing obfuscation. The tools and equipment are readily available, and, in view of the money saved for outside repair work and the longevity of the equipment, dirt cheap; almost any wrench will outlast almost any automobile. Working space can be a problem, but then space is always a problem, most of it being taken up these days by automobiles. The only really substantial investment Superconsumer will have to make, in order to save repair costs, is time. He might, for example, set up books in which he "pays" himself mechanic's wages. It'd be interesting to see what that would do to the Great American Cost-Per-Mile figures.

Or he might just say the hell with it. The hell with his share of that 13 percent of the GNP, the hell with his twenty-five cents out of every retail dollar, the hell with the costs on top of aggravations on top of costs. If he adds up the bill—honestly—he almost surely will, unless Superconsumer is either superaffluent or a supercarlover. As Lewis Mumford said, "The motorcar is treated like a private mistress, not included in the family budget no matter how extravagant her demands upon the purse." Books could not hold all the reasons why men take mistresses (and women take lovers); the reasons for which they discard them are superficially complex, but a certain fundamental truth underlies all the rationalizations: the love affair is over. And that is precisely what happened, at the end of the golden era, to the automobile.

CHAPTER 8

The Cost of Doing Business

The Priority Game

In 1955 President Dwight Eisenhower lent the full weight of his support to a nationwide "Safe Driving Day." The event was ballyhooed for months beforehand, almost as if it were Ike's personal idea. We would, it was presumed, continue to crash fatally at our usual rate up until midnight of November 30, but at the stroke of 12:01 on December 1, the nation was to join in an orgy of carefulness. There was vague implication that it might even be possible to go through a single day without any traffic fatalities anywhere in the U.S. Unfortunately, on the magic day while we were all tiptoeing around avoiding each other in our automobiles, the death toll from highway accidents rose by about 10 percent.

The results of the noble experiment were not heavily publicized. The effort did, however, serve to point up one of the many peculiarities about traffic safety in this country: the death rate seems to go up in some kind of bizarre relationship to the amount of attention that is focused on it. Since a less widely publicized dry run on Safe Driving Day had also yielded a spike in the statistics, the federal government abandoned exhortations to the public's sense of responsibility as a means of controlling the accident rate, lest it wipe out all its taxpayers.

The federal government's frustration was no greater than that of any other agency that has ever tried to deal with the highway death toll. The toll has a mysterious resistance to the most well-intentioned attack. For proof, one has only to look at the National Safety Council's record: Fifty-eight years of making "safety" the nation's most publicized cause (their estimate), 40 percent of the budget devoted to traffic safety, the endless media scare-campaigns (tapering off now, as we will see), and never a significant remission in the inexorable climb of the death total. Nothing seems to work.

The climbing death toll; we have almost stopped wincing at the statistics. Almost sixty thousand per year, more than a thousand a week killed, ten thousand a day injured, a billion dollars a month in economic loss. An obscene cost indeed, under any circumstances. The cost of doing business. We could cut the toll to zero tomorrow. We would simply have to stop all cars from moving (such a course would triple the nonautomotive death toll, of course—no fire trucks could move, for example). By the same token, a gruesomely positive face can be put on the statistics. The National Safety Council, a preponderance of whose budget comes from the automobile industry, has a favorite figure: the death rate for vehicle-miles driven. This figure has gone steadily down since World War II, and has held at under 6 per 100 million miles since 1957. The rate dropped to its lowest point in history in 1970, at 5.0 deaths. (The total number of deaths also dropped by about three thousand in 1970, as a result of the wholesale introduction of new safety equipment required by federal law in cars sold since 1968.)

As Nader has demonstrated, these statistics don't mean a great deal. While deaths per mile have gone down slowly in recent years, deaths per hundred thousand population have gone up slightly. "What this means," says Nader, "is that a motorist can expect to drive further in any given year without being killed, but he is just as likely as in previous years to be killed within that year." [1] In fact the statistics are remarkably uniform. As pointed out in Chapter 6, the number of deaths depends almost precisely on the number of cars that we put on the road. In only six of the past twenty-one years have deaths failed to follow the direction of the sales curve for new motor vehicles. The National Safety Council does not give much publicity to that line of thinking.

Federal intervention in automobile safety practices is about a million lives late, but that it is occurring at all is a remarkable tribute to private persistence in the face of massive corporate indifference. The industry has fought a long, expensive, and cleverly complex holding action against the notion that it had any responsibility for driver and passenger safety at all. Now that that battle has been lost, the industry is gearing as rapidly as possible to turn profits on the new safety equipment, which neatly turns the question back on the consumer. How much will you pay for your own safety? If past market response to safety as a sales tool is any indication, the answer is, not much.[2] It is curiously difficult to get the individual to pay extra for his own safety in a car. We are aware of the continuing death toll, we shudder at the thought of long drives on holiday weekends, we may occasionally suffer a moment of doubt even under perfect, traffic-free driving conditions. But somehow none of that has anything to do with using the car, into which we routinely hop, bustling from here to there, day after day. We hardly *ever* crash. . . .

The safety muddle would be funny if its ineffectiveness were not so tragic. Decades of hand-wringing alternate with brief bursts of application of a somewhat sanctimonious federal lash to the industry's indifference. We are currently in the lash period: both federal standards and industry solutions are so far quarter-measures pasted onto obsolete vehicles after the fact. Their beneficial effects may be real, but will be limited, slow to show measurable results, and productive of new and curious accident effects of their own (as will the concurrent upgrading of antipollution standards). All our technological expertise doesn't give us enough information to bring us omniscient planning, and complexities breed complexities faster than our engineering labs can schedule tests.

An example. The industry is currently plagued by failing engine mounts. The engine mounts are coming apart because of adhesive failures in materials that have been used successfully for a dozen years. The adhesives are now failing because recent car models are running under-hood temperatures as much as 50 degrees higher than for older cars. The under-hood temperatures are rising because of desperate cut-and-paste attempts to make large V-8 engines run cleaner, that is, give off less pollution. A broken engine mount can kill (usually, power brake hoses are severed when the engine mount lets go). When new adhesives are perfected, other unforeseen results will predictably surface. A very few of them may even be beneficial.

The frustration level is high among people who take on the job of doing something about traffic safety. The record of the past is worse than dismal, and the prospects of a sudden breakthrough to any real accomplishment are practically

zero. This doesn't have to be. If we are dead set on technological solutions, technology is currently available that could
bring drastic reductions in the death rate very quickly. We
will not soon see application of that technology, even though
the dollar cost, compared to the economic loss we now
suffer, would be comparatively small.

There are other costs, larger and more frightening than
mere expenditure of dollars, which will keep us from up-
dating safety technology. Political upheaval and corporate
realignment would be required. We would have to *change*.
We would have to revise both our vehicles and the way we
use them, have to revise the very way we regard automobile transportation. We have a system, already functioning, which is admirably suited for generating a trillion vehicle-miles per year in the economy as we now know it.
Unfortunately, it is arranged to do so at a known fatality
rate, acceptable or not depending on how sanguine one may
be about the cost of doing business. The system is particularly ill suited for reorganization or rearrangement of its
critical elements for purposes of preservation of life. To re-
organize for humane purposes might change the system in
unknowable ways. The result of this quandary is a poignant
demonstration of the difficulties inherent in that catch-
phrase of the late sixties, "re-ordering of priorities." Precisely
how much will we give up? If sacrificing a portion of that
complex system of cars, roads, drivers, costs, benefits, economic stimulation, etc., that leads to a trillion-mile year
could save lives, how much would we let go? If it could be
reduced to a formula, vehicle-miles sacrificed per life saved,
what politician would dare begin to apply the formula?

Back in the twenties, some safety flacks came up with the
slogan, "The Three E's—Enforcement, Education, and Engineering," as the solution to the highway toll for all right-
minded citizens. As Nader has pointed out, enforcement and

education referred to the driver, and engineering to the roadway; not for nothing have the car-makers kept a close watch (and an economic hand) on the efforts of the safety crusaders. Just to be sure, however, that no bets have been missed, it's worth taking a look at all three of the major elements of the traffic safety equation: driver, road, and car.

There's No Such Thing as Foolproof

The scene is a broad, smooth asphalt runway, wide enough for a dozen lanes of traffic. In the center, three lanes are marked off with white lines painted on the paving. Rubber traffic pylons are set up on the lines. Overhead are suspended three conventional traffic lights, one for each lane. A small sedan approaches the middle lane, running parallel, at 30 MPH. As the car draws near the painted lines, the center and right lane signals turn red, the left lane green. The car enters the middle lane before beginning to veer toward the left. It hits the first rubber pylon, sending it flying. The car begins to slew about, tires screeching, wavers momentarily as the skid is corrected, then tries to veer left again for the green light. It passes under the traffic lights still straddling the line between lanes. Failure; more pylons fly. The car goes around again for another try, as a man begins resetting the pylons on the lane stripes.

This relatively simple exercise was invented by Bob Bondurant, an ex-racing driver and automotive consultant who now runs an advanced-driving school in Santa Ana, California. The purpose is not to teach drivers the dubious skill of darting in and out of traffic lanes, but to demonstrate that the possibilities of driver control and reaction extend much closer to an emergency than the average driver realizes, and that training can delay the onset of panic. In the situation carefully constructed at Bondurant's school, the signal change occurs well before the physical capabilities of the car and the average reaction time of a normal driver have been foreclosed. Yet the driver was unable to accomplish the lane change that the signals asked for. Very few drivers can, in the early stages of such training. As the experience is repeated, the driver *will* become able to accomplish the change, and will do so at closer and closer intervals to the minimum possible warning time/distance. In the process he will learn that he can control a car well beyond the points in time and physical attitude of the car itself that he previously regarded as the irrevocable limits. He will learn the physical limitations of his own skills and of the car. Very few licensed drivers ever have such an opportunity.

"Most drivers don't drive into accidents, they abdicate," says ex-racing driver Denise McCluggage. Most accidents are avoidable through the conventional strictures—closer obedience to traffic laws, more rigorous vehicle inspection, more attentive driving habits, etc. But there is another area of possible avoidance: most accidents are avoidable right up through the last few feet before impact. The point at which the driver "lost control" according to the accident report is almost invariably the point at which the driver abdicated the responsibility of trying to save himself and the car. Panic. Training in emergency procedures can diminish the tendency toward panic, can give a driver a vital few more seconds in time and feet in distance in which to avoid disaster when it approaches. One might therefore suppose that such training would be a valuable requisite for driver-licensing in a nation that kills off a thousand of its citizens each week in traffic emergencies. No such training is required for licensing in any state; no such training is *available* except in the Bondurant school, in two or three other commercial ventures in the training of racing drivers, and in sporadic weekend racing-driver schools administered by the Sports Car Club of America.

Furthermore, the existence of any such training is regularly decried by the traffic safety experts. Much as that amorphous group denounces automobile racing—with considerable justification—as a glorification of speed and danger, and therefore an indirect contributor to the highway toll, the safety people also regard any emphasis on learning the limitations of a car's performance as tantamount to encouragement to those who would exceed those limitations.

The Bondurant exercise is only one of many which already exist or could easily be devised to help upgrade the skills of the citizen-driver. Liberty Mutual Insurance Company has built a skid-pad for driver training; there are half a dozen other similar facilities spotted throughout the country, although usually as part of tire-testing installments and thus unavailable to the general public. A few minutes of floundering about on such a skid-pad (flooded with detergents or other tractionless material) with or without an instructor can teach a driver volumes about vehicle behavior on ice or other slick surfaces, in perfect safety. The same thing can be accomplished—safely, again—on a snow-covered parking lot, if the lot is empty of other cars and an area free of floodlight poles is selected. Every driver whose travels take him within reach of snowy or icy weather *should* spend a few minutes each winter refreshing himself on the behavior of his own vehicle on low-traction surfaces. (But he is apt to be arrested for reckless driving if he conducts his research on a public parking lot, even an empty one.)

Every driver should be able to estimate accurately the minimum stopping distances of his car on every kind of road surface, if not from every speed the car is capable of then at least from those speeds at which he is accustomed to driving. (And he should be able to make those estimates not in number of feet, but in reference to visual landmarks.) Every driver should be able to run the sensory equivalent of computer formulas in his head, to judge acceleration distances and times for passing and for merging into heavy traffic. Every driver should know how much side-force his tires will take before they begin to skid, for every possible road surface—not in foot-pounds of energy but in feel, at the steering wheel and at the seat of the pants. Every driver should have clearly established procedures—habitual reaction, if possible—for dealing with fire, with the final seconds before an unavoidable collision, with the problems of escaping from a submerged automobile. Every driver should know the precise dimensions of his vehicle, not in overall feet and inches but in a clear sensory concept of the spatial relationships from the driver's seat. The driver should know where his car can go not only in the sense of its overall size but also in its ground clearance, especially for front and rear overhang; he should know what kind of unpaved terrain he can traverse, and at what speeds.

Unfortunately, not only are these skills not taught to drivers, but obtaining them can be illegal. Reckless driving. We are to drive our cars within their limitations at all times, of course. Do misunderstand what may sound like a campaign for dangerous behavior. I am not suggesting that we should practice near-crashes. I don't want Mr. Everyday Driver learning about skid behavior in his car while I am on the outside of the curve, or experimenting with stopping distances while I am trotting through a crosswalk. I am very much in favor of all of us driving well below the performance limitations of our automobiles at all times. But in every accident a car and/or driver has exceeded the limitations. (Many states automatically issue a speeding citation with every accident—"speed excessive for the conditions"—on the theory that if the car had only been going

185

slower, the accident could have been avoided.) I am suggesting that it would be appropriate to know what the limitations are, the better to stay below them.

It would be particularly appropriate somehow to accomplish such an upgrading of driver skills because, despite the accumulation of a great deal of information to the contrary, safety thinking in this country still holds strongly to two allied theories. The first, which is only about 50 percent wrong, holds that the driver and the driver alone is responsible for maintaining the safe flow of traffic. The second is that the driver is the only available point on which to work to reduce the highway death and injury toll, a theory which is purely self-protective, industry-promulgated hogwash.

It is inarguable that the driver has a great deal of responsibility in contributing to the safe flow of traffic, but there are other considerations. There is failure of equipment, poor roadway conception, poor roadway maintenance, rules and customs which actually violate both the physical capabilities of cars and the logical processes of their drivers, extraneous handicaps (dogs, cows, birds, small boys on bicycles, other drivers) to unimpeded progress, and weather and other acts of God which render safe operation impossible. When these are removed, then traffic safety does perhaps become strictly a driver responsibility. Interestingly enough, however, despite a recent upsurge in "no-fault" insurance, our automotive legal processes devote much time and effort, in collision cases, to deciding just which driver is at fault. This would seem to indicate that the driver held blameless had no responsibility for interruption of traffic flow.

The second theory, that the driver is the sole available source of access to improvement of the highway toll, could be dismissed as ludicrous if there were not so many responsible people—and responsible agencies—still maintaining it. The theory excludes much more than two thirds of the safety equation (the road and the car). It not only proceeds from that mythical point at which all of the external handicaps, hindrances, and natural disasters have already been removed, but it also stops at the instant of impact. (In fact, it stops well before impact, as we have seen. It stops at the instant of panic, of "loss of control." Loss of control can be caused by forces external to the driver also—principally by the car itself—so the theory isn't valid even for the very brief portion of the problem that it directly addresses.)

Ralph Nader has already documented the interlocking protectorate of industry-backed safety organizations and advisory bodies to lawmaking and regulatory agencies. He has also uncovered some of the more embarrassing attempts by these groups to shift the burden of responsibility for safety solely onto the driver's shoulders. A single example, from *Unsafe at Any Speed,* demonstrates the level of protection of the automotive public weal provided by car-industry-dominated thinking:

> . . . In March 1963 the motor vehicle bulletin of the Association of Casualty and Surety Companies noted that the "parking brake" of many new automobiles might appear firmly set but still allow rolling backwards freely. The association added that this could be especially dangerous if a driver parks his car in the family driveway, many of which slope. It explained that this hazard arises because of recent changes in the design of parking and emergency brake systems in nearly all passenger cars and in many light trucks. If the parking brake is set without the simultaneous application of the hydraulic service (foot) brakes, it noted, the bottom of the brake shoes are brought into contact with the drums on the rear wheels, but the shoes are not fully engaged. With the parking brake in this position, the association said, the car cannot roll forward, but it can move freely to the rear. If, on the other hand, the motorist is pressing his foot on the hydraulic brake while he is setting the parking brake, the shoe and drum engage completely and the car will not move.

The Costs

What did the association recommend? It urged the reader of this limited-circulation bulletin to get into the habit of applying the foot brake while he set the parking brake. "No problem can occur if a driver trains himself to do this," was the advice. Having told the reader how to adjust to a dangerous design, the association saw its task completed. It did not name the models which possessed such a hazard; it did not demand that the manufacturers change the design on future models and correct existing models; it did not notify appropriate state and federal officials, in spite of its knowledge of casualties proceeding from this hazard.[3]

What the insurance industry probably *did* do, if past performance is any clue, is raise the rates to cover the increased financial risk of insuring cars with such design flaws. On $11.4 billion in premiums per year (the figure is for 1968) the industry claimed to lose something like $170 million per year in the decade 1958–1968. The industry also claims an average yearly premium of $110 for the country's 105 million drivers; the DOT figures it closer to $170. I have no specific evidence that insurance rates were raised to cover possible damage resulting from the unsafe parking brake, but such a course would have been consistent with other insurance industry reactions to design dangers in automobiles. The result to the driver is that he not only gets an unsafe car, he pays extra for the privilege of driving it. And he's the fellow who is supposed to be responsible for maintaining traffic safety.

Driving safely is a relatively simple task as long as everything goes according to plan; the instant things stop going as planned, the task gets extremely complex. As we saw in Chapter 1, and will see again in more detail shortly, the automobile designers have devoted a great deal of energy and cost to making the easy part easier. Unfortunately, the concomitant result—as in increased weight and controls that respond more slowly—has been to make the complex portion

188

of the job infinitely more complex. This trend of startling contrasts extends further. As the entire mechanism surrounding private automobile transportation has simply swelled—in numbers, congestion, speeds, horsepower, complexity, sheer size and weight, in every conceivable numerical index as well as psychic load and legal responsibility—the human mechanism that is the operator has remained the same. Reaction times and capability for judgment have not increased. Training time has been marginally extended with the spread of driver-education courses in the public schools, but no valid indication has been found that such training accomplishes any real reduction in the accident toll.

I would not argue for a moment that better driving could not be an important factor in lowering the accident rate. I would argue that our attempts to obtain a higher level of driver skill and to instill in our drivers attitudes that would lead to greater highway safety have been directly counterproductive. Since the driver is getting blamed for the whole safety mess, it would help if he had some means of response to the blame. Unfortunately, in the trio of major elements in the problem of traffic safety, the driver is the one with no "industry" other than his government to represent him. And as far as the government is concerned, after the oil and insurance industries, the car-makers, and the road-builders, the citizen comes first.

Booby Traps

We will now pause in this tide of unrelenting abuse for a little cheer. Our roads are pretty good, pretty safe. We build too many of them, too often to the wrong places; we administer them out of corruption, and our building methods are invitations to graft; we repair our old ones too slowly (for

The Costs

the traffic that our car-centricity creates), and decorate our new ones with booby traps; we put our best ones where there are no people, and reserve our worst for those areas where congestion is so thick that even our best would not suffice. We spend entirely too much money on them, by any rational comparison with other national needs. But by and large, from a safety standpoint, our roads are not too bad. Safe roads cost more than we can afford, but we are busily collecting money so we can eventually smooth out the remaining heirlooms, bringing everything up to yesterday's standard. We are beginning to know what to look for, in safe highway arteries. (How the highway people love terms like "artery," implying that the lifeblood of the nation flows through their handiwork!) At the current rate of reconstruction and repair the whole mind-numbing 3.7 million miles should be adequately revamped for safe passage of automobiles just about the time that the automobile has completely outlived its usefulness as a system of private transportation.

The contribution of roadway to highway safety is a curiously negative one: the roadway is the environment where accidents occur, and thus where "safety" is lost. Bad roads contribute directly to accidents; good roads only somehow allow accidents not to happen. (Good roads also allow accidents *to* happen, of course. It is too much to ask of highway design that it completely foil our human and mechanical penchant for visiting disaster on ourselves.)

The parameters of safe highway design are not difficult to conceive. A certain minimum *constant* radius for all curves, maximum grades for the hills, expansive grassy areas at the shoulders without abrupt ditches. Dividing (but crash-absorbing) barriers between opposite directions of travel, where possible. Sufficient camber to road surfaces to provide rapid drainage of the pavement, but not so much curvature that cars will slip off an icy roadway. A surface texture that retains its tractive properties through maximum variation in weather. Smooth transitions between roadbed and shoulder. Adequate acceleration and deceleration lanes for entering and leaving side roads. Controlled, or at least well-marked, access. Clear marking (including reflective paint to mark the edge of the pavement, a lifesaver in fog or other conditions of markedly reduced visibility). Careful overall attention to lines of sight, blind spots, and visual obstructions so that maximum visibility is maintained over both directions of traffic, night and day. The removal of *all* obstructions impinging on the right of way, and a right of way adequate for traffic flow, emergency service, and escape areas. Route marking and information sufficient to keep the traveler informed of hazards, distances, services. Add your own personal crotchets; such a list is not difficult to make.

Unfortunately all highways aren't built across plains. Roads must deal with the terrain, and the more varied the terrain (in population and previous construction, as well as natural obstacles), the higher the cost. The reasonably clear principles of safe highway design run budgets ever higher. What we save in road costs we very often spend in lives lost, because when the principles are compromised, roads get dangerous very rapidly.

The danger is not often clearly identified, even in accident reports. Recent research into the causes of fatal accidents has shown that most fatalities result from a complex interlock of varying causes (which is another reason the oversimplification of blaming the driver is counterproductive—it serves to masquerade real causes for which effective cures can be found). In "The Case for Fast Drivers," Robert L. Schwartz examines in hair-raising detail a head-on collision in which three were killed, six others injured.[4] In the police records the cause of the accident was listed as speeding, with alcohol suspected as a contributing factor. A Harvard Medical School team painstakingly reconstructed the accident and found neither speed nor alcohol to be contributory. The real causes, according to the research team, were (1) bad equipment maintenance (an improperly repaired tire cut had let go at about 50 MPH on a four-lane highway); (2) inadequate driving skills (the driver of the car with the flat pulled toward safety on the verge, but then slammed on the brakes, which caused the car to dive back into traffic; (3) inadequate highway environment (no retaining barrier between opposing lanes of traffic); and (4) lack of restraining devices. (Here we shift from cause of accident to cause of fatalities: two of the three fatalities and half of the other injuries would have been avoided if all had been wearing seat belts. Whether the loss of control that sent the initiating car from fast lane to righthand verge, back across two lanes of traffic and a grass divider strip, and head-on into approaching traffic could have been avoided if the driver had been strapped in place in front of the steering wheel was not determined. It seems likely the erratic path could have been reduced.)

The desultory examination of road factors in such an accident, without the Harvard follow-up, can be imagined. In this accident, alcohol was originally listed as a contributing factor by police because one of the bodies was thrown from a car and landed among discarded beer cans—which the Harvard team determined had been at the scene for a month before the accident. Even a careful investigator would look to vehicle dynamics first for the cause of the accident, and if the roadway isn't the initiating factor (as in hitting a bridge abutment first, then ricocheting into traffic), it is quite likely to be disregarded. Well, sure, too bad that signpost came in through the windshield, but the fellow just picked an unlucky place to have an accident, right? It isn't as if the signpost *caused* any accident, and thus the highway design is exonerated, although the location of the post may have been a direct contributor in turning a bent fender into a fatality.

Still, we are learning. For all its faults, the Interstate System seems to be compiling a good safety record. Design standards have matured with the program, and the 90-percent federal backing has helped the states afford to enforce those standards in actual construction. Death-per-vehicle-mile figures for the Interstates are well below those for the rest of the nation's roads. It is impossible to prove or disprove the Nader contention about deaths-per-mile with regard to the Interstate. It may be that those swift, efficient through-way miles are manifestly safer, as logic would have us believe. It may be that logic is as inapplicable here as in other aspects of the automotive conundrum, that those swift, efficient miles merely generate more vehicle miles, allowing us to rack up more and more distance without materially lowering our actual death rate or raising our individual chances of survival. The Bureau of Public Roads was claiming in 1963 that the completed Interstate System, scheduled for 1972, would save 8000 lives annually. It isn't just the completion schedule that has slipped. Within three years of that claim the highway death toll had climbed by 10,000 lives; the climb has continued, to a maximum of 13,000—so far—over the 1963 figure. Two interpretations of these figures seem possible, both of them horrifying. Either the Interstate is not effective in reducing the national toll, in which case our $43 billion has been an investment in carnage as well as efficient travel; or the Interstate is as effective as the BPR would have us believe, in which case without it our highway death toll would have jumped an additional 8000, for an increase of 21,000 deaths per year over 1963.

The fallacy that has shaped highway design thinking from its earliest days—which is being weeded out of highway plans today—is the same that has exempted automobiles themselves from extensive safety engineering. The assumption is that if all of us would only drive sensibly—slowly and in control—and if highways were built to enable us to do this, then nothing bad would ever happen. And if it did, well, that was already after the accident had started; accidents are totally unpredictable, so there is little point in trying to help the situation after the fact, the "fact" being initiation of the accident. This fallacy has led to driver training that is primarily aimed at inhibition, at instilling fear in the driver rather than in teaching him skills. It has led to highway construction in which the primary consideration is pool-table smoothness of surface rather than a safe environment. This fallacy has also led to the creation of automobiles which provide every creature comfort except safety.

What Won't Work

If every car and driver in the United States were fitted with the following equipment whenever in motion, the highway death toll would be cut approximately in half. The equipment necessary: full roll cage; rupture-proof fuel cell; equal-action shock absorbers; premium-grade radial tires (with spikes in winter); three-point (lap and shoulder) restraining belts; crash helmets for all occupants; antiwhiplash head restraints; antilocking disc brakes. The most expensive piece of equipment listed is the last, which in its current limited availability costs about two hundred dollars per car. On a volume basis, as in a federal requirement that all this equipment be fitted to every car sold, the total cost for all could probably be brought under three hundred dollars, excepting helmets. The helmets would have to be purchased separately, as personal items, in order to get proper individual fit. Helmets are readily available now, at about thirty-five dollars. We won't wear them anyway, of course. (Motorcycle riders have sued for repeal of helmet laws as violation of their civil rights.) We won't even wear the lap-and-shoulder belts that are already fitted in late-model cars, even though only two crash fatalities have so far been recorded when lap-and-shoulder restraints were in use.

Meanwhile, the industry is alternately claiming, as it has since the twenties, that its cars are about as safe as they can be made, and insisting that it can't have new safety devices ready before 1973, or 1976, or ever. And the federal government is proposing air-bag passive restraints (which perhaps *can't* be made to work, ever) and speed governors and flashing lights and sirens that go off when a car exceeds a national speed limit—also for 1975 or 1976. Energy-absorbing bumpers, which will reduce sheet metal damage and the cost of repairs but will do very little to reduce deaths and injuries, are evidently items of higher priority than safety advances.

In fact, the crash-resistant bumpers may be the first federal design requirement to backfire seriously on the DOT. There is a great deal to be said for the shock-absorption value of all that soft, convoluted sheet metal up front which bends so easily and expensively. With crash-resistant bumpers, the bending forces may well be passed on to the occupants of the car, particularly if they are not strapped in place.

The list of mechanical features proposed above is somewhat arbitrary (as is the estimated cut in the death rate—but the available statistics on causes of automobile death indicate a rough accuracy). The specific equipment recommendations are simple enough. A roll cage is an internal welded-steel framework surrounding the passenger compartment to form a relatively crashproof cage of protection for the driver. (The two known fatalities occurring with lap-and-shoulder harnesses in place were caused by external objects encroaching on the passenger space.) If the driver is sufficiently restrained within such a cage, the cage acts as a safe compartment; surrounding sheet metal will absorb a great deal of the energy of the crash so long as there is structural integrity within which the driver can be kept away from the massive dislocations and displacements that result from a severe crash. The roll cage is standard equipment in stock-car racers, and with that addition, drivers have survived 180-MPH crashes with no, or minor, injuries.

The fuel cell concept also comes from automobile racing. Originally a self-sealing rubberlike bladder within the fuel tank was used; subsequent development has brought porous foam materials which prevent sloshing and surge in the tank (and thus prevent changes in vehicle balance, as well as fuel starvation), seal punctures, resist impact, etc. The point is simply to provide a fuel container which does not turn into a Molotov cocktail in a crash. The technology has been available for better than five years, and the cost is reasonable. No production automobile yet has a fuel cell.

Equal-action shock absorbers are a somewhat oversimplified attempt to overcome the results of decades of engineering concentration on soft ride, at the expense of handling and braking stability. The shock absorbers on most domestic cars devote 90 percent of their capability to absorbing bumps—compression of the springs—and 10 percent to the opposite movement, the extension of the springs as the wheel that has hit the bump returns to its normal position. The result of this arrangement is a soft ride on paper-smooth pavement, and a tendency to go out of control on rough surfaces. In severe cases, as under hard braking on uneven surfaces, such an arrangement can lead to "axle tramp" in the suspension (usually in the rear, where the weight of the entire axle is below the springs). When this happens, a kind of cyclical bounce is set up in the wheel. Since the wheel can only provide braking force when it is in contact with the road surface, and since the wheel is bouncing wildly, braking capacity is severely reduced. (Axle tramp is also what causes the washboard effect commonly found in gravel road surfaces and in asphalt paving near stop signs.)

The division of absorptive capability in a shock absorber is largely a matter of internal valving—50-50 shocks are no more expensive than the current 90-10, given a modest re-tooling investment. A better solution, still short of outright suspension redesign, would be extra-heavy-duty shocks with 50-50 action, but such a requirement would raise the cost, and probably would result in ride roughness that was unacceptable to the pampered public backside.

Some large American cars are now being equipped with premium-grade radial tires as standard equipment (Thunderbird, Lincoln). A complete discussion of tire differences could fill this book and still not exhaust the subject, but from a safety standpoint, a summary will do. Eighteen percent of the tires tested by the National Highway Safety Bureau up to May 1969 were faulty. The DOT reported in January 1969 that as many as two thirds of the new tires on the market had potentially hazardous defects. The regular standard-equipment tires supplied on new cars are very likely less dependable than these figures indicate; the manufacturers set minimal standards for original equipment tires, then purchase them from the lowest bidders. The authors of *What to do with your bad car* put it this way:

> *Tires tend to be more defect-ridden than any other single part of a car, and the defects generally have more disastrous consequences than other car defects.* Evidence of their frequency of failure can be seen along any superhighway—chunks of rubber and damaged guardrails are left behind, although the rest of the debris may be towed away.

The Costs

Defective tires can disintegrate at any time, regardless of age, price, or quality of the tire. Failure can be sudden and often total. Chances of failure are greatest at the precise moment when an accident would be unthinkably disastrous, when the car is filled with passengers and travelling at high speed.[5]

Premium-grade tires cost more because they have better materials in them and, one would hope, because they are more carefully made. Although the expectations of getting a defect-free premium tire are far from certain, the chances are better than with the lower grades. All radial tires are premium grade. The radials run cooler (heat is the tire's greatest enemy), wear longer, provide somewhat better traction on slippery surfaces, and will sustain greater side-loadings before skidding than conventional tires. Radials are also less susceptible to tread and ply separation. They provide a slightly stiffer ride, are a bit noisier than a conventional tire, and cost more. They are worth the extra cost. (On a per-mile basis, the cost is usually the same or less than conventional tires. Also, radial tires have less rolling resistance, require less horsepower, and therefore reduce air pollution.)

Three-point suspension lap and shoulder harness is now standard equipment, as are head rests. Crash helmets are but a foolish dream. Antiskid braking devices have been discussed at length in Chapter 1.

Such a list of safety "accessories" is woefully incomplete, and the features listed here have been selected primarily for low cost, easy installation within existing cars (only the roll cage would noticeably change the appearance of current cars; only the improved shock absorbers would noticeably change performance), and for prime effectiveness. Such a list is also inadequate because short of specific federal action the roll cage, fuel cell, and antilocking brakes will not go onto our cars; the manufacturers have already demonstrated an almost immovable resistance to putting a single dime's worth of quality into their products which isn't directly responsible for increased sales, and the industry is firmly convinced that "safety" won't sell cars. Indeed, the industry has consistently taken the stance that the mere mention of safety is directly deleterious to the health of the industry. No one in Detroit wants any possible connection drawn between their products and the mournful fact of traffic deaths.

Moreover, the tire and shock-absorber recommendations could almost be guaranteed to be reduced in their effect because although initial installation would have an immediate benefit for traffic safety, enforcement to require that the effect be maintained and extended would require supervision of replacement and maintenance of the equipment, which experience with state vehicle inspections, and with antipollution equipment, has proved almost impossible to achieve.

And, of course, people won't use belts. The very small reduction of the death toll in 1971 was probably because of the effectiveness of head restraints on later-model cars, the combined effectiveness of various other federal safety requirements (recessed knobs and levers, padded visors, side reflectors, etc.), and the miniscule percentage of belt-users who happened to crash. That resistance to seat belts, and the marginal improvement in the safety statistics, is what drives the federal safety people to the use of things like air bags as a solution to the highway death toll.

Letting the Feds Do It

The involvement of the federal government in the attempt to improve the safety of the private automobile has gone through an extensive evolution. Originally the government's only access to the safety problem was through its purchasing power, specifically through the General Services Administration, which each year buys and operates some 50,000 vehicles

The Costs

and makes the purchasing decision for the other 250,000 vehicles the government uses. No manufacturer was going to pass up a shot at fleet sales on that scale, and within limits— limits of foot-dragging, lobbying, and reciprocal acrimony— what the GSA wanted from Detroit, it got. Thus the GSA was responsible for the development of seat belts, recessed knobs and levers, padded instrument panels, four-way flasher lamps, exterior rear-view mirrors, etc., starting on 1966 models.

With the passage of the National Traffic and Motor Vehicle Safety Act of 1966, and the creation of the Department of Transportation as a cabinet-level organization the same year, the federal stake became more direct. The myth of safety and reliability in domestic cars was pretty well put to rest forever with the advent of recall campaigns with teeth in them, reaching a peak in 1969 when 7.5 million cars were recalled for correction of defects serious enough either to get the DOT onto the manufacturers' backs, or to cause the manufacturers themselves to begin to worry about liability. The imported car is not immune to recall, of course; in 1969, 400,000 of them were recalled, down from 552,000 the previous year. It should also not be assumed that recall orders issued simultaneously from Detroit and Washington represent the end of the problem. In the period from mid-1966 through 1969, the industry never achieved more than 70-percent effectiveness in recall campaigns, which means that out of a total of 13 million cars with defects serious enough for recall, approximately 3.9 million are still running around unrepaired—if these cars have not yet removed themselves, and their owners, permanently from the highways.*

* The latest mass recall—6.7 million Chevrolets for engine mounts—is not included in these figures. At the 70-percent rate, that brings the dangerous-but-not-repaired total up to an even 5 million cars.

The Cost of Doing Business

The industry's complaints about federal intervention in automobile design, safety oriented or not, have tended to center around the idea that nonautomotive people could not sensibly tell automotive people what to do, that bureaucrats —lawyers, academicians, and civil servants—were meddling foolishly in the province of engineers. Unfortunately for the argument, the industry's engineers have failed to engineer into the cars the safety that the public welfare seems to require—or they have been prevented from doing so by their own nonengineers, in sales, styling, and cost-accounting departments. The energy-absorbing steering column, for example, perhaps the largest single contribution to improving the crash-worthiness of the automobile, was engineered in the twenties, but it took pressure from the bureaucrats to get it into cars forty years later.

Detroit's argument is further weakened by the fact that none of the safety features conceived by the bureaucrats and then made into reality by those engineers has proved to be anything but a positive good—so far. Admittedly, some of them have been irritating (buzzing ignition locks), inconvenient (folding seat-back latches, draperies of shoulder harness), and marginally useful (side reflectors), but despite grumbling by the industry and public alike, none has yet quite backfired, creating more hazards than it cured. That this is so is a tribute to the engineering skills possessed by the industry, once it is directed. That the industry successfully dodged that external direction for more than sixty years is a national scandal.

With the exception of the aforementioned energy-absorbing steering column, head restraints, and lap-and-shoulder belts, federal requirements and industry solutions have so far been limited almost to minutiae. Recessed dash knobs— on underbraked four thousand-pound, 350-horsepower cars— represent a kind of safety nitpicking that seems unlikely to carve huge slices off the highway death toll. Now the feds are after bigger game, and they are after it with the peculiarly selective courage that characterizes political reform. In the early stages of this new burst of ambition on the part of federal safety officials, there is a distinct feeling of misdirected attention and painfully slow progress.

So far, little has been accomplished but the spread of confusion. A prime example is the idea of passive restraint. If Americans are getting killed from being dashed about inside crashing cars, and if they refuse to wear the lap-and-shoulder belts which would save them from this manner of death, then they must be saved from themselves by the DOT. A form of physical restraint would be devised that would require no action by the passenger to put into effect. The quickest, brightest answer to the problem of devising such a restraint seemed to be the air bag. Upon impact, a large plastic bag or balloon would be instantaneously inflated between passenger and dangerous nearby hard surfaces, such as instrument panels. The technology seemed to be available: sensors which could detect an impact, triggering an explosionlike inflation of the bag; plastic pillows which could withstand both the shock of inflation and the impact of flying bodies; devices to achieve the inflation within the first few milliseconds, and then the deflation, after the impact had been absorbed, to restore visibility within the car. There were of course severe problems to solve, but nothing that the industry, in the serene confidence of the DOT, could not overcome. A timetable was set up, requiring the airbags by 1972, then 1973, finally 1975—although the DOT's own tests of the device were scheduled to run through 1976. Working models of the air-bag system were demonstrated to the press.

Detroit said it couldn't be done. Nader accused the industry of yet another round of foot-dragging. An insurance company published an ad campaign built around the air bags, which built public interest in the device, and which also indirectly accused Detroit of malingering.

Detroit fought back, hard. Sensing devices capable of discriminating between collisions and inadvertent bumps—as in backing against a curb—were, according to the industry, beyond foreseeable technology. Inflation rapid enough to protect passengers at 30 MPH (sixty milliseconds) meant that the surface of the bag was moving toward the faces of the occupants at approximately 500 MPH. Ford researchers claimed that this would constitute a near-fatal punch in the face to, for example, a child standing with his face close to the instrument panel at the time the bag went off. Simultaneous inflation of front and rear bags, as for four passengers, caused a pressure differential in a closed car strong enough to blow the windows out. The noise of the inflation was likened to a shotgun shell going off in the front seat— almost enough to threaten permanent hearing damage, according to Detroit, or cause heart attacks. Small enough price to pay, said the DOT, compared with the damages of severe collisions; carry on with the research.

In the end two problems have almost killed air-bag development. One was plainly practical: the fate of eyeglass wearers, pipe-smokers, thumb-suckers, Coke-drinkers, passengers unlucky enough to introduce unmalleable physical objects between their faces and the air bags at the time of inflation. Nobody could figure out how to protect these people, and nobody wanted to saddle the manufacturers with the liability. Both DOT aides and industry lawyers shudder over the vision of an unfortunate car owner nudging a fence railing in a parking lot and thereupon being blinded by splinters from his own rimless spectacles.

The other problem was statistical. GM estimated that despite the best efforts of technology to provide 100-percent reliability, something like a thousand cars out of each year's

4-million-car production run (GM alone) would suffer inadvertent release of the bags. At turnpike speeds, such an accidental deployment was almost sure to *cause* an accident, in and of itself.

In late 1971, the industry won a year's delay—to 1976—in the federal requirement for passive restraints, but the DOT hasn't given up on the concept. Allied Chemical Corporation, one of four major developers of the air bags, now says it has licked the problems of excessive noise, injury from the bags themselves,* and the part of the reliability problem associated with making sure that the bags *do* work when needed. No comment yet on the other half of the reliability problem. Meanwhile the car manufacturers are busily trying to sell womblike interior bolstering, padding that virtually envelops the passenger when he steps into the car, as a less bug-ridden approach to passive restraint. DOT is a long way from giving up on the problem, but has at least backed down from its initial requirement designating the air bag as the single line of development. That, purely and simply, seems to have been a mistake, hamstringing more creative approaches.

As far as Detroit was concerned, it wasn't just the victim of a DOT mistake, it was the subject of total warfare from that agency. In addition to the passive-restraint requirement, the industry had been hit, in rapid succession, with stringent pollution controls, crashproof bumper standards, and open federal courtship of nonautomotive firms (including in that courtship sizable contracts) to get into the act with "safety cars." Detroit's response to the pollution controls was to announce that the 1975 requirement could not possibly be met, to obtain a one-year extension to 1976, and then to boast—superior engineering!—that the standards would be met in 1974. The boast seems to have been a bit premature

---

* But not from objects between bag and passenger.

(June 1971), since six months later the industry was talking about suing for further extensions.* The response to the demand for 5-MPH crashproof bumpers was not to redesign to avoid the ornate complexity that contributes so heavily to high repair costs in minor parking-lot tangles, but to plunge into the engineering of even heavier, similarly ornate front ends, indistinguishable from the ones that caused federal ire in the first place. These could be made to absorb shock only by extremely complex means, and added sharply to gross weights, but they preserved the jukebox "beauty" of the Detroit look. (It is unclear at this point whether the cars will meet federal requirements by deadline time, or the industry will pursue yet another postponement. The only thing that is clear, once again, is that in the industry view styling is more important than engineering, safety, or practicality.)

The response to the "safety car" concept—in fact, the concept itself—is a fascinating study in the mixed emotions, misdirection, and general confusion endemic in safety thinking in both Detroit and Washington. Safety cars have been built in the past by nonindustry interests, notably the Liberty Mutual Insurance Company, with considerable support from the government of New York State. None of the attempts has been particularly noteworthy, primarily because the creators never had the resources to do any kind of from-the-ground-up examination of the problems, and were therefore forced to start with existing cars. Thus Liberty Mutual's 1960 attempt, "Survival Car II," introduced such niceties as capsule chairs built to withstand 30-G forces, but added a great deal of weight to an existing oversize chassis, and retained stock suspension, stock tires, and the ordinary drum brakes that

* The suit was dismissed in mid-1972, the Environmental Protection Agency holding firm to the earlier schedules. The industry began immediately to talk about a complete shut-down in 1975—talk that might be likened to an economic nuclear deterrent, as soon as Congress starts counting the votes.

were clearly inadequate for the 1957 model with which the experiment began. The result might have protected its occupants in a crash, which was a good thing, as a crash was almost sure to occur—and the vehicle was a positive menace to other cars on the road.

A decade later, when the DOT began letting contracts to outside firms to construct safety cars with fresh ideas, the same situation existed. The automobile industry at first disdained to be involved, refusing to enter any such "competition" with outsiders. After Chrysler agreed to join Fairchild Industries in a $4.5-million prototype project, however (AMF was another contractor), Ford and GM announced that they were building safety cars to meet the federal specifications after all, and would, upon completion, sell the expert-insiders' versions of safety cars to the DOT for one dollar each.

Any real chance for fresh thought had already been foreclosed by the DOT itself, however: the specifications for the safety car contracts called for a 4000-pound car, 220 inches in overall length, 80 inches wide, 58 inches tall, with a 124-inch wheelbase, capable of accelerating from 30 to 70 MPH in 10 seconds, in which passengers would survive a 30-MPH crash without injury. Thus the DOT was asking for ways, by 1973, of making 1970 cars safer. The industry will of course cooperate, in 1973, by marketing 1970 cars, which are also 1960 cars. Other contracts have been let for "small" safety cars. Volkswagen is one of the contenders.

At last report, the safety cars so far taking shape are absolutely conventional automobiles onto which several safety "accessories"—and a lot of padding—have been piled. Rest assured, at the formal public unveiling of these experimental vehicles, estimated production costs will put the cars into the Rolls Royce class. No one has any intention of building one for the public.

Meanwhile in Detroit all is whirling confusion: nobody knows what to expect from the feds next; nobody knows how to make any of these earthshaking new requirements (such as bumpers that bump) *work* within the framework of the car and the business as Detroit has conceived it for the past twenty years. Nobody knows how to start thinking about new kinds of cars. The confusion is heightened by a kind of double-bind engendered by federal intervention. A top-level industry executive described the frustration to me in mid-1971: "We know we should be looking five years ahead. We know we are going to have to build smaller cars—our social consciences, our sense of citizenship tells us that. We can see right now that we are going to have to think about two-thousand-pound cars and fifteen-hundred-pound cars, and we think we can solve the problems on those cars. But we can't create those cars when we are still having to solve bumper problems on four-thousand-pound cars. Between pollution, bumpers, and crash protection, we are having to run as fast and as hard as we can with all the engineering talent and manpower we've got." [6]

It's an interesting notion for the customer to speculate about the next time he's shown a four-thousand-pound car as an accomplishment of superior engineering.

To put the federal government and the automobile industry into adversary positions is something of a misrepresentation, for all the acrimony being expended these days. In seventy years of automobiles the industry and the government, the safety agencies and public-service organizations, the press and the public—all of us—have learned very little about automotive safety, and have learned that little very slowly. We have learned, finally, that upgrading the quality of the driving is virtually impossible, and that it isn't enough; accidents are too complex always just to be avoided. We have learned that if we are going to move cars over the cityscape

207

and countryside at increasing speeds, we must somehow
provide an environment for that movement that, if it doesn't
actively defend cars against accident, at least doesn't actively
lead cars into disaster.

We have learned—statistically, if no other way—that the
automobile accident, like the poor, we have always with us: it
will happen, and seventy years of expense and energy poured
into campaigns based on its total avoidance have been
virtually wasted. It is a favorite argument of automotive
journalism—in a rare appearance as adversary to both the
industry and the government—that the solution lies in improving the accident-avoidance capability of the cars themselves, which admittedly is dreadfully bad. Much as I would
like to join my former colleagues in forwarding that argument (because it would mean better brakes and shock
absorbers, better handling, more interesting cars to drive), I
cannot in conscience do so. Raising the limitations of the
car's performance might, perhaps, slice off some bottom
fraction of the accident statistics. As the unbreakable bond
between the accident rate and the number of cars on the road
has demonstrated, the missing slice would be inserted somewhere else in the gruesome statistics. Accidents that happen
because the car's limitations are exceeded would still happen,
because the higher limitations would also be exceeded. We
would still crash, but now we would crash harder. If we
were going to drive within the car's limitations, we would do
so with the limitations we already have. To expect otherwise
is to go back to "Speed Kills" sloganeering, anticipating some
sea change in the character of the individual driver.

That leaves improving the crash-worthiness of the car as
the remaining means for making an appreciable reduction in
the highway toll. Suddenly the attempts of the feds don't
look quite so inept—and the seventy-year campaign on the
part of the industry to divert all responsibility for automotive safety onto drivers, highways, laws and law-enforce-

ment agencies, driver's schools, juvenile delinquents, drunks, addicts, criminals, would-be suicides, and the phases of the moon begins to assume the proportions of a monstrous industrial crime. At least that might seem to be a reasonable viewpoint to the families of the .5 million killed, the 1.5 million permanently disabled by the automobile in the sixties alone.

There are no simple solutions, of course, and improved crash-worthiness at the expense of everything else would very likely create new problems to take the place of old. The earlier proposal in this chapter for a safety car—NASCAR roll cages and helmeted passengers—is patently impossible, given our present attitudes about safety. Really massive federal intervention, not only into car design but even into our personal "rights," would be required to bring about such a safety car. Massive federal intervention would also be required to achieve any meaningful upgrading of driver-training methods or standards. The feds are already in the highway business, and we have national standards—but they apply only to 42,000 miles of the country's 3.7 million built so far.

Despite the inadequacy of improved performance—accident avoidance or evasive capability—as a sole means of reducing the accident rate, some benefit could be obtained by improving such capabilities as braking distances and steering responsiveness. Official federal attention to performance so far is limited to a requirement that the manufacturers publish acceleration and braking figures; the industry has responded by fudging heavily to be sure that their very worst products can meet their own quoted standards. At the very minimum, antilocking brakes would seem to be a reasonable requirement for all new cars sold. Firm federal action would be necessary to bring about that technological benefit in the foreseeable future.

Since the technology for antilocking brakes is already

available, a federal requirement for their installation would precipitate a production crisis, rather than an engineering crisis. Limited production capacity was the industry's excuse for the slow introduction of disc brakes, back in 1964 when that consumer benefit began making its way onto domestic cars. Eight years later, the production capacity seems still to be missing, although entire new automobile plants have been built to produce new body styles. If the antilock brakes were required tomorrow, the industry would raise a new howl about the stifling of technological development in other areas that would be caused by the—pardon the expression— crash program for brakes. Such a departure from the free enterprise system might indeed spare us from the development of the 1973 and 1974 equivalents of hidden windshield wipers and automatic cruise controls.

The public doesn't seem to want federal intervention any more than the industry does. Among our other irrationalities —such as our continuing purchase of four-thousand-pound cars in which to haul half-gallons of milk and loaves of bread, and refusing to use the safety belts which would save our lives—we refuse to examine the results of seventy years of nonintervention. We have been sold free enterprise more effectively than we have been sold self-preservation. Uncomfortable though it may make us, however, federal action has so far proved the only effective means of combatting the highway death toll. Perhaps, finally, our discomfort with government intervention has been overshadowed by our discomfort with highway slaughter. Both segments of public uneasiness are only small portions of the growing total revulsion with the automobile itself.

P. S.: Drunks

Approximately half of the 56,400 fatalities that occurred on the highways in 1969 involved drunk driving, directly or indirectly; the percentage was repeated in 1970 and 1971. There are seven million problem drinkers operating motor vehicles today. One of every twenty-five cars you meet while driving is being operated by an alcoholic. In a study in Minneapolis 131 drinking drivers who were killed in car accidents managed to take another 121 nondrinking drivers or passengers to the grave with them.

We tried outlawing alcohol once. We have tried to outlaw drunk driving, also, an effort which has worked just about as well as the Volstead Act. Surveys at known fatal accident sites have indicated that the odds against arrests of a drunk driver are about 1000 to 1. New fatal accident sites are turning up every day.

Now we have a drug epidemic. Drugs and their use are less easily detectable in the one-of-a-thousand times when an arrest is actually made. Many of the drugs—barbiturates, amphetamines, and tranquilizers—are perfectly legal on a prescription basis; others don't even require a prescription. Some of them bear admonishments not to drive or operate machinery during dosage, but there is little threat to the individual who wants to endanger himself and others in that manner. There are no breath-o-lyzers for antihistamines. We know very little about the effect of any drugs on driving performance. Law-enforcement personnel have hardly begun to adjust to the drug epidemic from the drug-traffic standpoint, not to mention the automobile-traffic standpoint.

It is tempting to leap to the solution: crack down on drunks and dopeheads. The method for the cracking is what is difficult to come by. There is even some doubt still whether it is law enforcement, rehabilitation, or a simple moralizing that is most effective as a means of controlling drunken and drugged driving. We have a great deal of work still to do in this entire field.

There is a growing body of evidence—flying in the face of more enlightened social theories—that get-tough crackdowns on drunk driving do work. Other nations which have adopted extremely severe penalties have cut their death rate. A new method of dealing with the problem has been developed in the Canadian province of Saskatchewan, which shows great promise. Any policeman can suspend any driver's license, on suspicion, for twenty-four hours. He simply pulls the suspected drunk over, tells him he's through driving for the day, locks the driver's car, and calls him a taxi. The driver may pick up his license and car keys twenty-four hours later. The driver may challenge the suspension, whereupon the police officer produces a breath-o-lyzer and checks for a blood alcohol content of .08 or over. If the policeman is correct, the license suspension stands; if the driver passes, he goes on his way, with, one assumes, an apology. *There are no follow-up convictions in either case.* In three years of operation of the program, highway deaths have been reduced by almost one third.

Efforts to toughen drunk-driving programs in this country, even at the level of television commercials aimed at focusing more public attention on the problem, have consistently been opposed by mental hygiene professionals and such groups as the National Institute on Alcohol Abuse. These opponents of tougher programs insist that such campaigns stigmatize a segment of the population, brutalize alcoholics, and discriminate against them. Alcoholics are people who are ill. Unfortunately, they are also people who kill other people by their driving habits.

It is beyond the intention of this book to propose simplistic solutions to such complex problems. Until the work is done, the research in, the information gathered—while the killing goes on—the single most effective protection against an even worse traffic record than we've already established would seem to lie, again, in crash protection. It would be different if, as Kenneth R. Schneider points out in *Autokind vs. Mankind*, we didn't arrange our cities and towns so that we usually *have* to drive to drink, as we have in most parts of this country.[7] Until we rearrange our society to avoid that problem, as well as to remove the pressures which cause us to seek so much chemical escape, we might as well turn our attention to saving as many souls as we can from the harsh and unyielding realities of statistical probability and the automobile.

CHAPTER 9

Fire and Ice

Killer of Polar Bears

It comes as something of a surprise that this machine which has killed our citizens, gobbled our natural resources, perverted our laws and moral structures, caused our cities to decay, absorbed our wealth, and misshaped the very contours of the countryside is now finally, seriously threatened, merely because of what it is doing to our air. With so many tangible evidences of the destructive cost of the automobile to choose from, and with a half-century of blithe unconcern about those costs as historical background, it seems almost whimsical of the public to choose to do battle with the automobile over an issue so insubstantial as the quality of the atmosphere.

But the public, in the form of a loose and internally cantankerous coalition of environmentalists, conservationists, scientists, and governmental agencies, has so chosen. That coalition has mounted the most effective challenge to the sovereignty of the automobile in its history. Barring unforeseen new scientific information—such as the revelation that what we've been considering to be air pollution is in fact some new kind of beneficial nutrient, a tactic not totally out of keeping with Detroit flackery of the past—the effect of that challenge will be to force the first substantial technological change in private transportation since widespread availability of the conventional car became a fact. The nature of that change is as yet unknown. Past experience would lead us to expect only a series of tentative half-measures and exploratory steps later to be rescinded for their unfortunate economic effect, and indeed, such measures are already contained in early directives from the various regulatory agencies. But there are indications that this time the resolution of the antiautomobile forces will not be diverted. The stakes are too high.

The seeming whimsicality of concern with air quality is, of course, no whimsy at all. The citizen can hope to survive the steady encroachment into his life of the other costs, can gamble his own care, skill, and luck against the statistical roulette of the traffic toll. He has in the past willingly, even enthusiastically, exchanged such vaguenesses as the "quality" of his life for what he conceives as unrestricted freedom of movement. But asphyxiation—and asphyxiation is indeed the issue—is the essential Freudian nightmare. Finally, a threat severe enough to overweigh the benefits, real and imagined, of golden-era-style automotive transportation. Scientists in California forecast the first mass mortality "incidents" for the winter of 1975–76.

The radio comedians began making jokes about Los Angeles "smog" shortly after World War II; it wasn't so funny to the public health officials and researchers who took on the task of dealing with the mysterious stuff. Dr. Arlie Haagen-Smit of the California Institute of Technology was on its trail in 1946, and is generally credited with the discovery of the photochemical process by which automotive exhaust combines with fresh air to produce the choking brown haze so familiar to Los Angelenos—and, now, to most other urban Americans. Results of Dr. Haagen-Smit's studies were published in 1953, a year after the earliest date cited by the Justice Department as the beginning point of an automobile industry conspiracy not to do anything about exhaust emissions.* (Dr. Haagen-Smit was made chairman of President Nixon's Task Force on Air Pollution in 1969.)

Between 1953 and 1970, as the haze spread across the land, what had earlier been regarded as only a nasty-looking irritant began to reveal some more serious consequences. The death rate from emphysema, for example, increased by 1000 percent in the U. S. between 1960 and 1968; even the polar bears in the Chicago Zoo contracted the disease. Emphysema seems to be directly related to air pollution. The U.S. Public Health Service issued a maximum safe limit standard for concentrations of lead in the air of ten micrograms per cubic meter; San Diego was already measuring eight micrograms. (The lead in the atmosphere must be assumed to come from leaded gasoline, although the Ethyl Corporation isn't quite ready to admit that yet.)

A spokesman for the Los Angeles Public Health Department has said that carbon monoxide levels in the city reached a point on occasions which would do heart damage and damage to unborn children. Los Angeles doctors began advising approximately ten thousand people a year to leave the city, seeking cleaner air. Smog Alerts were regularly issued to advise the city's public schools not to let children

* The Justice Department actually claimed that the industry knew that emissions could and should be controlled as early as 1952, but entered into a conspiracy in 1961, delaying installation of positive crankcase ventilation. The suit was settled in 1969 with a consent decree, as John Burby put it, "under which the automobile manufacturers denied they had broken the law and promised it wouldn't happen again." From *The Great American Motion Sickness*, Little, Brown, Boston, 1971, p. 80.

play actively outside, for fear of respiratory troubles associated with air pollution. The American Public Health Association estimated that badly polluted air in New York City was causing ten to twenty deaths a day. It was estimated that living in Manhattan exposed the lungs to the equivalent damage of smoking two packs of cigarettes a day; wags began suggesting health-hazard signs, *à la* cigarette packs, on bridges and tunnels leading into Manhattan. It wasn't too healthy on the mainland side of the tunnels either: smog damage to East Coast vegetable crops was estimated at $18 million a year.

The nature of medical research being what it is, there are few large organizations which would make outright statements about the physical results of smog exposure, perhaps because of the difficulties of running controlled experiments (where would they obtain experimental subjects who *hadn't* been exposed to smog?). Individuals were less bound by such formalities. Nader claimed that the contaminants found in exhaust emissions were associated with chronic bronchitis, lung cancer, and heart disease, in addition to emphysema. Scientists Barry Commoner and Clare Patterson—separately —expressed grave concern over quantities of lead in the air from exhaust emissions. A California health survey indicated that as early as 1956, 74 percent of the population of Los Angeles was affected by smog.

People weren't the only victims. A thousand-acre tract of ponderosa pines in the San Bernardino Mountains, eighty miles inland from Los Angeles, was discovered to be dying from air pollution in 1970. Orchid growers who fled the Los Angeles area in the fifties because of the air quality found that the smog had followed them to San Francisco by the late sixties. The U.S. Public Health Service estimated the cost of smog deposits in personal laundry and cleaning alone to run one hundred dollars per year per citizen in the

The Costs

Washington, D.C. area. Since Washington has no industry, it must be assumed that the air pollution there is caused almost entirely by automobiles. (General Motors, Ford, and Chysler aren't so sure about that, either.) In the major urban areas, while asthma and emphysema sufferers head for oxygen tents, the rest of the citizens watch nylon fabrics dissolve, building façades crumble, even—in a poetic sort of self-cannibalism—car paint corrode from the acidic effluvia put in the air by the cars themselves.

Specific damage from exhaust emissions is still hard to find. Carbon monoxide, of course, is directly and quickly fatal; the compound, which results from a faulty combustion process, has an affinity for the hemoglobin in the blood 210 times greater than does oxygen, and thus simply replaces the oxygen in the bloodstream of anyone breathing it. The other emissions are not so transparently dangerous. Unburned hydrocarbons (given off by gasoline vapors) seem principally villainous because the ultraviolet rays of the sun act on them via the aforementioned photochemical process to cause the filthy brownness of smog. Exhaust emissions also contain oxides of nitrogen and sulphur, the former from incomplete combustion, the latter from the combustion process, gasoline and oil additives, and contaminants. The oxides of nitrogen and sulphur seem to be detrimental to human beings in various subtle and not-so-subtle ways, including, in conditions of high humidity, the formation of airborne acids. Cars also spew particulate matter, and lead. Among the other kinds of particulate matter produced by the automobile is asbestos dust from brake linings, for which a direct relationship with lung cancer has been found. Lead poisoning is known to cause neurological damage; the problem seems to be in establishing the point of concentration at which poisoning sets in.

And the quantity of direct sunlight measured at the

218

Smithsonian Institue is 16 percent weaker than it was fifty
years ago. Scientists are just beginning to speculate about
what *that* trend means.

The attack on exhaust emissions is a particularly powerful
threat to the automobile because it strikes at the very heart
of the machine: at the internal-combustion engine itself. To
clean up automobile-exhaust emissions requires only the
absolute control of hydrocarbons before combustion, and
then the attainment of perfect combustion, which would
result in emissions consisting of water vapor, harmless carbon
dioxide, and inert nitrogen. But neither of these theoretically
simple tasks is easy. Precombustion control involves elaborate
carburetor and fuel-tank filtration systems, giving control up
to the instant of exposure of gasoline to the air which will
allow it to be combusted. (Thus it also requires absolute
control of the liquid in filling stations, refineries, tank cars,
etc.) Spillage, waste, evaporation, leakage, overflow, all
must be controlled. It is estimated that 15 percent of the
eighty-two million tons of motor vehicle pollution released
into the air each year in this country comes from this
precombustion source.

And, of course, perfect combustion is as unattainable as a
perfect vacuum or a perfect anything else. The automobile
engine was never a very efficient source of power, and the
excesses of the late sixties were achieved by increasing size
and gross power, and letting efficiency go hang, as anyone
who has paid a gasoline bill knows well enough. This meant
that by the time the pollution crunch came, each automobile
was spewing about fifteen hundred pounds of waste matter
into the air every year. Engineers were set to the task of
curing the situation without really changing anything, which
meant, basically, fiddling with the combustion process, step-
ping up the efficiency to cut down on the spew.

There are plenty of variables to fiddle with, even on a

relatively "frozen" engine design. Unfortunately, the automotive version of what-you-lose-on-the-roundabouts-you-make-up-on-the-swings quickly sets in. For example, one way to greater efficiency is to increase the amount of air that the engine gulps for every cubic centimeter of gasoline it burns. Most engines run most comfortably at about 11 or 12 to 1 in air/gasoline ratio. The slide rules said that 14.7-to-1 would result in a vast reduction of hydrocarbon and carbon monoxide emissions. At the leaner mixture, operating temperatures go up. When operating temperatures go up, not only do engine mount adhesives begin to fail, but the rate of production of oxides of nitrogen skyrockets. Reduction of two pollutants increases the third. Return to Go.

In short, the internal combustion engine is a filthy mess. There is one element of the technological community which cheerfully maintains that it can be cleaned up. Unfortunately, attempts to do so have so far not only created new problems within the engine itself, they have also seriously handicapped the engine from doing its appointed job. Hard starting, slow throttle response, sluggish overall performance, vapor locks, excessive spark-plug consumption, and valve wear have all resulted from the new tuning procedures aimed at making the big V-8's run more cleanly. This inconvenience and irritation to the consumer might be a small price to pay, if he was getting anything for his money (and rest assured, he is paying for it—estimates of the increase in car prices by 1976 to pay for pollution control equipment are now set at three to five hundred dollars per car). Unfortunately, spot checks of cars in actual road use since the earliest days of pollution control have shown that not only is there wide variance from new car to new car fitted with pollution control equipment, but the equipment is virtually useless unless maintained at a level well beyond the customary care that the public gives its cars. Despite new federal regulations intended to solve the problem, a late-1971 road-side test of 1971 and 1972 model cars in New York City revealed that better than 60 percent were already emitting excessive amounts of carbon monoxide, which is supposed to be the emission easiest to control.

Detroit's reaction throughout the rise of the pollution issue has been emphatically irresponsible. First the industry denied that there was any pollution, and insisted that the factories and power companies were causing it all anyway. When measurements—as from automobile exhaust pipes—indicated that there was indeed such a thing as automobile pollution, the industry then insisted that it wasn't harmful. Well, maybe carbon monoxide—favorite tool of suicides for decades—but none of the rest of the emissions could be proved detrimental. Finally, with burning eyes and stinging nostrils, the industry leaders gave up on the know-nothing approach and simply took refuge behind technological heresy: it couldn't be cleaned up. (A patent was issued for a crankcase-emissions control device in 1909.) When it began to look as if outside manufacturers would respond to increasing governmental concern over the problem, however, and produce working pollution control equipment which the car industry would then have to *buy* and install, the light dawned. There was profit to be made in this meddling madness that had overtaken the government! A demonstration of industry responsibility could now be launched. "Things are going to get bad for us too, you know," said one senior GM executive. "We *are* socially responsible. Sometimes I wonder whether these people don't think we've got some private planet staked out." ("These people" must refer to the ones who had to get laws passed to get the industry to respond in the first place.)

The legislation which accomplished this 180-degree revolution in industrial philosophy came to us, indirectly, from the same state that first found air pollution a serious social issue. California passed the legislation which led to "pollution control valves"—devices to reroute crankcase fumes back into combustion chambers—back in the mid-sixties, which was sufficient to cause Detroit to start building special "California-only" models. The laws, and the control devices, were mild enough to cause only minimal concern back at Motor City. But a quixotic California state senator named Nicholas C. Petris had bigger fish in mind; he wrote a bill in 1967 that forbade the sale of cars powered by gasoline-burning internal-combustion engines in the state after January 1, 1975. The industry laughed; the media laughed; California, the most car-crazy state in the union, laughed. The bill never got out of committee. Petris persevered, however; the next year he came back with the same bill, which was shuffled from the Transportation Committee to the Public Health Committee, which, looking at straight-line projections of fatal smog accumulations for about the same time the bill was to go into effect, took it a lot more seriously. The bill was reported out, actually passed the Senate, and started phones ringing all over Detroit. It failed in the Assembly, even in a watered-down version which called for a ban on the internal-combustion engine only if that device weren't cleaned up. But the precedent was established. Not only did a bill aimed at a clean kill of the automobile get halfway into law in our most populous state, but it got there with support ranging all the way from the nutball left through the conservative middle to the equally nutball right. It looked like an idea whose time was about to come.

Momentum. Federal clean-air standards, which had been limping along with the aid only of GSA standards, began clicking into place. President Nixon co-opted the environment issue in his inaugural address and his State of the Union message, coming down hard on the automobile. He followed that with three bombshells: a call for research in unconventional power plants for automobiles; representative sampling of production-line automobiles for compliance with emissions standards; and federal regulation of fuel composition and additives. HEW Secretary Robert Finch announced stringent new emission regulations for 1975. It was suddenly possible to attack the automobile directly. The climax came with the Clean Air Act of 1970, sponsored by presidential-hopeful Senator Edmund S. Muskie, which empowered the Environmental Protection Agency Administrator, William Ruckelshaus, to set ambient air quality standards.

Ruckelshaus did so, with what Detroit must have felt to be a vengeance: a reduction of already significantly restrictive 1970 figures for hydrocarbon and carbon monoxide emissions by 90 percent as of January 1, 1975; a reduction of similarly strict standards for emission of oxides of nitrogen, due to go into effect in 1971, by 90 percent as of January 1, 1976. At least part of the congressional enthusiasm for such strictures can be attributed to a careful reading of public response to the ecology furor which indicated that the time was ripe for a legislative slap on the wrists to the car moguls. Despite the appearance of all three presidents of the major car companies in Washington for a little personal lobbying, the bill passed the Senate by a vote of 73-0. Cynics were quick to point out that setting standards for 1975–76 gave Congress five or six chances to revoke the bill or weaken its severity, and that such possibilities increased the legislators' chances of keeping the automobile companies very attentive at campaign-contribution time. In the meantime, however, the industry considered that the Clean Air Act of 1970 set standards that were, for public relations purposes anyway, physically impossible to meet. The new law could even be interpreted as an attempt to legislate the private automobile out of existence.

Turning on the Nuts

A few pages back, reference was made to an element of the technological community which optimistically held that the conventional internal-combustion engine (ICE) could be cleaned up. There is, of course, another portion of that community which just as cheerfully dismisses the conventional power plant as beyond redemption, a dead issue, a lost cause. In that the anti-ICE folk consider the pro-ICE folk to be mossback conservatives, the division between them could almost be characterized as new-thinkers vs. old-thinkers—except that the new-thinkers are going all the way back to the infancy of the automobile, to Stanley Steamers and old ladies' electrics, for their "new" power-plant ideas. The demise of the ICE which the new-thinkers foresee—a demise encouraged by Nixon's own recommendations and by federal stimulation of unconventional power-plant research—has brought out of the woodwork most of the crotchety independent geniuses of the mechanical-engineering universe. Their efforts, ranging from natural-gas fuel for conventional engines through huge, high-speed flywheels to store kinetic energy, are conveniently dismissed by the manufacturers who have massive capital invested in ICE facilities. But despite the weight of authority behind a lofty dismissal from the people who have made the ICE a way of life, there is real merit to many of the alternative proposals.

Natural gas or liquified petroleum gas (called "gaseous fuels" by the GSA) provides the easiest, cheapest, and quickest approaches to a solution to automotive air pollution. (Methane gas, which can be generated from, among other things, human wastes, is similar—there's a man powering his personal automobile with chicken manure in England right now.) A conversion can be fitted to your car at the present for about five hundred dollars. It would allow you to alternate between conventional fuel and gaseous fuels at the pull of a lever. Immediately, you would reduce your own pollutant emissions by 90 percent, and get savings of about 40 percent per mile in direct cost of operation. You'd have to give up quite a bit of trunk space for the special high-pressure gaseous fuel tank, you might notice a slight reduction in power, you might have an occasional hard-starting problem; that's why both fuel systems are retained. (Gaseous fuel service facilities are not yet so ubiquitous as gas stations, also, so the gasoline system makes a good emergency backup.) The GSA already has test fleets running with gaseous fuel systems, and has verified the emissions and operating cost figures. Expansion of the experiment is scheduled.

Nobody knows how many nonconformists are already running around in cars and trucks powered by gaseous fuels, but the idea is hardly new—I rode in one in 1954, a homemade conversion to a Cadillac by a fellow who simply objected to gasoline costs. Engines specifically designed for gaseous fuels could in all likelihood overcome the power loss and starting difficulties, of course. Popular use of such power would bring down the cost of conversions quickly (at present every installation must be virtually custom-engineered). Gaseous fuels also eliminate most deposits of carbon on engine internals, and reduce sludge production, giving longer engine life.

So why don't we have a quick and emphatic total conversion? (It could be accomplished well before Congress has several more chances to water down the 1976 emission standards.) Well, Congress doesn't want to dictate a choice. Wants to give the car-makers a chance to pull this one out. Doesn't want to destroy the retail gasoline business (although the same super-powerful petroleum industry would reap the profits, and the retail side of the business would seem easily convertible). Wants to protect our precious natural gas reserves. (One source indicates that those reserves are a mere 250 trillion cubic feet, of which factory and home use eat up 20 trillion cubic feet a year now.[1])

Other alternative power sources run into similar problems. "Research Continuing, But Outlook is Doubtful," said the blurb on a *New York Times* story about steam research.[2] *Popular Science* automotive editor Jan P. Norbye surveyed for the *Times* various private efforts working under grants from the federal government or the automobile industry itself. (Sample: Ford Motor Company's munificent $4 million to Thermo Electron Engineering Corporation in Waltham, Massachusetts—to which Thermo Electron has had to add $2 million of its own.) Although, Norbye says, the steam engine is clean and silent, steam buffs shouldn't get unduly optimistic. "It is easy for steam-power enthusiasts to overlook the fact that the last and most modern series of Stanley Steamers were lightweight cars powered by 20-horsepower engines. *A car for the nineteen-seventies would need about 300 horsepower to give its 4,000 pounds adequate performance.*" (Emphasis supplied.)

He then goes on to describe promising contemporary steam engines which suffer from power outputs of only 100 horsepower (about equal to standard Pinto and Vega ICE engines, and not quite double the power of the Volkswagen). The well-publicized failure of millionaire inventor William P. Lear (car stereos, the Lear jet executive aircraft) to make good on his boast to develop a workable steam engine for automotive use by 1970 is examined in engineering detail; the success of Wallace Minto, who has a working steam prototype running in a Volkswagen bus, under contract to a Japanese car manufacturer (Nissan), is shuffled over quickly. The working prototype of a full-size steam car, demonstrated by its builders Calvin and Charles Williams to Senate Commerce Committee members in 1968 (who reportedly were impressed by the car's silence and swift acceleration) was completely ignored, without even a technological dismissal to explain why the car is impractical, if it is. A steam car probably won't work out anyway, concluded Norbye. "The disturbing factor is that although progress is being made on all fronts toward a modern steam car, there is still no guarantee that future steam-power systems will in fact meet long-term emissions standards." The source of this bleak view? General Motors.

General Motors included two ungainly steam cars in a line-up of twenty-six unconventionally powered experimental vehicles shown to the press in May of 1969. The purpose was a massive demonstration of the corporation's concern and sense of responsibility in the face of mounting criticism of the conventional automobile. All twenty-six vehicles were operable—barely. The steam cars, one built by GM and one by an outside contractor, were written off in press materials as too heavy, too expensive, and somehow, after all that work, unable to meet 1975 emission standards. Ditto, for one reason or another, for gaseous fuels, hybrid gas-electrics, turbines, ammonia-fuel engines, electrics, and various external combustion engines. Unfortunately for GM verisimilitude, none of the display vehicles would perform as well as existing independently built versions of the same types of cars. It was an interesting expenditure of engineering hours and profit dollars for propaganda purposes. It backfired. The automotive press saw through the ruse; the nonautomotive press seized on the novelties and ignored the engineering "failures."

The difficulties of electric cars have more to do with patterns of use than with technology. Working electrics exist now, in versions ranging from golf carts to full-size American Motors chassis-and-bodies, which a Detroit firm acquires minus engines, then fits with electric motor and batteries. There is also an "electric-car superhighway" between Detroit and Chicago—consisting of a series of plug-in recharge stations at Holiday Inns beside the existing highway. (The chairman of the board of Holiday Inns, Kemmons Wilson, is an electric-car buff.) None of the electrics will comfortably top 70 MPH; maximum range between recharges is less than a hundred miles, primarily because fuel cells, rather than batteries, are still too exotic for narrowly financed independent research to afford.

With a minimum of rearrangement of our automotive habits, however, inexpensive electric cars at their present level of technology could supply virtually all of our urban needs. The average American car trip is under ten miles in length, and the average urban speed is about 10 miles per hour, with 50 MPH maximum. If all the automobile trips that require speeds of less than 70 MPH and ranges of less than a hundred miles could be switched to electric power, the automobile air pollution would disappear almost overnight—and the increase in air pollution from electric power-generating stations would not, as the petroleum people claim, immediately expand to fill the pollution gap. Single-source pollution (as in one powerplant smokestack instead of one hundred thousand car exhaust pipes) is much easier to control. Nor would electrical capacity in crowded areas necessarily be swamped by the demands of all those exhausted electric-car batteries, if the recharging were done in what are now low-load periods, as overnight in the home garage. The power companies would even be able to use their sorely overstrained equipment more efficiently, by evening out generating schedules.

(An interesting offshoot of the electric car, already in

use in Swiss buses, stores energy in whirling flywheels. A plug-in source of electrical power is used to bring the flywheel in the parked vehicle up to operating speed; in use the vehicle unplugs, and uses the flywheel as a kinetic motor until it runs down. The vehicle must then be "recharged"—its flywheel electrically spun back up to speed—before further use. A meter within the vehicle translates flywheel speed into remaining energy, or mileage, just as a gas gauge does. One problem with such a system: the vehicle must be left "idling"—with the flywheel spinning—when not in use, or it must be "emptied" and "refilled" between each use.)

If the government and the industry are not courageous enough to force the reshuffling of oil industry technology sufficient to accommodate a switch from gasoline to gaseous fuels, they aren't about to adopt so drastic a course as that implied by the existing electric-car parameters. The closest the industry will approach a new direction in power plants is indicated by the present push toward two disparate but conventionally fueled engines: the turbine and the Wankel.

Pioneering work in automotive application of the gas turbine has been going on at Chrysler Corporation since the early fifties, and reached a point of development in 1962 that saw the company placing 203 specially built turbine-powered cars in the hands of "random" consumers, for general automobile use, to obtain a small but thorough market test of the product. After less than a year the cars, which had been loaned, were withdrawn. Reasons for the withdrawal and the subsequent disappearance of the vehicles were given as slightly excessive slow-speed fuel consumption, a lag in acceleration from standing start, insufficient engine braking, and a noise level that was unacceptable to some of the guinea-pig customers. The Chrysler turbine was two hundred pounds lighter than a conventional engine of comparable horsepower, had one fifth the number of moving parts, and gave overall fuel consumption rates comparable to its conventional competitors. It also had a clean exhaust—relatively so, anyway, at a time when concern about emissions was not the driving force that it is today. An indication that the acceleration and engine-braking problems could be solved is contained in the fact that a turbine-powered racing car came within seven miles of making a complete rout of the Indianapolis 500 in 1967. A minor transmission part failed three laps from the finish, after the car had totally dominated the field up to that point. The power plant was later banned from subsequent races as an unfair advantage. Turbine research has continued, and both Ford and GM have put large turbine-powered trucks into the test market. Independent firms are experimenting with passenger-car applications. Although internal tolerances are extremely critical in turbines, and there seem to be cost problems associated with exotic metallurgy and precision machining, it seems likely that those problems could be solved. But for the immediate future, engineering enthusiasm for the turbine has been muted by a quicker—and dirtier—solution: the Wankel.

The Wankel seems a product of the backyard-genius approach to automotive power, with the important difference that the establishment engineers now support the device. Patented by a German named Felix Wankel in 1954, the engine is closer perhaps to a mechanical turbine than to a conventional piston engine. Triangular rotors inside a roughly oval combustion chamber are driven by conventional (low-grade) fuel ignited by conventional spark plugs, and the rotary motion is transmitted directly to the central shaft. No heavy pistons go up and down, requiring heavy counterweights and complex balancing. The engine is extremely light in weight, mechanically simple, virtually vibration free, and powerful (on the basis of displacement, overall size, and weight) far beyond the dreams of conventional engine-makers. I vaguely recall an interview, in the early fifties, with a Detroit engineer concerning "cars of the future," always a popular feature-article subject. The engineer was asked whether cars a decade or two in the future would have engines located at front or rear. "Within twenty years," he replied, "power plants will be so efficient and so small that we'll be able to locate them in the glove compartment if we want to." Although the man was unduly optimistic—I think he was referring to nuclear power or some such pipe dream—the Wankel engine almost fits the optimism, once the hyperbole is knocked off it.

That the Wankel is the engine of the immediate future seems clearly indicated by the signing of contracts by GM for license to produce Wankels in passenger cars—approximately $10 million a year worth of contracts. The decision makes a good deal of sense to the industry's position, despite the high tariff: existing tooling and manufacturing equipment for conventional engines and components (especially automatic transmission equipment) is suitable for building Wankels. Ancillary equipment such as spark plugs, ignition systems, air cleaners, carburetors, generators, etc., is easily transferable to Wankel use. And hundreds of thousands of miles of field development in standard passenger-car form have already been done by prior licensees, NSU in Germany and Mazda in Japan.

In 1970 the engineering opinion at GM was about evenly divided between supporters of the gas turbine and Wankel enthusiasts; by late 1971, with the signing of the licensing agreement with Wankel, G.m.b.H., all indications were that the Wankel supporters had won. There were rumors floating about Detroit early in 1972 of tooling orders for a run of one to five thousand engines. The automotive press is already speculating on the designs for cars to be powered by them. Wankel-powered Chevrolet Vegas have been seen on the streets of Detroit.

Unfortunately, the Wankel is by its nature a very dirty engine, from a pollution standpoint, and original resistance to it was based on fear of the feds. Improved tip seals for the rotors, which serve the same approximate function as piston rings in a conventional engine, have materially reduced unburned hydrocarbon emissions. The Wankel runs quite well on low-grade gasoline, which eases the pressure resulting from the government's move to get tetraethyl lead removed from the bulk of America's gasolines by 1975. (The lead additive was brought on in the first place by Charles F. Kettering's high-compression engines. High-compression ratios require high-octane fuel to prevent "knock"— preignition—and lead was a cheap way to raise octane levels.)

Perhaps the final vote in selecting the Wankel to be our next mass-produced engine was cast by the pattern of the engine's emissions. High hydrocarbon output means low oxides of nitrogen. It was found that the hydrocarbons could be picked up well after the initial combustion stage, with a thermal reactor in the exhaust system. Doing so left the oxides of nitrogen levels low enough virtually to ignore. In short, although the Wankel is by its nature a relatively inefficient, high-pollution engine, its pollution characteristics can, perhaps, be controlled. Also, its reduced displacement (half to one third that of a piston engine for the same relative power output) will also help materially to reduce the gross volume of pollutants spewed into the air. It isn't going to replace the piston engine tomorrow, but it probably represents the next grudging step that the industry will take, once that industry is forced to give up its beloved pistons.

Thank You, Robert Frost

Once the air-pollution problem is solved (if it can be), we can go on to the next crisis resulting from the overproduction, overpromotion, oversale, and overuse of the private automobile. Perhaps it will be the imminent disappearance of platinum and nickel. Both metals are in short supply. Sources for them are politically questionable. Neither of these facts has stopped the experts from suggesting that they be used as basic components of catalytic mufflers and thermal reactors, to help extract the dangerous remaining pollutants from internal combustion engines after the combustion process.

Nobody knows yet what the effects of 100 million catalytic mufflers will be on the atmosphere. Nobody knows where we will get the materials for 100 million catalytic mufflers, how we will pay for them (they are very expensive), how often they will have to be replaced (present estimates are less than fifty thousand miles of useful life), where the replacement materials will come from. They are a technological solution which is loaded with whole new worlds of technological unknowns; we seem to be rushing toward them with our usual technological enthusiasm.

But maybe we will solve all those new problems, too. Assume for a moment that we can. Assume an industry that is totally socially responsible. Assume that the solutions are found: no more crises in environmental pollution, land rape, traffic death tolls, exhaustion of natural resources. The way completely cleared for unlimited expansion of the private automobile as the sole workable transportation system not just for the nation but for the whole planet. World-wide, up to the limit of the populace to pay for this private unlimited mobility. Whole new continents to conquer—with pavement, traffic lights, stop signs, parking lots, commercial strips. Snow tires for the Himalayas! Antifreeze for Antarctica! Dune buggies for the Sahara! The very thought is enough to make our salesmen's hearts start pounding.

Unfortunately, there seems little likelihood that we'll have a chance to fill out the invoices. In the unlikely event that the directly automobile-related crises evaporate to allow unlimited growth, we'll run out of fossil fuels to combust. One group of doomsday scientists predicts that the production of carbon dioxide—from *clean* combustion—will cause a "greenhouse" effect, preventing the planet from allowing enough heat to escape. So we'll fry. Another group says that, on the contrary, the particulate matter—even benign particulate matter, i.e. dust—that we are now spewing will blot out the sun. We'll freeze. "Some say the world will end in fire, some say in ice," as Frost put it.

And a third group—or maybe it is composed of the more pessimistic portions of the other two groups of doom-seers—says that neither will make a difference. The rate we are burning fossil fuels has already overtaken the balance of nature, and we are generating carbon dioxide faster than we are oxygen. By the year 2000 the available oxygen supply will be reduced by 25 percent. (One car, driving from Santa Monica to Pasadena, burns up more oxygen than the total population of Los Angeles County breathes in the same forty-five-minute period that the motor trip takes.)

So we do smother, after all. If population growth doesn't kill us off by famine in the meantime. If the bomb doesn't go off before that.

Making fun of the prophets of doom is almost as entertaining as the delicious terror of contemplating the doom itself. In the meantime (before the doom catches up with us), no serious citizen can question the advisability of doing

what we can to forestall the apocalypse. Pollution control—
changing the character of the automobile to lessen its destructive effect—is an essential step in that postponement.
Sure enough, controlling the automobile's drastic environmental effect *does* change the character of the car, and
changes the public attitude toward it. Stopgap though the
effort may be, emission control is clearly a minimum step
to help us survive the time period necessary to phase the
automobile out of our economy and our lives. For the first
time in history, the public supports the stopgap, if not its
necessary eventual result. Funny—all smog was at first was
a *stink*. But it tipped the balance. It made us see, finally,
that the automobile is the enemy.

235

PART IV

The Death
of the Automobile

CHAPTER 10

The Slaughter
of the Buffalo

The time span covered during the writing of
this book contained four extremely significant events in the
post-golden-era life of the automobile: the UAW strike of
1970, the worst car sales year since 1961, the price freeze
and Phases I and II of Nixonomics, and the largest selling
month in the history of the automobile, October 1971, when
one million new cars were sold in the U.S. A saga of rags
to riches; the New Bonanza lies just ahead. Unless somehow we find the wisdom to stop before it.

The strike against General Motors in the fall of 1970 was
an ironic period. That massive corporation was quivering in
frustration, under fire from all sides for its excesses of the
past, ready to launch what it considered the first hopeful
wave of the cars of the future—the Chevrolet Vega, small,
simple, almost rational, a counterforce to those past excesses.
It was prevented from reaching the hands of the public in
any appreciable numbers by the strike. With the expensive
settlement of that strike, GM began grinding out cars as if

possessed by the Furies, and in a sense it was: those new cars were being dumped into a bottomless recession.

Few realized the seriousness of the industry's mid-1971 situation. By announcement time for the 1972 models, the backlog of unsold new cars stacked up in dealer lots and at distribution points across the nation had reached 1.5 million, the most depressingly gross total of unwanted cars in the nation's history. Despite the production miscalculations implied in that kind of tag end to the model year, the new 1972's, virtually unchanged and slated for price increases of from two hundred dollars per car upward, were clanking out of the assembly plants at near-maximum production rates. Meanwhile imported car sales, more a solid measure of discontent with the domestic product than any endorsement of Old World Craftsmanship, were continuing to rise: in bellwether California the imports were booming along at over 40 percent of the market.

"Autos Back From the Brink," said *The New York Times*, when President Nixon announced the price freeze, the revocation of the 7-percent excise tax on new cars, and the 10-percent surcharge on imports. The Nixonomics came after trend analyst Albert Sindlinger had forecast "a complete collapse of the domestic market" for automobiles; Wall Street car-industry analyst David Healey labeled the action "the auto industry relief act." The results were immediate: a million cars sold in October—and forecasts for a 12-million-car year in 1972. Back from the brink, indeed—and a long way from the death of the automobile, it would seem.

And yet, and yet. There is little real indication that this early-seventies surge signifies anything other than a momentary adjustment in the snowballing misfortunes of Detroit. We will see 1973 as the year of the bumper, 1974 the year of the passive restraint (except that will be postponed, perhaps indefinitely), 1975 the year of the catalytic muffler/

thermal reactor; even the dubious benefits of the Wankel engine are yet several sales years in the future. Nothing here to stimulate a burst of renewed consumer interest; lacking that, Detroit will ride along on the minimum base demands of the population, rising and falling with the economy, a semifrozen set of supercorporations. Friendly government kicks to the economic wheel won't continue to help much, in that state of health.

A regular litany was forthcoming from the industry during the sour year prior to the price freeze: "The love affair between Americans and the automobile is *not* over," they kept saying, the very emphasis and repetition enforcing the public sense that undoubtedly something huge and awful, in the way of economic trends, was being covered up. Retiring GM Chairman James M. Roche, otherwise an eminently unquotable man, expanded the denial: "It's just turned into a marriage." Marriages, by comparison to love affairs—at least in the advertising scheme of things—are dull, dull, dull. "People are simply beginning to look for other values from their cars," another executive explained—"simplicity, utility, even austerity." He must have blanched as he said the words, for the prospect strikes fear in Detroit. "You take the value out of a car faster than you can take dollars off the price," has long been an industry adage. What it really means is that cheap, small cars have almost no profit margin when produced in this country—by Detroit methods.

What such comfy talk of marriages and utilitarian automobiles overlooks—thanks in part to the artificial stimulation of Nixon's economic fiddling—is the pervading sense among the public that anything we do with regard to cars is wrong. Perhaps we are not yet a nation driven to consumer strikes by social conscience, but it is a rare and insensitive car purchaser indeed, in the early seventies, who can totally shrug off his sense of guilt at adding to the problem, rather than working toward a solution, in indulging his taste for private transportation. Even if a million of us did have our rationales ready in October of 1971, we knew with dead certainty that they were rationales. We can expect nothing so surely, in coming years, as an ever-rising sense that the automobile is somehow antisocial. There are no forces gathering, in the foreseeable future, to work to reverse that sense. There are multitudes to enhance it.

It is that sense which stimulates my radical friend to discount Nader as a tool of the establishment. Paying the costs for emission control and crash worthiness will raise the expense of car ownership and operation. The rising costs will further disqualify the economically disadvantaged from freedom of movement, raising higher the walls of the ghetto trap, accelerating the exodus from the transportationless hinterlands *into* that ghetto trap (where decaying mass transit marginally increases economic opportunities). The rising costs will also severely limit the freedom of movement of another growing element of society, one closer to my friend's immediate concerns. These are the non-achievement-oriented New Culture, that loose amalgam of communards, New-Left activists, posthippie antiestablishmentarians, "dropouts," and other intentionally poor who are intent on constructing the Alternate Society. That clapped-out two-hundred-dollar Volkswagen bus which has become their anti-Detroit symbol will simply be legislated—or rather regulated—off the roads. They will consider this limitation of freedom of movement to be a form of political repression. They will be correct.

Thus the paradox of the automobile compounds itself: attempts to save lives and to save the planet become instruments of political repression. An offshoot effect will put the economically disadvantaged (intentional or not) into older, hence less safe, ecologically destructive cars, while the affluent will move with admirable good citizenship into newer, socially benign machines. For the Haves to invest their hard-earned money in lowered traffic tolls and reduction of pollution while the Have-Nots are spewing contaminants into the air and killing themselves—and taking others with them—in highway crashes will exacerbate the polarization that is already splitting our society apart. It is equations such as this which generate such loosely flung terminology as "genocide" on the part of the repressed. The ecologists tell us that the rats that bite the babies in Harlem are part of the ecology too.

Nowhere does the sense of the destructiveness of automobiles grip harder than in the cities. "I can tell you one thing, the cities are finished," said the elder Henry Ford, back in the twenties. Possibly he had in mind a gentler automotive effect, but he was a prophet indeed when he uttered those words. Stewart Alsop used the same quote to head a deeply pessimistic *Newsweek* column, in which he ran through the elements which spell doom to the cities in the near future.[1]

The car makes the suburb possible. It is pleasanter to live outside the city than within it. The affluent move out to the suburbs, eroding the tax base of the city. Meanwhile the poor are moving into the city—fleeing a collapsed farm economy, the transportationless hinterlands, the indignities of the South, whatever—and increase the need for city services. The city services, stretched thin by the growing population, are further diminished by the shrinking tax base. The poor are taxed more severely in an attempt to bridge the gap, adding to discontent. Discrimination, illiteracy, crime, drugs, spring up. The poor culture rewards different accomplishments than does the rich, and moving to the suburbs isn't one of them. Census reports are registering middle-class white population losses in all major cities—15 percent in

The Death of the Automobile

Manhattan, 30 percent in Detroit, 40 percent in Washington—and the incoming poor more than compensate in numbers, but not in tax base. Former Census Bureau Chief Richard Scammon forecasts an accelerating exodus of business offices and factories from the cities, which will further erode the tax base, which further reduces city services to the poor, which further accelerates the crime and despair which chase the affluent away.

The destruction of the cities by the automobile is not limited to congestion and the lack of parking spaces. The automobile is the key element in turning the cities of the future, in Scammon's forecast, into urban models of the Indian reservations, as Alsop put it, "kept alive by the state, but ruled by a kind of internal jungle law. The surrounding middle-class suburbs would be heavily guarded (as some are already), the chief function of the guards being to protect the middle-class majority in the suburbs from marauding bands from the cities."

There are, of course, denizens of the cities who refuse to accept so dismal a scenario, who are fighting manfully to resist the force of old Henry I's prediction. (If they fail, my designation of the railroads as the supreme example of a throwaway economy is seriously inaccurate, since we will then in effect be throwing away the cities, too.) Among them are dozens of embattled mayors, any one of which would welcome with tears of gratitude a workable method of denying automobiles access to his inner city. Those fellows know that more parking spaces are not the answer.

There are few who don't know that cars are a disaster for the cities. There are few who have missed picking up the pervasive sense of swelling excess, of destructive distortion, surrounding automobile transportation in all its facets—the roads, the laws, the costs, the cars themselves. The pressure is not relieved by twelve months of sagging sales. The public conscience is not eased.

244

The Slaughter of the Buffalo

Detroit has puzzled its way through periods of low public regard in the past, reflected in unsold cars. ("You Auto Buy Now," said the show windows—for a brief while—in the Eisenhower recession of 1958.) The previous sales slumps have been economically based, and there is, of course, a strong economic effect behind the dismal 1970 sales slump also. But there is a great deal more to it. *Future Shock* author Alvin Toffler calls it a revolt against psychological packaging; if that is all it is, Madison Avenue can be depended upon to have antipackaging on the shelves within six months. (And, in fact, it is happening: every supermarket now has—at outrageously high prices, packaged with coy ineptitude—an organic food display.) But I think that the buyer resistance is stronger than that, less accessible to the blandishments derived from motivational research. It is in fact a revolt against the very assumptions which would plunder motivation in search of sales. It is composed not only of horror at the collapse of the cities, at safety and pollution scandals; it is much more than a timorous hesitancy in the face of an economy so schizoid that both inflation and unemployment are generated with equal virulence.

To call it a revolt against psychological packaging only skims the froth of the malaise; it is a deeper sense that nothing works any more. We build roads which make traffic, mount civil-rights campaigns which intensify segregation, declare war on poverty and make the poor our victims. Into the sole comprehensible measure that we have of our economy, we throw the actual costs of treating the nation's tragedies. As Ralph Waldo Emerson once reported, down-easters in Maine rejected a new lighthouse for the deleterious effect it would have on the salvage business.

We also measure our standard of living on the basis of gadgets that serve little primary purpose, deluge us with secondary ill effects, and don't work anyway. It is an insignificant portion of our lives, perhaps, but their failure has telling effect. A substantial contributor to the growing rage at the automobile has been the consistent shoddiness of that product, a shoddiness colorfully demonstrated by the government's recall campaigns. The implications contained in the industry's response to those campaigns are devastating: if the automobile industry is not, in its blithe unconcern, actually trying to kill its customers, it is not trying very hard to avoid doing so. The implication is perhaps unfair, but it is repeated again and again in the manufacturers' stiff resistance to remedying the causes of documented fatalities.

No other possible interpretation of this resistance is left to the customer than this: shoddiness of assembly and unconcern with final product are the guiding philosophy of the industry. Working back from the premise, the past two decades of frivolousness and waste in the industry's product become a clear expression of the industry's attitude toward its customers. The avalanche of social costs coming due in the seventies would be bad enough even if their cause—the car—were a genuinely worthy project. When the cause of those rising costs is demonstrated to have been cynically manipulated to worsen the costs, then it becomes purely insupportable. The industry has consistently assumed that its customers would never see that manipulation; it has assumed that the customers could be manipulated as readily as the products have been. Part of Detroit's current shock stems from the failure of that manipulation.

The consumer revolt is, in the end, a revolt against arrogance. In the American self-image, no sin is greater; it invites public retribution. We can expect, for example, that it will not be enough that James M. Roche remain, in the public eye, simply the man who had to apologize to Ralph Nader. The anger is larger than that; we can be expected, as a people, to consign him and his fellow automotive moguls to a special niche in public memory. The men who perpetrated the golden era of runaway automobile merchandising will join those other American rogue-villains who, in the pursuit of their niches, managed to wreak visible destruction on a land even so large as this. The buffalo hunters fit the category. The exterminators of the Indians. The lumber barons, strip miners, railroad magnates: the professional rapists of land, water, air, souls. The competition is keen for the dubious honor, but we are beginning to see that perhaps the car-makers are the ones who have destroyed the most of all.

You Can't Get There from Here

There are hopeful elements in the otherwise unrelieved gloom of the aftereffects of the golden era. The emergence of federal intervention in safety and pollution control as a viable political course of action will help in the future, if it can't undo the damage of the past. It is perhaps not unreasonable to pin considerable hope on the small cars, the new "subcompacts." In order of appearance they are Gremlin, Pinto, and Vega, from AMC, Ford, and GM respectively, plus Chrysler Corporation's imported Colt and Cricket, and in coming months a host of small trucks from Japan, produced under licensing agreements with American manufacturers who can't hope to compete with Japanese labor costs. The imports won't do anything to help the balance of payments, but the cooperation between U.S. and foreign manufacturers ought to help stabilize the dollar.

The small cars do represent a step toward rationality in automobiles. They represent an immediate gross savings in natural resources at the manufacturing stage, requiring less steel, glass, aluminum, etc., per unit. The smaller engines use about a third as much gasoline as do our standard

The Death of the Automobile

V-8's, which should help save those dwindling petroleum reserves the oil industry is always worrying us with. (Perhaps the savings will wipe out the danger to our national security. Then we could withdraw some of the outrageous oil-industry tax breaks which are supposed to encourage exploration and developments of new sources. *That* would help—substantial tax income from virtually a new source, to help pay for some of our more human needs.)

The reduction in gas consumption carries with it an automatic reduction in pollution, simply on the basis of volume alone. Add what we can now expect to be reduced pollution from such developments as the Wankel, and suddenly the sunshine starts to break through the smog-clouds. (Although consumption of gasoline just shot back up. A Wankel one third the size of a V-8 may produce the same power as the V-8, but it doesn't yet do it on one third the gas.) Translate the reduction in size into increased room on the highways and in parking lots, and *that* pressure is partially relieved. Add the federal safety and crash-worthiness requirements—for all the current confusion surrounding them, still decidedly a worthwhile gain. It almost begins to sound as if we can keep our cars.

The seduction of small cars is so great—relieving anti-Detroit animosities at the same time they seem to offer logical solutions—that my intention was to propose here one more red-herring solution: the eighty-cubic-inch limit. That engine displacement would be about two thirds that of a standard Pinto or Vega. The case can be made for a rigid final limit to maximum car-engine size, federally applied. Why not, while we are at it, take a really *huge* swipe at the problem and limit them to a neat and simple eighty cubic inches? The low horsepower reliably available from such an engine size would quickly pull overall car size and weight down to match, as manufacturers struggled to retain what they have come to regard as acceptable performance for American traffic conditions. (A level of performance which the Volkswagen does not, in their view, meet.) The attendant small-car advantages—to the social fabric of the nation, if not to the notions of status and prestige of the individual car owner—would immediately accrue. New materials would be investigated, new technologies created as the makers pushed to replicate in miniature the grossnesses of the golden era.

The technological stasis would be broken wide open: no moral judgments, no intricate formulas, no glacial pace of controlling legislation, sliding backwards two feet for every food gained. Just *zut!* Eighty cubic inches. As of this date. It wouldn't even be necessary to legislate the old cars away, as they would quickly enough fall apart and be gone from the highways forever.

With universal small cars (maybe even the Universal Small Car?) we would find most of our congestion problems quickly easing. Then we could indeed keep our cars. We could keep them until there were . . . how many? Two hundred million, twice what we have now? Twice that?

After you've synchronized those traffic lights so the road can hold 30 percent more cars, and then 30 percent more cars show up, you still need to build a new road. Simplistic solutions tend to turn very simplistic. Particularly when they tread the same beaten paths that led to the problem in the first place. Other nations have taxed horsepower or engine size, which is only just. If you want to go faster, accelerate more swiftly, haul greater loads, take up more space than your fellow citizens, you can damned well pay for the privilege, not just to the manufacturer but also to the state that builds the roads where you perform your excesses. Such a system of taxation is no total solution—none of the industrialized nations where the automobile has

gained broad acceptance is more than a decade or two behind us in problems of congestion, pollution, and highway
death toll—but at least it doesn't subsidize the prime offenders in the problem areas.

Taxation does represent a means to a solution of many
automobile problems, as we will see. Building smaller cars
(thinner, shorter, lower) does not. Proceeding in the direction of the present technology—even with the occasional
minor deviation of a Wankel or a turbine engine—does not.
Obviously, we will have to look to the marvelous new technologies to come, for our salvation.

When the Magic Works

Oh, how I love cars, have loved cars. Some of my most en-
joyable moments have been spent streaking over back
country roads (yes, I admit it, at illegal speeds) reveling
in power, speed, freedom, taking delicious pleasure in being
a mild social criminal metaphorically on the lam. I have
also enjoyed quiet hours delving mechanical automotive
innards, petting my technological triumph of the moment.
I still snatch up the latest copy of *Popular Science, Motor
Trend, Car and Driver*, as I have for twenty years, to read,
to dream about the automotive marvels now being conceived. Automotive journalism promises me wonderful cars
in about five years: agile, economical, swift, safe. It is always five years. And five years, and then five years. (See
Chapter 8, Note 6, for the 1942 version of this promise.)
When the cars get here, they weigh four thousand pounds
and have all the agility of the Great Barrier Reef. All that
is over now, Detroit is telling us, always, regularly over
those twenty years. We've changed, they say. It'll take a
while, of course. Amortization costs. Capital investment. The

economy. Federal regulation, which slows up the technological advances. But you'll see.

I see four-thousand-pound 1976 Chevrolets. There is something that seems to go awry between technology as it is
envisioned and technology as it is realized. NASA seems
to be technology envisioned, while Detroit is technology
realized. NASA can do *anything*. It is strongly oriented toward visible, identifiable goals; it operates virtually on a
cost-no-object basis; it is forced to deal with the outer fringes
of available knowledge, which tends to be marvelously lib-
erating. NASA focuses sharply on achieving its goals, protecting the lives of the astronauts, and obtaining scientific
data, all of which it does well. It ignores economy, pollution
(how the enviromentalists winced at the detritus left on
the moon!), and such petty details as the advisability of
understanding earth before exploring space.

Viewed in these same sweeping categories, perhaps the
car industry is not so different after all. It too focuses sharply
on its goal, which happens not to be providing economical,
efficient transportation for the masses, but profit. Not safety,
not preservation of national resources—and certainly not
the frontiers of technological knowledge. It is easy and fun
to demonstrate, with example after example, Detroit's stolid
ignorance of the world's technological advances, the dreary
way that the product of the industry fails to measure up to
the image, so carefully created, of superior engineering. It
is a paper tiger. The only indication of even a whisper of
interest in technological mastery in the automobile industry
comes in the advertising copy; in fact, the industry is
heavily committed to technological stasis. The food-dragging
in Detroit is not so metaphorical.

Japan supplies confirmation. That nation has entered automobile manufacturing virtually from scratch in the past
ten years, and is the most serious competitor Detroit now

faces in its own market, with an annual production of over 4 million cars a year. Japan started with the philosophical clean sheet: no crippling amortization costs for existing facilities, plenty of capital for new ones, the world's technology to draw on, labor costs one sixth of ours or less. Despite their reputation as copyists rather than innovators, the Japanese have shown themselves to be brilliant technological creators, not just in cameras, electronics, heavy industry, and shipping, but also in the closely allied (to automobiles) manufacture of motorcycles.

Yet from that clean sheet have come cars that are only mildly evolutionary in concept, very little better than Japan's direct competitors in equivalent product sizes, with only the slightest market edge—except in price. The innovative brilliance has gone into production, rather than product, engineering. Where the profit lies. The cars that will scratch my car-buff's itch will be designed only by the media (and never produced). The industry couldn't care less.

Where technology now shows signs of making great leaps forward is in an explosion of antiautomobile uses. Thus we will save the cities, the technologists say. Mayors are presently in the same peculiar position as printers. Printing technology has expanded exponentially in the past fifteen years, and the printer who is in the position of making capital investment is deluged with choice. Which of the new systems will work best, fastest, cheapest, will last longest, will fit into my existing system? No one knows. Similarly, city planners are deluged with widely diverse mass- and rapid-transit systems of the future, ranging from electronic highways which merely guide (safely, and at tighter, space-saving intervals) conventional automobiles, to 400-MPH underground tubes that whoosh passenger capsules about like the change-makers in department stores. Monorails, rubber-tired subway trains, private two-passenger rail cars, moving sidewalks, heli-buses, even the Provos' free bicycles are being suggested.

Pause to sucker for the technological dream game. Shall we visit Dallas, where we can sample moving sidewalks, or go to Memphis to try their plug-in electric carts? One can imagine a future when each city has its own characteristic mode of inner-city transport, contributing materially to the special ambience of its home. Added richness to the travel experience; San Francisco's cable cars are a tourist attraction in themselves, as well as a working mass-transit system (a system, incidentally, that indicates that the technology needn't be all that futuristic).

All of them will work. It is pointless to prescribe or predict with regard to the dozens of mass-transit systems now being proposed. There is really no question that, given enough money, our technologists can make them function. Some of them will perhaps even work as adjuncts to the private automobile. These systems *have* to work; despite Stewart Alsop's gloom, the urban/rural population split is pushing toward the 95/5 percentage point. Whatever the composition of that urban population—upper, middle, or lower class—it will be huge, and it will have to have transportation or the cities won't collapse, they'll explode. Mass transit can carry up to forty times the number of people per hours per lane of traffic that a highway can.

There is also no question but that the new systems will be expensive. But the only remedy to total paralysis in the cities is to provide workable mass transit that is clean, comfortable, economical, and safe enough to lure people into using it. The automobile lobby is fond of trotting out statistics on the decline of mass transit to show that Americans have already voted with their feet, proving that they just won't use that facility. It can safely be predicted, however, that at that point in time when Americans must reserve space on the highways for the use of their cars—say two weeks ahead of embarkation on a trip—there will be a reversal of this trend we have already "proved." That day is not too many 10-million-car years away.

Of course a great deal of planning must be done. Faced with multi-billion-dollar investments in the transit systems of the future—multi-billion-*tax*-dollar investments—the cities can't allow things just to develop, to spread (as the automobile has) any way that profit lies. The inability of any force short of federal intervention to materially affect the automobile safety and pollution situations has demonstrated the need of external viewpoints, external controls. Diversity is fine, but we must be sure the parts fit, the puzzle goes together. As the technology gets more sophisticated (and it will get more sophisticated), as loads and speeds imposed on these new systems increase (and they will increase), more and more expertise will be needed. All of these systems can be made to work, but they can't be made to do so willy-nilly. Control, planning, regulation will have to be very carefully established (we cringe already, awaiting the first 350-passenger jumbo-jet crash). Otherwise, *chaos*. As with the automobile.

John Burby analyzes the existing chaos of the American transportation muddle in *The Great American Motion Sickness*. He demonstrates the need for external intelligence, for overall planning of transportation systems that mesh. For regulation of the automobile, certainly, but also of the rest—private aviation, inland canals, the lonely surviving railroads, even Defense Department contracts that eventually feed into the nation's transportation system (such as the C-5A). All of it must be regulated. The book also convincingly demonstrates the outright failure of the Interstate Commerce Commission, and the need for *removal* of all federal regulation of that portion of the transportation system. Well, as

The Slaughter of the Buffalo

Old Lodgeskins say in *Little Big Man,* sometimes the magic works, and sometimes it doesn't.

As my anti-Nader radical friend is quick to point out—paranoia has its uses—it all fits in. A good place for federal regulation to begin might be with automobile styling. The stylists claim to be working five years ahead of the public taste, laying down on the drawing boards now the curves and curlicues that will accurately mine the public pockets half a decade from now. Suppose they miss. Suppose they so misjudge the mass whim that the industry (its fortunes forever tied to sheet metal) has a serious losing year. If the industry goes truly sour, in our present economic balance, the stock market and the GNP do likewise. If the economy collapses, the government is in big trouble. Obviously, for our own stability—and in the interest of more intelligent planning—it is best that the government take steps to insure that five years from now, X-number of buyers will want X-number of products in X-quantity. Left to the vicissitudes of public taste, the economy could fall from under us in any given styling year. We must, obviously, find a way for the government to plan/regulate automobile styling.

Or perhaps it would be more efficient for the government to regulate public tastes. (Perhaps Washington could arrange for us to like tail-fins again in 1977. In 1957 they were all the rage—God knows why—and that seemed to be a pretty good year, all things considered. Not so much congestion and confusion. Maybe we can get those days back again.)

Pardon the silliness: technology *is* political. The planned society necessary to make an explosively expanding technology work is a frightening bargain. The complexity looks, at this point, to be unavoidable. The more complex the technology becomes, the more certain is the need that it be

The Death of the Automobile

controlled and turned to socially ameliorative uses (else we have learned nothing from the environmental crisis). The more certain the need for that control, the more evident that that control must be from the top downwards. Not that such control is any new development, but the recent acceleration in the expansion and extension of that control has been remarkable. Even the automobile industry, staunch defender of free world markets (because of extensive foreign holdings, including several European automobile manufacturing concerns), gulped collectively, swallowed its scruples, and gratefully embraced the economic controls of the Nixon administration—or at least that portion of those controls which imposed a 10-percent surcharge on the sale of imported cars in this country, and wiped out the excise tax.

Computers—fruit of the technological vine—will make it happen. Enough good minds feeding enough good data, enough attention paid, and it will be possible. Atlanta will know, by the time the order is placed for the hardware, how many commuters will have to be moved to which locations in which lengths of time. It won't seem as convenient as the car—we automatically discount in our own cerebral memory banks that time wasted looking for parking spaces, just as we discount the true cost-per-mile figures for operating the machine—but the pressures will be eased. Not immediately. The pressure has to build a while yet, before we will be willing to allocate the tax dollars. But it will build, bringing the Alsopian gloom as well as the suburban flight, until we are ready. Then when the government tells us the solution, sells it to us in terms of dollars per body per mile moved, even sketches in "cost-benefit" figures that deal in windows unbroken, riots cooled, muggings averted, we will push the money through the wicket and smile. Gratefully.

As will the automobile industry come to embrace federal regulation of safety and pollution. We are already being softened for the blow of rising car prices, with lugubrious statements from industry figures predicting increases on the order of 50 percent—from $2000 for a small car to $3000 by 1975—to pay for the new equipment. As surely as three-dollar seat belts cost twenty-four dollars (and up) when installed by the car manufacturer, then the passive restraints, pollution controls, and working bumpers of the immediate car-owning future will be retailed at a maximum profit. (Have to pay for all that research that went into them, right?) We will be paying, in effect, a Nader Tax—but it will go to the industry rather than to the government which levied it. Detroit will soon be *selling* us clean air and lowered highway death rates—if the solutions work. And we will have no choice, if we choose automobiles, except to pay.

And all of Detroit's current grumpiness, all of the ongoing recalcitrance, the irate appearances before congressional committees and the ringing statements by company presidents about impossible federal deadlines and politicians getting in the way of engineers—is simply an expression of Detroit's distaste at being forced to break the technological stasis. (It was a pretty sweet little 8-million-cars-a-year operation we had there, until the feds started messing it up. You never had to spend a nickel except to fiddle around with a fender line once in awhile, trying to swipe some percentage points from your buddy across the street.)

The proof lies in the immediate postregulation response. You want technology? We'll give you technology, in spades. You just tell us where it has to plug in, what the pieces have to fit, and we'll give you all the technology your money can buy. Of course we'll have to lay the new technology on top of our old technology (amortization costs, you know), but we'll come up with the new technology. We'll deal with *all* the complaints. We'll pound a technological plug into every hole: pollution, safety, congestion, urban decay, junk-car disposal, dwindling natural resources, blight, squalor, trash, psychic dislocation, all of them. Lots of plugs for lots of holes. "We created the pollution problem and we'll *solve* the pollution problem," says Ford President Lee Iacocca, to thunderous applause.

And, he might have added, the problems the solution causes. There is little doubt that the lure of the rewards to come in industry profits, plus the stimulation of federal intervention as a potential threat to those profits, can bring better machines, that Detroit can fill all the visible and predictable holes. (The unpredictable ones may be another matter.) Nobody ever said Detroit couldn't build a better bad machine.

The Death of the Trip

The force that will finally finish off the automobile as the basis of our transportation system still lies unrevealed in the future, of course, and I have few clues to its identity, although some educated guesses are possible. It could well be a ponderous technological overcomplexity that will drive prices totally out of reach, forcing the private citizen, already staggered by the Nader Tax, to reevaluate his own transportation needs in new terms. More conventional taxation is due to increase markedly in the immediate future. We will surely recognize, shortly, that the automobile was responsible for the total decline of public transportation, and represents one of the few remaining sources of revenue substantial enough to pay for bringing that institution back to functioning life. European gasoline prices are boosted by taxation to circa sixty cents a gallon (and public transit is uniformly excellent). Japan taxes engine size so severely that over-180-cubic-inch engines add 40 percent to the cost of a car in taxes alone.

The Slaughter of the Buffalo

The automobile seems to represent an endless source of revenue generation, a role that could contribute to its own demise. The foreign nations are behind us in automobile-centered problems because they taxed early, limiting the growth of private automobiles. It seems likely that we will soon find it necessary to attempt to tax ourselves back away from the problem. The solution sounds a bit elitist for our democratic blood, but it fits our style better than anything so drastic as the outright ban that probably represents a more desirable solution. Use-taxes for city streets sound unreasonable? The parking bandits in New York City are already getting seventy-five dollars a month and up, which is exactly the same mechanism except for where the money goes, what it accomplishes.

Changing consumer habits may be enough to revise radically our patterns of automobile ownership and use, if not to wipe out the machine entirely. One such change Alvin Toffler calls "rentalism." Many city residents are finding they can avoid car ownership entirely, simply renting when the extended need arises. The savings in out-of-pocket expense, on a long-term basis, is immense. An interesting side effect of the rental phenomenon, originally surfacing in the computer industry, is that it dumps squarely back on the manufacturer the problem of product longevity and serviceability. There is absolutely no need for the customer to put up with any kind of unsatisfactory original condition or service when he can simply turn in the product and rent another for the same cost. Rental-car owners will be less inclined to sucker for psychological trimming, keenly interested in reliability, and absolutely immune to the emotionality of product loyalty. The effect could even bring back product engineering.

For the foreseeable future, the likelihood that the automobile will simply be replaced by some other new transportation technology seems dim indeed. We've had our fingers burned on not a few new technologies in the past, and can be expected to move slowly and suspiciously toward a commitment to a new gadget on a scale that will represent a total replacement of our hundred million vehicles.

We already have, however, the technology to supplant most of the automobile's function—and have it manufactured, distributed, installed, paid for. Personal communication can and perhaps will supplant the automobile eventually, not by superior performance of the automobile's function, but by diverting us away from that function. In the face of the clearly insurmountable problems that an ever-expanding automobile population presents, our futurists are beginning to see that it is mobility itself—that simple original notion that we so quickly mastered and then went on to other things—that is the enemy. The range of spokesmen who are mulling over the idea in public print is remarkably wide. Sociologist Paul Goodman perhaps represents the reputable anti-establishment extreme: "The first question about transportation is not private cars and highways versus public transportation, but why the trip altogether. I have not heard this question asked either in Congress or in City Hall. Why must the workman live so far from his job? Could that be remedied? Why do I travel 2,000 miles to give a lecture for an hour . . . ?" [2]

For the other side of the abyss between anti- and pro-establishment forces, nobody could be a better spokesman than the director of research for General Motors, Paul Chenea: "When you stop to think of how much traveling you do which you wouldn't really do if you could accomplish the job some other way. Just think of how much travel you could avoid if you could look at a guy when you talk to him on the telephone. I'm not really convinced that everybody's got to go everywhere all the time. There must be a better way than this. . . ." [3]

When the director of research for the largest transportation company in the world says perhaps we shouldn't move around so much, it is mobility itself that is clearly identified as the culprit. Dr. Chenea will be joined in the near future by what will amount to a world-wide chorus—the same kind of swelling organ tones of piousness and moral exhortation that have unfortunately characterized a great deal of the environmental protection movement. Don't go, the voices will say. Stop. Consider alternatives. Stay home. Phone instead of going. (The phone service shows signs of collapsing already. We have yet to discover the communication equivalent of exhaust emissions, but it is hardly cynical to suggest that we probably will.) Okay, we are a buzzing, jittery, flighty human race; maybe we can spin off some portion of those jitters in increased—dare we hope for improved?—communication. Talk, don't drive.

Visual phones, access to data banks and computers, transmission via phone of graphic materials—these will increase slightly the effectiveness of electronic rather than mechanical travel. As we have created a new class of the technologically unemployable in the recent past, we might well profit by creating a class of professionally unmobile in the future. It is unlikely that such a sea change in American custom will spring lightly from the public-spiritedness of the citizenry. During one of New York's subway strikes, Mayor Lindsay issued a public plea that all Manhattan workers not "absolutely essential" please stay home; the result was an historic traffic jam, as every citizen rushed to the office by car to prove his indispensability.

Neither new gadgets nor new social and economic classes are sufficient, really, to break the pattern. Nor will we give up our cars for moralistic reasons, no matter who or what would thereby be saved. It has been suggested that the automobile must be abandoned if we are to survive. Yes, of course—just as we must stop having wars in order to avoid killing so many people. We will not exhort ourselves out of

The Death of the Automobile

the automotive trap any more successfully than we stopped highway crashes with moral imperatives. No appeal to our reasonableness or our humanity will finally demobilize us.

The automobile will die when its use becomes unbearable. It would be comforting to end on a positive note, to suggest some new attraction that will pull us from our cars by increasing human possibilities, but we've run out of room—and, perhaps, time—for that. When the moment comes—as it will, as surely as tomorrow's polluted dawn—when movement threatens, when to go carries a greater psychic cost than to stay, then we will stop. The automobile has made a powerful beginning in the creation of an environment in which such a threat is integral. Every day new elements click into place: the risk, the cost, the delay, the bother, the crowding and congestion. The rage. When the destination diminishes as the task of getting there grows, when the endless prospect of unrelieved blight conquers the remaining vistas, when no conceivable *place* holds any hope of being different from any other—when all of America becomes Woodward Avenue—then we will stay home. What new toys—surrogate sports cars—will fill our time is beyond imagining. But there will be time to fill, a great deal of it, when none of it is spent in automobiles.

One possibility lies waiting in the wings for our discovery, if we have the wit to seek it out. When Alan S. Boyd became the first Secretary of Transportation, one of his first official acts was to decorate his new chambers. On one wall, he hung a large photomural: it showed a pair of well-shod feet. It's a transportation solution that hasn't had a great deal of technological support in recent years, but it might be the salvation of us yet.

Franconia, N.H., January, 1972

Notes

Chapter 1

[1] Charles F. "Boss" Kettering of General Motors *really* started the horsepower race, with a paper in 1947 describing experiments with engines of higher compression ratios than the then-current 6.5:1. The high-compression V-8 became the basis of the golden era of the industry. It also brought the development of high-octane fuel, with resultant higher costs, and leaded gasolines, heavy contributors to air pollution and principal obstacle to the use of catalytic mufflers to clean up the internal combustion engine.

[2] Car prices, and car profits, are a source of great mystery—see Chapter 7 for details. I've used $600 gross per car from an article by Brock Yates called "The Grosse Point Myopians," *Car and Driver*, April 1968. A report from the Senate Subcommittee on Antitrust and Monopoly entitled *Administered Prices—Automobiles* documents fleet sales to state and local governments at prices up to $800 below dealer cost, which would indicate room for a $600 gross figure with some to spare.

[3] Sales figures, too, are a source of a great deal of confusion in automotive reporting. Unit sales may or may not include trucks; manufacturer figures (cars shipped) may differ from dealer figures (cars sold), which may also differ from registrations. The figures here are from the industry itself, *1971 Automobile Facts and Figures,* published by the Automobile Manufacturers Association, Inc., Detroit. R.L. Polk & Co. uses registrations as a primary source, and pegs 1955 passenger car sales at 7,942,125.

[4] *Car and Driver*, April 1970.

[5] "The Senseless War on Science," *Fortune*, March 1971. Lessing goes on: "More important, out of that war came the impetus to get the U.S. fully engaged in doing basic science on its own. From having won only a sparse dozen Nobel Prizes in the forty years up to 1940, U.S. scientists went on in the next thirty years to win 45, *and take first place among the nations.*" (Emphasis supplied. This is the first instance of nationalistic scorekeeping for the Nobel Prize that I've run across. I thought the practice was reserved for the Olympic Games.)

[6] *Unsafe at Any Speed*, Grossman, New York, 1965.

[7] Most automotive innovations find their way onto commercial vehicles first.

Notes

Lawrence J. White, in *The Automobile Industry since 1945* (Harvard University Press, Cambridge, 1971) attributes this to a higher level of technical sophistication and a stronger interest in performance, rather than appearance or prestige considerations, among commercial vehicle buyers. White lists automatic transmissions, power brakes, power steering, diesel engines, and, likely soon, gas turbines, among technological innovations introduced first on trucks and buses.

[8] Burby, John, *The Great American Motion Sickness*, Little, Brown, Boston, 1971, p. 111.

[9] A.B. Shuman, "Reflections on a Three-Pointed Star," *Motor Trend* Magazine, October 1971.

Chapter 2

[1] Although the unit-body is intrinsically more crash-worthy, federal attention to that ghoulish consideration contributed to its demise. General Motors was using its notorious "X-frame," a structure which provided almost no protection against side impacts, in conjunction with a body subunit. Although the corporations stoutly denied that there was any structural weakness in the X-frame (and the competitors just as stoutly whispered that the cars were deathtraps), adverse publicity led GM to search for a more protective package. The perimeter frame was one solution; steel beams in the car doors was another, which the industry now seems to be adopting generally. At any rate, the phase-out of the X-frame in favor of the perimeter arrangement took place for all GM cars except the specialty Buick Riviera by 1965.

[2] Nader, p. 214. When meaningful technological change does occur in the American automobile, very little effort is made toward sales capitalization of the fact, probably because Detroit reads the American automotive tastes as conservatively as possible. Front-wheel drive was introduced on the Oldsmobile Toronado in 1967, on the Cadillac Eldorado later (same mechanical works). The customer still must be virtually an industrial spy to discover that the change—astonishingly radical for Detroit—exists. General Motors didn't introduce front-wheel drive until engineering had made the feature all but indistinguishable in performance from the rest of the line. Little has been made of it in advertising and sales promotion. It is confidently assumed that many customers have purchased front-wheel drive and don't know they have it. Reports of cars with tire chains or snow tires fitted to the wrong wheels are the source of sardonic glee among filling-station operators.

Once bitten by the unconventional Corvair (rear-engine, air-cooling, four-

264

wheel independent suspension), GM is twice shy. Besides, in industry myth-ology, if not in public memory, there is still a considerable residue from the whisper campaign about the inherent dangers of front-wheel drive that reputedly drove Cord out of the automobile business before World War II. Wouldn't it be poetic justice if those rumors had been started at GM?

3 Nader, p. 218.

4 *The Great American Motion Sickness*, Little, Brown, Boston, 1971, p. 75.

Chapter 3

1 Brock Yates, "America's Sweetheart," *Car and Driver*, March 1971.

2 Inside dope—sworn to as gospel truth—claims that the real reason a Chevrolet Caprice even exists is *not* to broaden Chevrolet's product line, but to give its top executives something to ride home in. A GM decree in the early sixties required division executives to use their own products, which meant that the chauffered Cadillacs that the heads of Oldsmobile, Pontiac, Buick, and Chevrolet were using for commutation had to go. Most of the other divisions produced suitable luxury products, but the poor executives at Chevrolet had to ride in—oh, the shame of it—Impalas. So the Caprice was created. Gospel or not, there is a ring of truth to it: long-legged John Delorean, head of Chevrolet, is reputed to have caused to be constructed a stretched Caprice body on a Cadillac limousine chassis for his daily trip to the office.

3 Random House, New York, 1970.

4 Hal Higdon, "The Big Auto Sweepstakes," *New York Times Magazine*, May 1, 1966, p. 97.

5 For 1972, Detroit swung back in the other direction in horsepower mea-surements, going to a "net" figure obtained with accessories and exhaust systems, and the engine in the form in which it actually exists in the car. The result is a drop in advertised horsepower, for example, for the 350-cubic-inch Chevrolet V-8 from 250 to 165. The latter figure is a more ac-curate representation of what the customer has been getting all along. The move was aimed at distracting federal attention from scary-sounding out-puts, but represents no real horsepower loss, simply another kind of mea-surement.

6 There are marginal advantages of one kind of spring over another, prin-cipally depending on things like mechanical layout and available space. Advertising of springs started when the noisy old leaf spring—now layered with plastic to prevent metal-to-metal contact—began to give way to coils. "Full coil spring suspension" probably conjures up visions of mattresses in

Notes

the customers' heads, and connotes a softer ride. What it actually means is that with all the other clutter, coil springs was all there was room for.

7 Four-wheel disc brakes would be better than front disc brakes, of course, but there are production and cost problems in putting discs on all four wheels, so most American manufacturers give up 50 percent of the disc effectiveness and keep drums on the rear. The limited-production Corvette sports car is the only domestic car with four-wheel disc brakes. Since weight transfer forward under braking puts more load on the front brakes than the rear, that's where the discs go.

8 Those compacts represented a kind of high-water mark in technological experimentation in the domestic industry. The Corvair was air cooled, rear engined, and had four-wheel independent suspension. The Pontiac Tempest had a transaxle (rear-mounted transmission) for better weight distribution. The Olds F-88 and Buick Special shared a revolutionary aluminum V-8. The Corvair is totally dead now, of course, and of the others, nothing remains but the nameplates.

9 Dial Press, New York, 1971, p. 4.

10 Robert J. Cole, "Why the High Cost of Auto Insurance," *New York Times,* April 4, 1971. So the '72's had the new bumpers, and the Insurance Institute for Highway Safety tested them: average front-end damage from a 5-MPH collision with a barrier was $231 (*New York Times,* January 19, 1972). Back to the old drawing board.

Chapter 4

1 Lawrence J. White, in *The Automobile Industry since 1945* (Harvard, Cambridge, 1971, p. 214) lists forty "cases in which one or two companies clearly led in the introduction of innovation." Of the forty, only eleven appeared first on the more expensive cars. At first glance it would then appear that the industry is doing the bulk of its innovation on cheaper cars, democratically making advances available to the poor, rather than the rich. In fact, however, the practice only means that all innovation is held up until ways are found to bring the production costs down and the profitability up.

2 *Ibid.,* p. 44.

3 "The Grosse Point Myopians," *Car and Driver,* April 1968.

4 The shock of the Detroit civil war of 1967 did not, of course, go unnoticed by the automobile industry. Most of the top officials of the major car companies are dutifully enrolled in charitable and public-service work, and the establishment of the National Alliance of Businessmen, a massive program to find jobs for half a million hard-core unemployed, was led by car-industry executives. The effect of the program in Detroit has been the

Notes

waiver of conventional job-entry requirements, more lenient standards on performance measurements such as absenteeism, etc. In the first year of the NAB program, 146,000 people found new employment; 88,000 of these remained on the job a year later. The average period of unemployment prior to accepting the new job was six months to one year. Unfortunately, the economic downturn of subsequent years cut harshly into the program's effectiveness.

The reaction time—in 1968, after thirteen years of glorious prosperity, followed by a devastating riot on home grounds—seems a more meaningful index to industry social consciousness. In a generally laudatory piece on G.M. entitled "For Roche of G.M. Happiness is a 10% Surcharge," (*New York Times Magazine*, Sept. 12, 1971), William Serrin discusses GM racial policies during and before James Roche's chairmanship: "For example, under his [Roche's] leadership, the number of blacks employed by the corporation rose noticeably. Minority-group workers (most of them black) now make up 15.3 per cent of the work force, compared to 13.3 just before Roche took over in 1967. There are about 5,000 black white-collar employes, 3 per cent of the total in this category. There are 15 black dealers, compared to two before Roche. There is even a black on the corporation's board of directors, Dr. Leon Sullivan. Under Roche, G.M. has also donated funds to build low-cost housing and placed money in black banks.

"All this may not sound too impressive, until one examines the corporation's previous record . . ." Serrin says, and quotes a former GM publicity man: "Ralph Bunche could literally not have gotten a job as a janitor in those days" (the early sixties).

No mention is made by Mr. Serrin of the salary levels of the five-thousand black white-collar workers, but similar studies of the situation at Ford Motor Company seem to indicate that admission to the lowest rank of white-collar positions is about the maximum expectation a black might reasonably hold. Mr. Serrin also fails to note that the black addition to the GM board came only as a direct result of the intensive "Campaign GM," a stockholders' revolt—for "corporate responsibility"—led by Ralph Nader.

[5] For a further look at whether automobile sales push or are pulled by the national economy, see Chapter 10.

[6] *1971 Automobile Facts and Figures,* Automobile Manufacturers Association, Inc., 320 New Center Building, Detroit, Mich. 48202.

[7] My quotation is from Mintz & Cohen, *America, Inc.,* Dial, New York, 1971, pp. 258–59. The authors explain that the correspondence first surfaced in 1952 in *United States of America v. E. I. du Pont de Nemours & Co., et al.,* U.S.D.C. N.D. Ill. Civil Action No. 49C-1701. The correspondence was made public when it was Exhibit 220 of the Hearings before Subcommittees of the Select Committee on Small Business, United States Senate, 90th Congress, Second Session, *Planning, Regulation and Competition: Automobile Industry—1968.*

Notes

[8] Mintz & Cohen, p. 6. The internal quote is from "The Massive Statistics of General Motors," *Fortune*, July 15, 1966.

[9] I am indebted for this point of view to columnist Bruce McCall, writing in *Car and Driver* in February 1970, and expressing rather surprising sentiments in a more-often-than-not captive publication. For a more typical car-magazine view, see Brock Yates's column, November 1971, in the same magazine, in which Yates attacks Nader as a power-hungry demagogue, chiefly dangerous, as best I can tell, because his style of dress and sense of humor don't measure up to Yates's standards.

Nader leaves few people unmoved, in one direction or another. A radical friend of mine has suggested that the man is a kind of witless tool of the establishment. By focusing attention on safety defects, Nader has forced government intervention in car design. The intervention is going to serve to drive car prices further upwards, and to cause a stiffening of such regulations as vehicle inspections, which will effectively ban the older, cheaper cars from our highways. Thus Nader's consumerism will eventually help Detroit sell more new cars with more expensive safety accessories and other modifications. It's an interesting point of view to try to sell to the probusiness element, which is currently busy accusing Nader of being an agent of Godless Socialism. The view is examined further in Chapter 10.

Chapter 5

[1] Juan Cameron, "How the Interstate Changed the Face of the Nation," *Fortune*, July 1971.

[2] *Superhighway—Superhoax*, Doubleday & Co., New York, 1970, p. 36. Ms. Leavitt is particularly effective in detailing the Byzantine intricacies of the road-building lobby, in particular in the area of interlocking directorates and joint committees. I am heavily indebted to Ms. Leavitt for a great deal of the information in this chapter.

[3] A kind of native awareness of the divisive nature of roads is in evidence in rural America, where patterns of exploitation are at least more genteel and subtle than they are in the ghettos. Laurence Lafore, in "In the Sticks," *Harper's*, October 1971, described an interesting variation of the divisiveness of roads in Iowa: "The roads run sternly to compass points, as they do throughout the Midwest, where the ground rules of civilization were laid out by engineers in advance of settlers. . . . A few years ago, the Iowa legislature, after much debate, repealed a law forbidding the highway commission to build what are called 'diagonals.' After a few years a new bill was introduced to reestablish the ban. It was specifically aimed to prevent laying out a new interstate highway, from Des Moines to Minneapolis, on

a straight-line northeast southwest. The sponsoring legislators were determined to preserve the tradition, even at a cost of several right-angle turns, several score of added miles, and several million dollars. The avowed reason for this was the violence the diagonals do to section lines; since property lines are all rectilinear, a farmer through whose land the interstate would run at an angle would find his fields cut into separated triangles. It is rational consideration, stemming from a belief—now in fashion again—that land is more important than highways." The farm vote is, of course, a more significant factor than that of the ghetto, or even that of the conservationists.

4 *The Great American Motion Sickness*, Little, Brown and Company, Boston, 1971, p. 19.

5 *Ibid.*, p. 91.

6 March 19, 1969.

7 Leavitt, p. 107.

8 Burby, p. 311–12.

9 Leavitt, p. 46.

10 Burby, p. 95.

11 Cameron, *Fortune*, p. 81.

12 Leavitt, p. 226, quotes a Bureau of Public Roads highway research engineer on the subject of public hearings: "The public should be heard but it doesn't mean you have to follow what they say. Engineers are professionals just like lawyers and doctors. Does the community make the laws? Do you take a vote in the community to see if you need an operation?"

13 *Earth Tool Kit*, Sam Love, ed., Pocket Books, New York, 1971, p. 105.

Chapter 6

In general, I've drawn quite heavily from two magazine articles for this chapter: Brock Yates's "Beep . . . Beep . . . Beep . . . Jingle," *Car and Driver*, February 1970, and Robert L. Schwartz's "The Case for Fast Drivers," *Harper's*, September 1963—which was reprinted in *Car and Driver*, February 1964. Enthusiast magazines naturally reflect their audience's fondness for fast cars and fast driving. Although the campaigns they carry on against speed control are therefore somewhat self-serving, they do provide an external viewpoint on the problem, from outside the narrowly guilt-ridden sphere which seems to control traffic-management thinking in this country. Since seventy years of guilt-based legislation hasn't worked very well, the fresher view seems worth considering.

1 Lead editorial, *Car and Driver*, June 1970.

Notes

2 "The Case for Fast Drivers."

3 Yates's monthly column, *Car and Driver*, November 1969.

4 Lead editorial, *Car and Driver*, June 1970.

5 "Beep . . . Beep . . . Beep . . . Jingle."

6 *Harper's* identified Robert L. Schwartz, author of "The Case for Fast Drivers," as a journalist, entrepreneur, and motorist with "a license free of speeding arrests." I can't say the same. In the interests of proving non-objectivity, I've attempted to reconstruct my own arrest record, to document the source of attitude in this chapter if nothing else. I suppose I have been, from time to time, a "fast driver," although Schwartz maintains, "There are practically no 'high-speed drivers' as a constant group; a man's own driving speeds vary more from hour to hour or from day to day than they do from those of other motorists. A man killed at 40 MPH today on a rural highway was going 65 MPH yesterday—and he was safer then by 300 percent."

At any rate, in twenty years of driving, my own depressing score:

1955—Ruidoso, N.M., radar, limit 45, speed 55. Clear, dry highway, light traffic, night. $10.

1956—Hereford, Tex., radar, limit 55, speed 65. Clear, dry highway, light traffic, night. $15.

1957—Paradise, Tex., pursuit, limit 30, speed 45. Clear, dry rural town 4-lane, light traffic, day. $15.

1958—Rankin, Tex., radar, limit 55, speed 70. Clear, dry highway, no traffic, night. $20.

1965—Pennsylvania Turnpike, radar, limit 65, speed 75. Intermittent rain, moderate to heavy traffic, night. $20.

1966—Queens, N.Y., pursuit, limit 35, speed 45. Empty Long Island Expressway, early Sunday morning. $15.

1970—Troy, Vt., radar, limit 60, speed 70. Clear, dry highway, very light traffic, day. $20.

1971—Bethlehem, N.H., pursuit, limit 60, speed 70. Clear, dry Interstate, very light traffic, day. $20.

Two other comments about this display of wickedness. In five of the eight occasions, I was within half a mile of a speed-limit change. And during this tawdry twenty years, I've had one accident: a roll-over at 50 MPH (speed limit 60) in a rainstorm, with no injuries. (I also crashed on a racecourse once—and oh yes, a lady ran a stop sign and bent one of my fenders at about 5 MPH.)

I really think I deserved the pinch in Pennsylvania. After all, the pavement *was* wet.

7 David Skedgell, "Car Thefts: The Billion Dollar Headache," *Car and Driver*, March 1971.

Chapter 7

1 "The Okie Charmer," *Car and Driver*, November 1967.

2 Lawrence J. White, *The Automobile Industry Since 1945*, Harvard, Cambridge, 1971, p. 106.

3 Second only to the "list price" in customer abuses is the "dealer preparation" charge. All of the manufacturers provide lengthy predelivery inspection forms; many dealers engage in artful editing of the form, knowing from experience which items they can omit to save shop time with a minimum chance of incurring customer complaints. It is very likely that the preparation charges that a customer pays are insufficient for proper preparation of the car at a fair price. Dodge, for example, requires (or suggests) an eighty-six-step check-out procedure, which includes such time-consuming tasks as checking accelerator pump link adjustment, carburetor linkage adjustment, tracing wiring circuitry, measuring front-end height, toe-in, and headlight aim, checking dwell angle, ignition timing, and ignition advance—in other words, operations that are included in a normal tune-up procedure.

Many dealers have come to regard the preparation procedure as another excuse for sloppy workmanship by the manufacturer, referring to the new cars as delivered from Detroit as "do-it-yourself" kits. In any event, both manufacturer and dealer would certainly appreciate any of the postshipment final assembly costs that the consumer is willing to pay.

4 The manufacturers strive to maintain the myth of a free, competitive market, and to this end are sure to utter a barrage of press releases about things like competitive price structures around new-model time. Actually, it is very simple: GM sets the prices, and Ford and Chrysler follow. Period. To maintain the myth, however, the onerous task of announcing new-car prices is rotated among the manufacturers just as the UAW rotates its beginning bargaining points among the manufacturers every time a new contract comes up. The maker who announces first is testing the water for the entire industry; if there isn't too much flak from government over the new prices, the other makers fall into line. If there is considerable pressure, manufacturer number two will announce lower prices, and manufacturer number one will pull what the newspapers are fond of referring to as "an embarrassing rollback" on the first prices announced. Somehow, everyone survives the embarrassment.

GM domination of the price policy is self-evident. The firm has had better than 50 percent of the market for more than twenty years, and is also the most profitable. (GM averaged a 20.67 percent rate of return on its net worth between 1946 and 1967; the rest of the industry averaged 16.67—all

271

Notes

figures from White.) The industry desperately wants to avoid a price war, since GM would obviously win such a struggle. For a detailed study of price-setting policies, see White, pp. 109–16.

5 White, pp. 118–19.

6 White, pp. 119–20.

7 *Look Magazine,* National Automobile and Tire Survey, 1965.

8 John Barbour, Associated Press, "The Auto in USA," *Boston Globe,* November 13, 1971.

9 Maintenance costs in the earlier years of a car's life are extremely sneaky. Volkswagen's excellent reputation for service in this country is peculiarly self-replicating. The car is simple, and the mechanics well trained, but there is something else going for the nameplate. The car's reputation for good service sticks in the owners' minds, and makes them get the car serviced more frequently. Dealers, service managers, advertisements, sales literature all put heavy emphasis on routine maintenance, and good routine maintenance of course enhances the car's service reputation. During the car's most successful years in this country, when waiting lists for new VW's were six months long and dealers were functioning primarily as order-takers rather than salesmen, a dealer inadvertently spilled the economics of the whole mechanism to me. If a new VW purchaser followed the recommended service schedule religiously, he estimated, the owner would spend about three thousand dollars for service, in the first fifty thousand miles, on what was then a sixteen-hundred-dollar car. A very good piece of business for the dealer. A very sharp method of insuring the car's reputation for good service in the bargain.

10 "Encounter with an Athlete," *Sports Illustrated,* September 27, 1971.

11 Car/Puter, Inc., a division of United Auto Brokers, Inc., 1603 Bushwick Ave., Brooklyn, N.Y. 11207.

12 Grossman, New York, 1971. The book is extremely good on sources, addresses, legal forms, explanation of legal machinations for obtaining satisfaction, etc. The reader is advised, however, to take the section of the book which concerns the basic mechanics of an automobile ("How Your Car Works") with a grain of salt.

Chapter 8

1 *Unsafe at Any Speed,* Grossman, New York, 1965, pp. 265–66.

2 "In 1956 Ford sold safety—and Chevy sold cars," is the refrain in Detroit. It's an interesting legend, tied up in the larger world of politics. Chevy had a bright new (face-lifted) model for 1956, and Ford was

caught out, without a hot competitor. In an effort to recoup, Ford General Manager Robert S. McNamara pushed safety. The 1956 Fords had a deep-dish steering wheel, safety door latches, padded seat-backs, and "swingaway" rear-view mirrors as standard equipment. Customers could order seat belts (the first U.S. car to offer them), padded dashboards, padded sunvisors, and an external rear-view mirror as safety options. The move was abetted by an extensive "Lifeguard Design" safety theme to the year's advertising campaign.

Chevrolet outsold Ford by two hundred thousand cars for the year. Midway in the sales year, industry leaders, including some in-house competitors of McNamara at Ford, mounted a coup attempt to remove McNamara as head of Ford, on the grounds that publicity connecting the industry and its products with highway death was treasonous. The coup didn't quite succeed, but the advertising campaign for safety was dropped, and the legend that safety doesn't sell was firmly established.

In fact, in view of the 1955 success of Chevrolet, the momentum from that year, and the failure of Ford to respond in 1956 with substantial improvement in the car itself, that 200,000 difference in sales is not a particularly unreasonable gap. (The 200,000 difference has been matched or exceeded by Chevrolet at least fourteen times since World War II.) Moreover, the effort was no test of safety in the marketplace, since not only was the campaign killed in midyear, but Ford had underestimated the demand for safety options so badly that dealers were unable to get many of the options that customers ordered, and the factory was back-ordered on safety equipment for several months of the year.

[3] Pp. 252–53.

[4] *Harper's*, September, 1963.

[5] Grossman, New York, 1971, pp. 40–41.

[6] Private conversation—but for a repeat of the sentiments, I refer you to an article in *Better Homes and Gardens*, October 1942, in which the coming glories of the post–World War II car were described:

> But in Detroit engineers point out what nonsense it is to use a ton and a half or two tons of gas-eating, road-hammering machinery to haul one 160-pound man around. They say that right now they can design and mass-produce a car that weighs a third to half less than our 1942 models, that rides on air and goes half again as far on a gallon of gas and yet offers more space and comfort inside.

One might speculate at length on the reasons we had to wait thirty years—for the introduction of the Pinto and Vega—to see that prediction come true—and then only in part. I doubt the delay mystifies many automobile manufacturers.

[7] Norton, New York, 1971, p. 175.

273

Notes

Chapter 9

[1] Ralph E. Lapp, "We're Running Out of Gas," *The New York Times Magazine*, March 19, 1972.

[2] "Wanted: Space-Age Steam Engine," May 16, 1971.

Chapter 10

[1] "The Cities Are Finished," *Newsweek*, April 5, 1971.

[2] "Confusion and Disorder," *Earth* Magazine, August 1971.

[3] John Burby, *The Great American Motion Sickness*, Little, Brown, Boston, 1971, p. 33.

Index

Index

Index

Index

Index

Index

Index

Index

Index